K.M. ROBINSON

THE CONSPIRACY OF JACK FROST

THE CONSPIRACY OF JACK FROST
Copyright © 2021 by K.M. Robinson.

Published by Crescent Sea Publishing.
www.crescentseapublishing.com

Cover designed by Cover A Day.
www.coveraday.com

To my dad.
Thanks for making me watch all those survival shows and teaching me what to do out in the wild. It certainly helped for this book!

PROLOGUE

He was a force of nature.

He could warm your soul like the sun and then bury you in ice the next second.

He was more destructive than any universal element has ever been or could ever be. It was his way, to be like a hurricane crashing upon the shores, or lightning splintering everything in its path.

He was a force.

But he was *my* force.

And in the end, it didn't matter, because he disappeared, just like the weather always does. Here for one brief moment and gone the next.

His name was Jack and his love for me was like a flood, now frozen over.

My fingers are cold—so cold I think I might miss the vicious tingling of an hour ago. Now I can't feel anything, like phantom limbs sitting at the end of my throbbing palms, my fingers dancing against my body, slamming painlessly into my legs as I walk.

My gloves, lined with fake fur, do little to warm me. I miss Jack's warm hands in mine, protecting me from the storm. It's too cold to survive, but my stolen moments with Jack give me the only hope I have left.

I live in a snow globe—at least that's how Jack describes it.

Each crunch shatters my ears, exploding around me. Each step makes me want to fall to my knees and scream.

Would there even be a noise if I tried?

Our world runs in cycles that change like a person shaking one of the snow globes we found in the storage room in the bunker when we were kids. Two days of Spring, a week of Summer, four days of Fall, followed by a month of Winter. Most days, I wouldn't mind if our world fell off whatever shelf it is sitting on, smashing the cycle.

Suddenly my ears go out, like the life was sucked out of a room. There's no ringing, no pain, but the entire dynamic of my surroundings has changed, like a motor dying. Nothingness sounds far more vicious than what I now realize hadn't been 'nothing' at all.

There. The light is ahead, its glow reaches out to me, calling me, persuading me to move faster. As if my legs could.

Shattered breath pours out from my lips, blue as Jack's eyes. He will be waiting for me. His arms will be warm when he drags me into the bunker and sits me by the fire. He insists I stay inside, but the moment he leaves, I go too. We can't afford not to.

"Genesis!" His voice is clear and calm, but his eyes betray him even from this far away.

He lets me approach, tracking my every move until I'm fifteen feet from the door. He comes to me, quickly and slowly all at once. Jack's fingers linger on my shoulder until we reach the dip in the hall.

We descend down the ramp into the tunnel, the blue lights transfixing my thoughts as he guides me.

"You shouldn't have gone out," he says harshly.

"We don't have time to wait around, Jack. This is about survival."

"Someone needs to watch the little ones," he protests,

his warmth traveling through my coat. I can't feel it, but I know it's permeating my skin and sinking into my bones.

"Eliza is perfectly capable of watching them." My voice shakes as my teeth start to throb. The tunnel is by no means warm, but the dramatic difference between the howling wind and the still cavern is shocking.

"It's dangerous out there."

It's not like I had gone all the way to the mountains. I hadn't even gone that far into the forest.

"It's dangerous in here too, Jack." I trudge along behind him, feet refusing to move. "We have no idea what's going to happen out there..."

"Come sit down," he whispers. Raising his voice, he adds, "She's back!"

Little snow-children gather at my feet as I sit, bundled in their heaviest blankets. Coats are in short supply and the days of snow are too fierce not to have warmth at all times. Jack lets me stay in mine in front of the fire that Eliza tends. He drops *his* on the boy at my feet.

"Anything?" she asks.

I shake my head. I have no answers.

"Gen, Gen!" Nicholas whimpers at my feet. "Tomorrow is Spring."

His smile trembles on his face as if the entire world is depending on the weather changing tomorrow. In fact, it does.

"Yes, Nicholas, tomorrow should be Spring. I hope it comes true."

We need it to come true. We haven't been able to find food for two weeks. The snow always lasts longer than the other seasons.

"We have two whole days of Spring and then a week of Summer." He announces, satisfied with my answer.

A week *if we were lucky*.

I give him a weak smile, my face just starting to thaw. He grins back and huddles against my knee. All the children are trained to gather against the person who just walked in from the storm to share body warmth. They cluster around us and melt us. The ice drips from my boots and Nicholas slides back, his arm reaching around me, moving his warmth. I can't help the sigh that escapes me.

Jack's eyes dart immediately to me to see why I made the noise, but just as quickly they move beyond me to Nathaniel. He grimaces in a way that only I can tell.

Nathaniel eyes me before shooting a look to Jack. Without a word, Jack reaches down and pulls me up. The children at my feet scatter, drawing their blankets around them once again.

Pushing passed Nathaniel, he drags me away from the room, into one of the storage rooms. It's colder than the main rooms where we all sleep and live, but it's private.

"Are you okay?" he whispers as his hands fumble for my zipper.

I nod. Every muscle in his arms tightens under my hands as he works.

"What did you find?" he asks, barely glancing up at my eyes.

"Nothing. I found nothing."

Pushing back the thick fabric of my jacket, he wraps himself around me, pressing his chest to mine. Warmth floods me.

"Did *you* find anything?" I ask.

"A bit of food, that's all. At least we'll eat tonight."

His face hovers over mine, forehead brushing lightly against me. It tickles as we sway together.

"Are you okay?" he whispers again, eyes closed.

"I'm okay, Jack," I assure him, hands migrating to his chest to absorb his heat.

"You shouldn't have gone out there. It wasn't your day."

In the Winter storm times, we divide up the work, only allowing a certain number of people to go out for a specified amount of time per day. Jack and I have never been good at following rules.

"We don't have a lot of time to waste, Jack. We have to figure this out. The Winter days have been getting longer and harsher. We can't withstand much more of this."

"We'll find a way. One that doesn't involve you getting yourself killed out there."

"You would have found me," I say quietly, smiling. I knew he would; he had done it before.

"You're going to get us *both* killed, Gen."

"Oh, please, Jack, you're the only one of us that is *going* to survive this place."

"Don't say that." He looks hurt.

"Guys!" Eliza's sharp voice outside the door makes us both jump. "We've got a problem!"

Ripping apart from each other, we race out of the storage room, my jacket still resting around my shoulders where Jack left it. Rounding the corner, we find Perrin holding a knife.

"No..." I gasp, knowing behind him sits one of our own, about to lose an appendage.

"How did this happen?" Jack asks, able to see around the doctor.

"*How do you think?*" Eliza snaps. "He was out there too long."

Eliza has never been good with blood and carnage. That's why I left her to watch the children. She wouldn't fare well out in the real world.

"Oh gosh!" she gasps as Perrin moves closer to Nes. I grab Eliza's hand and spin her out of the room before her brother begins the amputation. Frostbite is particularly nasty.

We're down the hallway before he screams and Eliza doubles over. Hauling her upright I force her back to the main room. The children will have heard the scream and no one prepared them.

Nicholas scampers over to me, throwing his arms around my legs. Lilly follows, clinging to my thigh.

"Eliza, sit." My command springs her into action and she scoops up some of the children and ushers them to the fire to tell a story over the chaos.

The moment Nes passes out is a relief and all grows quiet.

"Nes?" Nathaniel asks, sidling up to me.

I nod, brushing my hand over Nicholas' hair. Nathaniel nods back, sighing deeply. When one of our own is *hurt*, it's bad. When one of our own is *unrepairable*, it's worse. Nes will be useless to us for weeks as he learns to function without whatever Perrin is relieving him of.

"We have to keep him from ending up like Lewis," Nathaniel says quietly so Nicholas doesn't overhear.

I give the boy a push and send him to sit by the fire, his nerves having calmed.

"We won't let that happen." I look up to Nathaniel as he leans against the wall with one shoulder. "Nes will be okay."

I push away from him and walk back to the operating room. Blood pools on the floor and table, but Perrin has finished his work. Freshly stained fabric is wrapped around Nes' hand, concealing the wound. He's passed out from the stress.

"How bad?" I ask.

"Three fingers. We saved the rest," Perrin answers, darkness clouding his gaze. His eyes never leave the floor.

"He'll be okay." Jack's voice is deep and solemn as he wipes his hands on a towel. "He's strong. He'll make it."

I nod. Nes has always been a fighter, always been strong. Jack wouldn't let anything happen to him. He cared too deeply for the people here to let them be lost to us.

"Go," Perrin orders as Nes starts to stir. I've been in the room for the notifications before and quickly take his advice to leave. I don't need to see that.

Stepping outside, I slip my jacket off. Jack nods in approval. We've trained ourselves to endure the coolness of the bunker without bundling up too much. If we kept our coats on like the little ones do, when we step outside, it would do us no good. Jack wraps an arm around my back and pulls me toward his hip.

"What is going on out there?" I ask, knowing he doesn't know.

He sighs as he guides me down the tunnel.

"Something is changing, Jack," I lead, "Winter is getting harsher. We can't find food; the temperature is dropping. Jack, we can't survive like this."

"I know, Gen." His voice is low and frustrated.

"What if Spring doesn't come? Or what if Summer only lasts a day and we're back to this cold?"

"We'll be okay."

"But what if we go right to Summer and skip Spring all together-could we handle the severe switch?"

"We'll be okay," he says a little louder.

Jack is an eternal optimist. No matter what happens, he believes the best—he's usually right. He firmly believes there is always a way and if anyone can find one, it's him.

"We don't even know what we're facing here—"

"We'll be okay," he insists, interrupting me.

He also doesn't like it when I'm not as optimistic as him, but at least one of us should be practical. We're a good balance for each other in that respect.

"How do you know, Jack?"

"I just do, Gen," he snaps. "We'll be okay."

"You can't possibly know for sure." My voice comes out in a whisper.

"But I do, Gen. We're going to be okay," he whispers back softly, apologizing in his own way for snapping.

I drop it. Arguing won't help. Besides, I trust Jack. If he believes we'll be okay, we will be. He's proven to be right more than once over our years here. As Jack always says, he follows the data.

"Tomorrow will be Spring. I'm sure of it. It's how it

always works." He nods firmly. "Until then, though, let's get you taken care of."

"If you're trying to feed me, don't bother." I can survive until tomorrow when the snow is gone and we can find food again. I won't let Nicholas or Lilly or one of the other children go without just so I can have something. Those of us old enough to understand, ration everything, making sure the kids have enough to survive, splitting the rest between us. We take turns going without.

"It was mine," he says, tucking food into my hand. My stomach betrays my bravado, making the corner of his lips tug upward. "I saved it for you."

"But..." My protest fails as he pulls away into the main room and walks toward the fire, leaving me with the gift in the hall. I consider sneaking it to one of the children, but Jack sacrificed for me and I don't take that lightly.

I eat quickly and join the main room, taking a seat by Eliza who eyes me.

"Three," I whisper, drumming my fingers just once on my knee, making her suck in a breath. She nods, knowing it could be worse.

"So, did we find anything outside?" she asks, sliding a little one off her lap as the wave of children waddle over to sit by the fire on the far side of the room for the third part of their daily lessons.

"No, I think we all came back empty handed."

"I don't think Jack was too happy with you." She glances at him as he talks with some of the older boys. Eliza smiles when she turns back to face me and finds what she calls "my look."

"Do we have a plan yet?"

"Jack says Spring will be here tomorrow."

"Nicholas *says* Spring will be here tomorrow. Jack *knows* something is changing," she corrects.

"If he believes it, then so do I."

We shouldn't be questioning it at all—this is the way the seasons have always been. But the slight shifts have some of us uneasy. Little things are changing.

"And if it doesn't?" she questions.

"We'll find a way."

"Like Nes did?" Eliza is rarely bitter, her tone surprising me.

"Ladies," our heads snap up at the voice.

"How is he, Perrin?"

"Resting." Eliza hands him a lap blanket as he sits.

"I don't know how you tolerate it." Eliza glances at me as she shifts to be closer to her brother.

"Training." He closes his eyes. "How is it going in here?"

"They've settled down." She motions to the kids, "A little warning would have been nice."

Perrin mumbles an apology.

"How long until Nes is back up and running?" I ask.

"A bit. He'll learn quickly, but no more Winter until that heals up." Perrin's gaze shifts to where Nathaniel is walking in the door, carrying a bucket of snow. He pauses and nods for help.

When no one moves, I rush over. He doesn't wait when he sees me move and I follow him into the next room. Steadying the pot, I pause as Nathaniel transfers the snow to be melted.

"At least we aren't running out of drinking water." He grins for the first time today.

We step back, allowing the machine to work, cleaning and purifying the water.

"I think we should do a second batch." He steps back out of the room. I wait at the end of the hall for him as he steps out to retrieve a second bucket of snow. We repeat the process, depositing the snow into the heating machine.

"Hey," he stops me as I go to leave. "Next time...try these."

I catch a pair of gloves right before they hit me and raise an eyebrow.

"Theoretically, they will keep you warmer."

"*Theoretically?*"

"Fine. They work." He stalks out the door, frowning.

"Good to know."

"You want to tell me what happened out there today?" he asks without turning around.

"Not particularly." I stride behind him. "I was just out a little longer than I should have been."

"Your boyfriend seemed pretty worried." He glances at me.

"Wouldn't *you* be if *your* girlfriend were out longer than she should have been?" I reply, "I mean, just look at what happened to Nes."

"Nes got lost. You don't get lost."

"I could have."

"You didn't. I know it, Jack knows it, and you *certainly* know it. So why did you do it?"

I sigh. "Honestly, I wasn't sure if Spring was coming and I couldn't waste time. We're out of options, Nathaniel. We need food. Now."

"Yeah, I get that, but sending a bunch of us out there to retrieve your body wouldn't help that situation. We'd still have no food and one less person to help look for it. And who knows what could have happened to the search party, especially if things got worse."

"I've got it, *thanks*." Jacks easy voice fills the hallway.

He leans against the wall next to the door to the main room, casually folding a map. He puts it into his pocket as we approach. Nathaniel nods briefly as he walks by.

"I don't know why you let him bother you like that." I brush against him, leaning into his arm.

"I don't like the way he looks at you." The only time

I've ever seen Jack jealous was around Nathaniel. Funny enough, the two are friends.

"Well I'm not interested in him, so you can stop worrying."

"I know you're not...I still don't like it."

Before I can say anything, he adds, "We're going out early tomorrow, you want to come?"

"Yeah." Of course I do. I need to know if we'd been cursed to an eternal Winter like in the story Nathaniel once told the kids.

"Good, we're going out at dawn. We should get to sleep soon. If it's Spring, we'll have a long day ahead of us."

"Even longer if it's Winter," I mumble.

"We'll know soon..."

CHAPTER 2

Blue light greets me when I enter the hallway, dressed for Winter, but ready to peel off a few layers should Spring surprise me. The halls are quiet, all of the children still in bed.

"Ready?" Jack takes my hand, noticing the thick gloves I have on. "It will be Spring," he assures me.

We step up at the end of the hallway, the last stretch rising to the surface. I hold my breath as the guys open the door, blinding light filling the dark hallway.

When I let it out, I check to see if my breath crystallizes in the air, smoke filling the space. No white puff, no cold blast. Spring.

We all shed our outer layers, leaving them on the floor by the exterior door. The sun, miraculously, is up, beating brighter than normal for this time of day. Green replaces the brightness of snow and flowers push through the dirt.

"Two days," Jack whispers. Two days until Summer... two days until food.

"Spread out," Adam commands. He nods to one of the

younger boys to inform Eliza to take the children outside once they wake. In the limited warm weather we keep them outside as much as possible to soak up the sun to stay healthy. He darts off.

We split into teams, my group heading west, the sun at our backs. I feel it warming me through my jacket, creeping up my neck, making me shiver. Once we reach the perimeter, we split into further groups, fanning out.

"I'm sorry if I overstepped yesterday," Jack says when we're alone.

"You're concerned. I understand. I would do the same to you."

"*Would?*" he grins, making me giggle.

"Fine, I do. A lot." I slide my hand into his. "You disappear so much. I always worry you'll come back like Nes or Lewis."

"I wouldn't do that to you."

"I know...but still."

He reaches over and kisses my temple.

"Like it or not, you're stuck with me, Gen."

I sigh, drawing out the decision between the two options. "*Like*...I suppose."

He spins me around into his arms.

"Well, if you're so uncertain, allow me to convince you."

So slowly it's almost painful, he covers my lips with his, scorching my skin where his touch mine. His hand makes its way to my neck by way of my shoulder, trailing across it until he reaches my hair. Cradling my head, he pulls me closer and I wrap my arms around him. When I can't stand it any longer, I quicken our kiss and he responds by pulling me tightly to him.

As my hand tangles in his hair, he sighs against my lips, making me tighten my grip on his light locks. Jack pulls away and smiles at me, eyes locked on mine.

"I told you it would be okay." He grins, making me want to smack the look off his face...or kiss it off.

"I never should have doubted you."

His eyes flicker for a second as his lips tick up into a mischievous grin. "We have work to do."

"Fine." I pretend to sigh and roll my eyes, but they're already roaming over the earth, looking for any signs of food to take back to the bunker.

"We should split up...to *search* of course," he added before I can make a joke about finding a new boyfriend. Jack reaches out and squeezes my hand once. "One hour?"

"One hour," I agree and veer away from him.

Leaves are on the trees, buds just starting to appear. Tomorrow they will be ready to bloom into Summer. Adam and a few of the other leaders will be fishing and looking for other game. The scouts will be checking the terrain to make sure nothing has changed. The rest of us will search for food, but won't find much. The Summer days are best for collecting.

A bird sings somewhere, chipper enough to make me wonder if it somehow missed the devastation of Winter, though I don't know how that would be possible. The whistling moves as it flies from tree to tree.

An hour passes quickly, with nothing to yield for my efforts. The walk back is always longer than the walk out, but with Jack by my side, it goes quickly enough.

Outside the cavern, noise fills the air. I catch sight of Eliza and Perrin corralling the children.

"Genesis!" a young shriek demands my attention.

"Nicholas!" I yell back, swinging him onto my hip. He crashes into me. "You're awfully big for a six-year-old."

In truth, he's small, but he doesn't need to know that. I ruffle his dark hair and grin. "You're going to have to start holding *me* pretty soon."

"No." he grins.

"Yes." I nod, insisting it should happen.

I can't believe it's been two years since Nicholas arrived at the bunker. The years start merging together after awhile.

"Did you find anything?" Eliza asks as she approaches with Lilly on her heels. It would be interesting to see if Eliza could remember any question other than that one.

"Did you expect us to?" I ask playfully. She raises an

eyebrow at me, unwilling to scold my sarcasm in front of the children.

"Better luck tomorrow," Jack promises, patting Lilly on the head. "Are you having fun, sweetie?"

Lilly nods, tossing her blonde pigtails.

"Can I play with you tomorrow?" she asks.

"I have to go look for food tomorrow," he reminds her, crouching down to her level as she begins to sulk.

"But you *never* play with us outside." Tears threaten to burst like the rivers of water that *should* come from the melting snow when it switches to Spring but never actually happens as she pouts.

"I play when I get home," Jack counters, flicking her pigtail in hopes of making her giggle.

"For five minutes," she protests, arms crossed across her chest.

"You can either let Jack and Gen go look for food, Lilly, or you can starve to death while they play around for all of Spring," Eliza reminds her, a warning slipping into her voice as she continues to smile at the girl. "Do you want to die?"

"No," Lilly looks away, lips pursed.

"Do you want the rest of us to die?" Eliza continues, wanting to make her point.

"No," Lilly rolls her eyes dramatically.

"Then you get to play with Nicholas while the grown-ups are gone."

"They're not that grown up," Lilly mutters under her breath.

"Excuse me?" Eliza chides. Instead of backing down, Lilly gathers herself up and turns back to her caretaker.

"I said, they aren't that old."

"They are compared to *you*," Eliza's eyes spark a dark, twisted color. "Unless you'd like to start helping with the food preparation, young lady, I suggest you remember your age. Skinning a rabbit will make you think twice."

Lilly pales at the suggestion.

"Let's go play, Nicholas." She grabs the boy's hand and the two run off, Nicholas watching us over his shoulder.

"Well, that was pleasant," Jack comments.

"I didn't see *you* handling it, Jack," Eliza challenges. She's not usually one to take that tone with people. She must be just as worried as I am that Summer isn't going to last. Despite Jack's memory, the last Summer was so short, and Fall was so long. He called it a glitch, but it doesn't make sense except that things are changing.

"I had them out all day," Eliza backs off, realizing her sharpness was misplaced. Apologies have no place in our lives, and we certainly don't have time for them, even if they *did* matter. "I thought that maybe tomorrow, I could have them work on collecting things."

Starting the children with their training early is incredibly important. We teach them how to help each other survive in Winter and thrive in Summer.

The older they become, the more responsibilities they are given. Learning to collect things—even small things like flowers—is a step in the right direction.

"Great idea," I chime in. "Have you checked on Nes today?"

Eliza shakes her head.

"I've been out here all day. Perrin has been with him though. I'm sure he's already started teaching him how to work without his fingers."

"Are *you* okay, Eliza?"

"I will be." She nods before moving away to begin to gather the children and bring them back inside.

"She'll be okay. She'll help him," Jack gives me the most sincere look he can muster.

"We should check on them."

"We should."

Jack offers me his arm, leading me into the bunker. The immediate temperature difference prickles against my skin as I glance down. Someone had picked up our outerwear that we left on the floor and returned it to where it all belonged.

Blue dances along the walls as we make our way deeper into our home, footsteps echoing off of the concrete walls. The air is stale, but every once in a while you can catch the scent of the outdoors—*freedom*—as it hides in the corners and lurks in the shadows.

"Genesis, Jack," Adam nods to us as he steps around the corner, directly into our path. "With me."

Changing course, we veer to the right. We quickly catch up to Adam, nearly stepping on his feet to keep up as he moves quickly down the hall. Adam isn't particularly tall, but his gait is as wide as a giant's.

He darts into a room where Nathaniel and Perrin are already waiting. Jack and I take a position in the corner, angling ourselves so that we can lean against the wall and still engage in conversation.

Adam's wife, Kalley, sits in the corner, listening. She's always been a quiet one.

"We need to talk about Summer," Adam starts, "Last time, Summer didn't last for the full week. We have to prepare in case it gets cut short again."

"It was only by a day, Adam," Jack protests. "It was still enough time."

Across from each other, the two look like they could be mirror images. If Adam weren't sitting in the chair, he would be about the same height as Jack. They share similar blond hair and muscular but lean builds from years of hard work and lack of food. Even their personalities are similar, though that may have something to do with Adam mentoring Jack since we were children.

"But we can't be sure of that, Jack," Adam responds, rubbing his hand against his chin. "Things are changing here. We can't always assume that it will fall into the same patterns."

"This has happened before. It's in the record books," Nathaniel adds, trying to be helpful for once. "It goes in cycles. Things are stable for a long, long time, and then things start to change. If we don't adapt, we could die."

"They didn't all die before," Perrin reminds us, crossing his arms.

"And Perrin would know. He's the one who studied all of that," I fold my arms, mimicking Perrin's pose.

"The point is that we need to start strategizing," Adam redirects. "We need a solid plan for getting as much of this handled as possible, as quickly as possible."

"What are you proposing?" I ask.

The light flickers on the far side of the room. We have a limited amount of power in the bunker—just enough to keep a few lights on to see and run the water purifier. Flickering is not unusual.

"I think we need to get the younger ones involved. They're already putting it into practice. Maybe we give them an area near the bunker and have them do the work there."

"And what if something changes and they get lost? What if night comes early or the weather morphs without warning? Do we really have the manpower to handle protecting them should something happen when they're spread out like that? We certainly can't afford enough of *us* to watch them and Eliza can't monitor all of that land by herself."

Kalley looks up, knowing I didn't include her. Eliza spends more time with the children than anyone else, but Kalley bounces between helping outside and watching the children.

"It's one thing to have the kids in the yard under the supervision of one or two people, but to let them go out in the meadow and woods? I don't think that's wise." Jack backs me up.

"What else can we do?" Adam asks.

"What if we work longer hours?" Nathaniel proposes. "There are things we can do in the dark. We have flashlights and lanterns and the moon stays brighter in the summer.

"What if we just take turns doing night shifts and just rotate. That way no one is exhausted, but we all give up a little rest to gather more resources faster than we had before." I suggest.

"Not a bad idea," Adam rubs his chin again, processing the information.

"We can work out a schedule and each take a few extra hours every other night. We can gather in the dark without it being a problem." Jack looked around the room to see what the others thought.

"It's not like it's Winter, so it won't be cold. We can make this work," I announce.

"I'll see if Nes is up to working on a schedule for us," Perrin pushes off of his chair and heads toward the door. "He needs something to keep his mind occupied anyway."

"How is he, Perrin?" I call after him.

"He'll be okay, Genesis. He just needs a little time to adjust. Send Eliza to see him when you run into her, will you?"

I nod as he retreats through the door backward, still watching us. He gives a brief wave before ducking out.

"Don't even think about it," Jack warns me as I turn back to the group.

"I didn't say anything." I stare at him.

"You didn't have to," he grins at me. "We all know you were going to suggest starting this little plan tonight, but it's still Spring and nights are cool. We are not risking anyone not handling it well and becoming useless to us for Summer work."

"It doesn't have to be *everyone*," I object.

"Well it's not going to be you," Jack smirks at me.

"I'll go with you, Gen, if you want to go out tonight," Nathaniel smiles innocently at me.

"Have you guys seen Lilly?" a voice interrupts us from outside the door. Eliza hurriedly enters the room.

"No, why?" I respond, shifting away from the wall.

"I can't find her," Eliza looks worried. "I sent Azra to look for her, but neither of us can seem to locate her."

"She came in with the group, didn't she?"

"I saw her walk in, so she was definitely inside," Eliza lingers in the doorway like a scared deer. "Can you help us look?"

We all bolt toward the doorway, but I catch up with Eliza as she leads the way down the hall. She turns to talk quietly with me as we walk.

"Do you think she's outside?" I ask.

"I don't see how. She couldn't open those doors even if she tried. She's got to be in here somewhere."

"We'll find her, Eliza," Jack promises from a few feet behind us. "We should split up."

"I'll go check with Perrin and make sure she didn't slip into medical," Nathaniel announces, peeling off from the group.

"I'll take the supply room," Adam slows his pace as we near the hallway he will need to take, "Eliza, why don't you go check in the main room again and make sure she didn't find her way back to the group. Check in with Azra too."

"Gen, why don't you take the boiler room? I'll go down to the basement," Jack suggests. I nod as he backpedals and retreats back the way we came.

"Oh, Eliza, Perrin wants to see you when we're done with this. No rush, though."

"Okay," she says absent mindedly as she jogs toward the main room. I stop short, turning into the boiler room.

"Lilly?" I call. Only the clinking of the machine answers me. "Lilly, are you in here?"

Clink, clink. Clink.

I duck under a large pipe from the machine, checking to make sure she hadn't curled up for a nap under the warm machinery. We would need to gather more wood for burning during Summer too, I noted.

"Lilly, you're not in trouble, you can come out."

I knew she wasn't in the room, but I make the effort to check anyway. Once I have swept the space, I move toward the main room, hoping someone had found her.

"Gen!" Nicholas shouts. "Lilly is missing."

"I know, bud, but we'll find her. Can you do me a favor though and keep the other kids entertained? Eliza doesn't have time to help watch them right now."

The boy nods, running off to sit on the outside of a group of children who are entertaining themselves perfectly fine without the quiet boy.

"She's not with Perrin." Nathaniel sneaks up behind me, making me jump.

"She's not in the boiler room," I respond with my own update. "Or the storage room. I checked there too.

"I'm going to go help Jack downstairs. You should check the records room."

"On it," he announces as he spins on his heels toward the door.

"Eliza," I raise my voice enough for her to hear me.

"Boiler, storage, medical all clear. I sent Nathaniel to records and I'm going to help Jack. You coordinate when the others come back."

"Azra just went to records," Eliza calls to me.

"Oops," I shrug. Nathaniel will either help her or pick a different space to search, so it doesn't really matter. "Maybe take a post in the hall and direct?"

Eliza nods, waving me off as she makes her way to where I was standing. I turn and head toward the staircase.

My steps sound hollow as I crash down the stairs quickly, taking them two at a time. I drag my hand along the wall for balance, but with nothing to grab on to, if I trip, I won't be able to spare myself a significant amount of bruises.

The door flies open harder than I meant when I pushed it. It crashes into the wall making Jack jump as high as the water in the river over the rocks in the waterfall in Spring right after the snow melts.

"High-strung much?" I tip my head playfully before squinting my eyes. "What are you doing?"

Jack is along the wall, hidden behind a counter unit sitting out from the wall oddly. He drops something from his hand, kicking it with his foot to hide it. My brow furrows as I approach him and I consciously remind myself not to scowl.

I've learned not to push when he's being secretive

about things. I usually found out within a few hours, but on his terms. It's usually something sweet from my boyfriend.

"I was just going through some things to make sure she didn't get herself locked in while she was playing." He shrugs casually. "I'm almost done though. What are you doing?"

"I came to help."

He gives me his best let-your-boyfriend-handle-this look.

"I've got it," he says quickly, turning me toward the door before pausing. "Well, actually. The only thing I didn't check yet was that corner. If you want to go over there, I'll go check the safe room and then meet you back with the group."

The corners of his eyes are tight, but there's an easy smile on his face. Jack shoves his hands in his pockets, shoulder raised just slightly higher than they normally sit in this position. Something feels off, but it could just be because he's worried about Lilly. I am too.

"Okay," I finally agree, releasing him. He grins and leans in for a quick kiss before taking off to the door. His steps slap behind him as he bolts up the stairs.

Gifts aren't something we can easily give in the bunker, but Jack has always showered me with the present of doing things so I won't have to. He's done it even since before we started dating. In fact, Jack has taken care of me since the moment I arrived at the bunker all those years ago. It's sweet the way he looks after me. It's even more attractive when he takes on tasks for the others too—something he is acutely aware of.

The back corner is cluttered with pieces of broken furniture and equipment. There's no way Lilly wedged herself in there, but I search anyway.

The basement is cooler than the rest of the bunker. Even during Summer, it stays cool. We occasionally bring the kids down if it gets too terribly hot, corralling them near the door so they don't get hurt on anything, but we force them to stay outside as long as possible in the few short days of warmth that we get.

I trip over a metal iron, rusted over from years of neglect. It scrapes off on my boot leaving orange flecks on the toe of my footwear. I growl in annoyance.

"Graceful," Nathaniel smirks at me.

"Yes, well we can't all have Jack's reflexes," I retort as I turn to face the door.

Azra laughs sarcastically next to Nathaniel, elbowing him. She's always been a fan of pitting Nathaniel and Jack against each other.

Before Nathaniel can roll his eyes, noise across the room makes us all turn.

CHAPTER 3

My hair slaps me in the face as I turn to face the wall. I'd blame a rat in the wall, but the bunker was free of pests and had been for as long as I'd been there.

A second noise—a scuffling sound—prompts us into action. Azra reaches the area first, glancing around to locate the now-quiet source. I nearly collide with Nathaniel, misjudging the distance between us.

We move items around, searching for the source of the disruption.

"Guys," Jack says a moment later from the doorway, interrupting our search. "I found her."

Lilly sits on his hip, arms wrapped around his neck as he holds her. She buries her head in his neck shyly.

"Lilly, thank goodness," I exclaim. "Where have you been?"

"I found her in the safe room. She must have worked her way in and then she fell asleep, didn't you?" He turned to her, bouncing her on his hip to try to make her giggle. When she finally looks up, he winks at her, succeeding in his mission to make her laugh.

"Come on, let's take her back upstairs." Jack nods to the stairs he is standing on, flipping his light hair out of his eyes.

"Something moved over here, Jack," Azra protests.

"Moved?" Jack repeats, stepping into the room. Realizing he's still holding Lilly, he changes his mind and steps back, protectively wrapping his free arms around her waist. "What do you mean?"

"There was a crashing noise and then it sounded like something was moving."

"That's strange. There's nothing down here." He frowns. "Nathaniel, are you messing with them?"

"I was standing right next to them," Nathaniel grumbles, glaring at Jack from across the room.

"When was the last time that you heard it?" Jack asks icily.

"Whatever it was, I doubt it's still here," I jump in, hoping to downgrade the impending storm between the men. For being friends, they sure fight a lot. "Let's take Lilly back."

At the sound of her name, she ducks into Jack's shoulder again, hiding her face. I rub her back as we walk up the stairs so that she knows we aren't upset.

"Oh, come on, Lilly, it's not that bad," Jack sings,

trying to get her to stop sulking. "Consider it an adventure. You like adventures, don't you?"

She nods against his shoulder.

"So pretend you are a Springtime Fairy like in that book Eliza reads to you. You ventured out into the somewhat-unknown in search of a magical treasure to save your fairy friends.

"But the evil Snow Monster was lurking," he drops his voice low to add to the drama, "and cast a spell on you, making you sleep so that you could not save your friends.

"Just in time," Jack lurches forward, making Lilly's eyes go wide before she giggles, "the brave Ice King found you, pulling you into the safety of his arms as he carried you back to the fairy forest. He dropped you in the middle of a Summer garden, your fairy friends rushing around you to welcome you home after your brave journey."

He spins her around, stopping in the middle of the hallway. Azra yelps, narrowly avoiding colliding into him. She grumbles as she skirts the pair.

"Now, Springtime Fairy, it's time to put you back in the garden. Let's go."

Jack has always been so sweet with the children. I've seen him sneak his food to them before when he thinks no one else is looking. I worry about him when we're short on food and I see him giving so much of his away quietly. I don't know how he stays as fit as he does. He should be skin and bones by now.

"We found her," Jack bellows as he saunters into the main room. He grabs her hands in his, pulling her away so that her feet kick out in a large arch over the other children's heads before lowering her to the ground.

Lilly skips over to the fire that has been started up for the evening to keep the room warm. She babbles to the others, telling them Jack's silly story with a few of her own improvements.

"Where was she?" Adam asks, joining us from where he had been talking to Eliza just inside the door.

"She got into the safe room and fell asleep," Jack laughs it off. "She was a little spacey when I woke her up, but she's doing fine."

"Well, at least that's one problem solved."

"Two," Jack grins. "We have a plan for our Summer work too. We'll be fine. In the meantime, we should probably get these children fed."

I WATCH Jack slip out of the room, quietly picking his way around sleeping bodies. Some nights I would follow him and we'd sit in the hallway or storage room and talk or play games. Tonight I don't. I know he needs space sometimes.

Instead, I roll over to face Eliza. Azra and a few of the girls were sleeping in the main room with the children tonight, leaving my friend to get some uninterrupted sleep. She's sleeping quietly on the floor under her blanket.

Knowing it will be awhile before my brain decides it's tired enough to sleep, I kick my blanket off and silently make my way around several dozen sleeping teenagers. To be fair, some of them were older, but anyone over thirteen was given the responsibilities of an adult, and we just count everyone as part of the same group.

Adam snores loudly as I walk by, starting at the sound he was making. He jerks forward, nearly waking up, but quickly settles again, rolling over on his side. I bite my lip to keep from laughing.

Once in the hall, I pause to decide where to go. Everything in me pulls me toward the door. I pad down the hallway, grabbing a coat to throw around my shoulders should the night air be chilled.

The door creaks quietly as I open it, slowly letting in the moonlight. The pale reflection glints off the concrete walls of the tunnel. My lungs practically jump outside of me at the first sniff of fresh air and I calm their efforts to vacate my body by lowering myself along the doorframe, one leg inside the bunker, one out.

When the door swings shut on me, I reach over and wedge a rock under it, forcing it into place. The trees, now fuller with leaves, sway in the soft breeze. I watch the landscape shift under the movements of the shadows from the clouds. Everything is an illusion in our little snow globe of a world.

A shadow catches my eye, gliding across the flat plane outside of the bunker.

Jack?

He's wearing dark clothing, making it hard to see, but it's definitely him. The moon glints off his pale hair, making me sure it's my boyfriend.

Jack disappears behind the gentle slope of a hill.

Do I follow him? We specifically said we wouldn't go out foraging tonight.

"Can't sleep?" Nes asks, taking a seat next to me on the ground. He rests his bandaged hand in his lap as he folds his legs under him.

"How are you feeling?" I ask, no longer worried about going after Jack. This is too important.

"Okay," he says sadly.

"What happened out there?"

"I don't know, Gen," he looks at me earnestly. "It was the strangest thing. It was like the earth shifted. I should have been able to find my way back, but the snow kicked up and everything iced over. I've never seen anything like it, Gen."

He looks away, gaze following the darkness into the tunnel.

"Coming back should have been easy," he murmurs.

"Things happen. You can't beat yourself up over it."

"It was like the snow sucked me in," he swings his gaze back to me. "Like it swallowed me whole… Like it was possessed by the desire to destroy me. I'm not sure how they pulled me out. When they found me, I was covered almost completely in a snow bank. Todd and Kris had to carry me back. I barely remember any of it."

"At least they found you," I added, pulling him away from his traumatized state. "It could have been worse."

"It could have," he agreed.

"How is Eliza doing with all of this?"

Something snaps near the meadow. We both watch for signs of an oncoming animal. Whether it's a predator or something we could use for food, it would be a good idea to take it down if it comes into the opening.

The tall grass sways, but the animal never approaches.

"She's fine," Nes says when we relax back against the doorframe.

"She was pretty upset," I mention.

"When is Eliza *not* upset over things like this?" he jokes, finally smiling a little. "Anyway, she'll be fine. *We'll* be fine."

"I'm glad you have such a good attitude over this, Nes."

"Worried I'd end up like Lewis?" he gives me a look.

"Maybe a little. You've seen what this place can do to us."

"There has got to be a better way to live," Nes says quietly. "We're trapped and all we can do is survive."

"At least we *are* surviving."

"Barely," he holds my gaze a little too long, as if trying to prompt me to start another conversation. I feel like I'm missing something.

"You heard we have a plan for Summer?" I ask, trying my best to read his mind. I clearly failed.

"Yeah, Perrin told me tonight," he sighs. "It's a solid plan. Wish I could help."

"You'll be ready to help by next Summer," I assure him, nudging his foot.

We stare out at the silvery grass, dancing under the stars that dart in and out of the passing clouds. The quiet hum of the blades moving on the breeze is all we can hear.

After awhile, Nes turns back to me. He catches me yawning.

"Ready to go back?"

"Apparently," I laugh.

Extending a hand down to him, I pull him up by his good arm. We walk inside, securing the door behind us.

I wait for Nes to settle back down on the guys' side of the room in his new spot next to Perrin before I find my way back to my blanket. I shouldn't have abandoned it for so long—it's cold as I slip under it. I shift toward Eliza, drawing on her heat to warm me up. It was cooler outside than I realized.

Sleep quietly creeps in, tightening its hold around my body like ice over the river in the middle of the night before the switch to Winter.

"Here, look," Jack says, pointing to the ground. "Look at this."

"What did you find?" one of the boys asks.

"The plants are starting to grow. We should be able to start harvesting those tomorrow.

"And at least we have *these* until then," Kris comments, holding out some of the small game we had caught earlier in the day.

"Speaking of which," Jack takes command. "Why don't you take those back to the bunker, Kris. They can start cooking while we finish up."

Kris nods. Several of the older guys follow him, carrying tonight's dinner with them. Jack turns back to the group.

I wander a few feet away as he shows the kids what to look for. This morning, we had all agreed to let the twelve-year-olds help in the search for food this time, but that also meant we had to teach them. Jack and I spent the better part of the day educating them on what to look for. The plan was to send them with the kids that were newer to gathering and have them work as a team, that way we didn't lose our valuable hunters to babysitting.

The kids watch him with rapt attention. Their eyes follow his every move. Jack notices too and starts adding some dramatic flare to his lessons. If there were any snow on the ground, he might have picked it up and thrown it in the air as if he were sprinkling fairy dust from that story he told Lilly.

Overnight, the flowers had blossomed on every tree and bush. The bees rushed around, pollinating them. I eye one as it buzzes too close to me.

The sun peeks through a tree, temporarily blinding me as the light hits my eyes. I blink as green fills my vision.

"The temperature is rising," Azra says, sidling up next to me. "And I don't just mean your man."

I pretend to glare at her but fail miserably.

"That's because it's almost Summer," I remind her.

"Thank goodness for that," Azra peels off her long sleeve shirt, leaving her blue tee shirt in place. "I need to work on my tan."

"You're the only one of us *with* a tan, Azra."

"I can't help it that I was born this way," she teases.

"The point is we have work to do tomorrow. Are you on first shift?"

"Yeah. You?"

"Yes, ma'am. I guess we get to go out together." She pauses for a moment, planning ahead. "We should make a plan. I have to head down to the river anyway, why don't you come along?"

"Sure, I'm not doing much here anyway. Let me tell Jack."

He looks up as I approach him, his eyes sparkling in the sunlight as it hits him through the trees. Unlike me, he never blinks at the light.

"Hey, beautiful." His grin takes over his entire face.

"Azra and I are headed down to the river. You okay here?"

Jack pulls me into his arms, wrapping his fingers around my back. I try not to giggle when his hair sweeps across my forehead as he leans into me.

"I will die a slow and painful death if you walk away from me right now," he teases. "These flowers will grow over my grave as my ice-covered heart stops beating the moment you leave. If you go, you are ending me right here and now."

"You're going to wilt away and leave the kids here to learn how to gather supplies on their own?" I look at him skeptically.

"Fine," he replies dramatically, rolling his eyes. "I'll

get them back to the bunker and then I'll collapse outside of the door and you'll find my cold, dead body waiting for you. You'll spend all of Summer and Fall crying before you buck up and handle Winter."

"Eh, maybe just Summer," I shrug, "I like the Fall leaves and I'd hate to miss them."

"You'd pick leaves over me?" I have to bite down on my tongue to keep from giggling over his mock disdain. He spins me out of his arms. "Be gone, woman. You're too much of an Ice Queen for me. I need to find someone with a warmer heart."

"I hear Shanna is looking," I suggest with a deadpan face.

His face goes slack. Jack waits to see if I'll crack first, but when I don't, he launches himself at me. I turn just before he collides, his chest slamming into my back. Jack lifts me off the ground, spinning me in a circle as several of the young girls giggle at our antics.

He kisses my cheek before releasing me, giving me a shove.

"I want you back at the bunker in one hour," he shouts, grinning at me while pretending to parent us.

"Yes, boss," Azra pretends to hiss at him. Then she adds slyly, "I'll have her back by midnight. Gotta go!"

Azra grabs my hand, pulling me away quickly as we laugh. Jack shouts about returning in one hour in the background as we walk away.

Along the way, we plan a few places to focus on during our evening work. The forest is a great place to find food, but it would be easier to get lost at night. The meadow would likely be a good choice for finding grains to make bread. A number of berry bushes grow on the outskirts of the area that we plan to visit as well.

"I saw you and Jack go out last night," Azra mentions as we step over a stone wall that is so low that we don't know its purpose. "Have fun?"

"We did go out, but not together. I'm not sure where he went. I saw him skulking out into the night, so I'm assuming he went to do a little scouting before we put the Summer mission into play."

She nods, accepting it. Jack was known for being incredibly responsible with everyone else, but willing to take big risks when it came to doing things himself.

"I ended up talking to Nes."

"Oh? How is he handling things?" She eyes me from the side, willing me to say he's okay.

"Much better than I expected."

"Thank goodness, I couldn't handle that again."

The rush of water from the river gushes in the distance. Usually, we can't hear it from this far away, but in the complete stillness of late afternoon, nothing is muffling it.

"We should probably bring some fish back while we're here," Azra adds.

"Isn't that why we were coming anyway?"

"Well, honestly, I thought the cattails might be ready. We could definitely use more of those."

"Good thinking. That will be easy to carry back too. If you want to handle the fishing, I can start collecting the cattails, assuming they're ready."

Over the years, we've started storing up things like cattails for later use. Cattails are especially helpful because there's not much that goes unused.

"Does that sound weird to you?" Azra halts quickly, her hair swinging in front of her. "That sounds weird, right?"

The closer we walk to the river, the louder it becomes. I had thought it was because it was quiet out and the sound had carried, but she's right—something is different.

We look at each other before sprinting ahead, wanting to see whatever we would be facing quickly. I lean forward as I climb up the hill, stabilizing myself on the incline. Azra is quicker than I am as she darts up over the grassy slope.

"Just go," I call, freeing her to run faster. She darts across the hill and disappears over the side.

I skid down the far side of the hill, feet nearly catching over the tall weeds at the bottom. I push off at the last second, launching myself into the air as I hurdle over the obstacle in my path.

"Genesis," Azra's voice carries to me over the crashing sound of the river.

This is bad.

CHAPTER 4

Water gushes over the natural sides of the river, cascading onto the grassy shore. To the left, water shoots over a rock, creating a waterfall showering into the already rough waters of the river. The edges of the water calm slightly, lapping on the grass by our feet. Cattails jerk back and forth as the water pushes them down, looking like drowning men.

"What in the world?" I breathe.

"This is going to be problematic."

We both gasp as the water spurts higher over the rock near the waterfall. The motion translates into wet shoes for us as the water splashes further onto the land to accommodate the extra rush of water.

"We have to find out what is causing this," I say scrambling toward the ledge that leads to the rock on this side of the waterfall. Azra swings wide, preparing to climb a tree for a better view.

I scramble up the wall of rocks to the top of the precipice, hands slipping each time I touch a wet rock. When I finally reach the top, I find that the main waterfall has expanded to twice its size, gushing down to the pools before the small drop that leads into the lower half of the river. The rush is so strong, it could easily knock me off of the wall next to it. I shuffle away, careful not to slip on the dripping rocks.

The spray from the falls hits me in the face, stinging like a million bees against my skin. I can't see what is causing the flow.

"Can you see?" I yell, twisting back to find Azra in the trees.

"No! I have no idea what it is!" she yells back before scrambling higher into the branches. "It doesn't look like it's blocked."

When she returns to the ground, I join her.

"Whatever it is, we have to stop it. If it floods out the end of the river, we won't have anything to forage tomorrow."

"What do you want to do?" Azra grimaces as she notices my hair plastered against my face from the spray of the falls. My entire outfit is soaked.

"We need to get help. You're faster, just run and I'll catch up."

So much for collecting cattails.

We rush away from the river, back the way we came. I scale the hill, quickly glaring at it as I force myself up its slope. Azra pulls ahead once on the top of the hill and bounces down the side. By the time I reach the bottom, she's got a strong lead. I slow, knowing she'll reach the others before me—an effort to conserve my energy. If something is blocking the river causing the extreme amounts of water down this path, I'll need my strength to help clear it.

When I can no longer hear the river's rage, I slow. My clothes are sticking to me, making an annoying sucking sound each time I take a step. I pull my shirt away from my chest, leaving my skin feeling suddenly cold. I try to wring myself out as best as I can.

After a few minutes, Jack appears over the horizon.

"Where's Azra?" I ask.

"I sent her to the bunker for reinforcements. What's going on?" Jack's brow furrows. I turn, falling into step beside him.

"The river is running over. We climbed the waterfalls to see if there was something obscuring the water's path but we couldn't see anything. Azra even climbed up in the tree to check."

"And you...went for a swim?" Jack questions, taking in my appearance.

"I climbed the ledge. *That's* how bad the spray was."

"Wow, seriously? I was waiting for you to tell me you fell in. If Lilly could see you now, she'd be convinced you turn into a mermaid every time you come out here and have been hiding it from her."

"It's not that bad," I protest. Maybe it *was*.

"Here," Jack lifts the bag off of his shoulders and rummages inside. "Put this on."

He hands me a light jacket. I wrap it around my shoulders, knowing it wouldn't help.

"You ready?" he asks, lowering his stance to run.

I nod and we take off toward the river. I'm running so hard that I don't even hear the rush of water as we approach. Jack grabs my hand as we advance on the hill, pulling me up one side and holding me so that I don't slip down the other. We come to a crashing halt at the water's edge.

Nothing.

Everything is calm and peaceful.

The water has calmed down, quietly flowing along its banks, the only evidence of its breech is the mud resting on the grass. A bird flies overhead, chirping as if nothing were out of the ordinary.

"I don't understand," Jack turns to me.

"I..."

The mud doesn't even reach where I had been standing before, as if it had all dried in the twenty minutes since I had left. Even the mud along the edges seemed partially dried.

"Jack, the water was up to *here.*" I point to the ground where we were standing. A sudden thought hit me. "*It dried faster than I* did. How is this possible?"

When I glance at Jack, he's holding his face very even,

not showing any emotion. I expected confusion. *I* was confused.

"You might be right about the patterns changing, Gen," he finally offers. "We're going to have to prepare in case Summer really *is* short."

A nervous look creeps onto his face as his jaw tightens. The optimist is beginning to worry. He turns, surveying the river.

"Show me," he directs.

I guide him to where we had observed the flood, describing what Azra and I saw. He nods, asking questions when needed. I watch as my boyfriend kneels to the ground, touching the drying mud with his fingers.

"This is definitely not normal."

"What's happening?" Nathaniel yells, slowing to a walk just steps from us. The rest of the group crests the hill. He frowns. "This does not look like a flood."

"It stopped." My eyes sweep back to the gentle waters. "And it dried up."

"What in the name of Springtime is this?" Azra yelps, bounding up to us. She looks shocked.

"I think it's safe to say," Jack addresses the group, "that things are changing. Genesis and Azra saw a flood here."

He motions to my still-drying clothing.

"But when we returned, we found this." I nod to the calm water. "The water was up to here and then it dried before we returned. It's only been twenty minutes."

"It was an insane amount of water," Azra adds.

"Which suggests that we're right and the cycle is changing," Jack concludes. "We don't know what this means for us, but we have to be prepared in case Summer doesn't last."

"Or if it doesn't come at all," Nathaniel adds quietly.

"It will," Jack says icily—a warning. "Summer will arrive."

Azra makes eye contact with me. We both know what this means.

"There's nothing more to see here. Adam will be anxious to hear about this. Let's go back to the bunker," Jack instructs, turning the group around.

"You okay?" he asks quietly as he wraps an arm around me, not minding my damp hair.

"It's just so strange, Jack. How does something like that happen? It's not like the temperature particularly picked up. We still have a few hours to go before it switches over to Summer, so it's not like it escalated. This just doesn't make sense."

Jack looks like he's trying to puzzle it all out. In a world where things were fairly dependable, this was anything but. As someone who relies on things being dependable, this is throwing Jack.

"Sometimes there's just no explanation for this kind of thing. I mean, we can't exactly control the weather, Gen. If we could, it would be Summer year round and we'd have plenty of food and wouldn't have to live in a bunker all the time."

"You just want to live under the stars, don't you, Jack?" I tease, bumping into him with my shoulder.

"It wouldn't be so bad, would it?" he asks.

"It would when it rains." I bat my eyelashes at him.

"Well, we don't have to be outside *all* of the time. Just out of that bunker."

"I know, you like your space. You and your secrets."

"I do. Far too many people poking their noses into your business in that place."

"And yet here you are, one of the leaders of *that place*."

"Someone has to do it." He points out a rock ahead of me so that I don't trip.

"Well, you do it wonderfully, Jack. Everyone adores you and you work so hard for them. Speaking of," I pause. "Where did you run off to last night?"

"Hmm?"

"I saw you sneaking off last night while I was sitting outside the bunker."

"I didn't see you leave," he frowns.

"I left after you. I went and sat outside the tunnel because I couldn't sleep. I saw you wandering off after you told *me* not to run missions early. I ended up chatting with Nes though, so it's fine."

"Oh, that. Well, you know me, lots of secrets," he playfully refuses to tell me. He winks flirtatiously at me.

"Fine, I'll find out sooner or later though."

I'd just have to be careful about getting the information out of him without him realizing it.

I SHUDDER as the sun radiates against my back. The warmth feels incredible and I linger in it before bending down to set my basket in the collection zone.

Our meeting with Adam when we had returned from the river had resulted in the entire team planning to give up sleep for as long as possible without dropping from exhaustion. We left early this morning to do as much work as possible before the sun sets and we pause just long enough to eat enough to keep us going.

One of the younger teens rushes into the collection area, clearly out of breath. He bends down to scoop up the load of supplies I had just delivered.

"Hi, Gen," he pants, turning on his heels. "Bye, Gen!"

"Slow down a little, Kai, we don't want you to collapse."

"Too much work to do, Gen," he calls. "But if you really want to stop my suffering, I'd rather be out there with you guys."

"Soon enough, kid," I yell back, but he's likely already out of earshot.

In the distance, I see another younger teen running

toward the collection area, a never-ending chain of worker ants delivering supplies back to the bunker so that we don't have to waste precious time moving it ourselves.

"How's it going, Genesis?" Perrin casually walks up to me.

"Good, I found those things you needed. Kai just took them back to the bunker."

"Ahh, beautiful. Thank you for your help."

"No problem. Anything else I should keep my eye out for?" I ask, brushing the dirt off my hands from where I had to dig up a specific type of root for one of Perrin's treatments. It amazes me what he's learning to do for us over in medical.

"Just more of the same, if you come across it, thanks," he smiles at me. "Listen, if you're done, Jack wants to see you. He's in Section Twelve."

"Thanks, I'll head over. Are you going back in?"

"I have a few more things to collect," he slides his bag off his shoulder as the teen reaches us. "This is delicate. Please put it directly in my office on the main table and try not to jostle it too much. Thanks, Zach."

Zach mumbles a response before slinging the pack over his shoulder and taking off toward the bunker.

"Did I *not* just tell him be gentle with that?" Perrin sighs.

"That *is* gentle for a thirteen-year-old boy, Perrin. Oh

wait, I forgot, you've always acted like you were forty-seven. My mistake, you wouldn't know."

"Ha, ha. Very funny, Genesis. See if I wrap your bleeding hand the next time you walk in after taking your glove off and cutting it on ice outside."

"Jack will help me," I counter, smirking at him.

"Ordinarily, I'd point out that boyfriends are the worst ones to trust when it comes to handling injuries, but he's the only one I *do* trust around here to get something like that right." Perrin laughs. "Better get going. He's waiting."

I hurry back toward the woods, branching off at certain markers to reach the correct location. We had thought ages ago to mark off the woods into sections so we could locate each other easier, especially in case someone gets lost in the winter.

"Hey, babe," Jack looks up as I approach. "I'm going to need a hand."

He's bent over something on the ground, fiddling with it as I walk over.

"It's not going to bite me, is it?" I ask cautiously.

"I hope not," Jack says seriously, making me panic long enough for my foot to return to the earth with my next step.

"What are you doing?"

"Hold this," he ignores me, handing me a rope. I take it from him.

He stands up, leaving his circular contraption where it

rests on the ground. Jack leans back, on his heel, shifting his weight to one hip as he crosses his arms smugly.

"Pull that," he instructs. When I don't move, he emphasizes his words with a sharp nod in the direction I should be tugging on the rope.

My eyes follow the length of the rope to where it's tied around a rock several yards away. I give an exaggerated sigh as he freezes, refusing to balk until I cooperate.

Leaning back, I pull on the rope until it becomes taut between my arms and the rock. No matter how hard I pull on it, the rock doesn't move.

"Is there a point to this other than seeing how strong your girlfriend is?" I ask, still jerking on the rope.

"Watch," he says, untangling the rope from my hands.

He maneuvers himself into the same position I had been in and strains against the rope.

"It's not moving, right?"

"Right," I reply cautiously.

"Now, watch this," he says, dropping the rope to the ground. He turns his attention back to the circular device he had been playing with when I walked up.

A second rope is attached, wrapped around part of the device. It too stretches to the rock. Jack grins as he cranks a lever on the side of the device that looks like a tiny version of a Ferris wheel from one of the books in the bunker.

Slowly, the rope tightens. Then, with each turn of the

handle, it begins to inch the rock away from its resting place, doing the work we could not.

"It's the leverage, you see," Jack explains. "I have a plan."

"To pull rocks over?" I ask, amused.

"No, girlfriend, not to pull rocks over. It's for the bunker."

"You're going to pull the bunker over?" I gasp, feigning shock.

Jack steps aside so that I can test the device. I turn the handle, moving the rock bit by bit, not nearly exerting as much effort as before when I couldn't move the rock at all.

"You're in rare form today, Genesis. Apparently someone isn't worried about Winter coming soon."

"I thought we had a week of Summer, *insistent one*," I challenge as the rock tips at an unnatural angle.

"We do, but not long after that comes the snow."

I mimic his earlier pose, shifting my weight to one foot so my body is leaning away from him as I cross my arms.

"And just how do you propose to use this rock removal machine this Winter?" I forget to hide the flirtation in my voice and over emphasize my words. He responds by leaning in and grinning. I might have to evade him if he tries to distract me with his arms around my waist.

"It's not a rock removal device, Gen," he grins wickedly but stays in place. "It's a snow removal device."

I open my mouth to ask how he aims to tie a rope to snow but he cuts me off, waving his hand in the air.

"Not like that," he replies, knowing where the conversation was going. He always *could* read me like a book. "It's for the bunker exit outside the tunnel. It's hard enough getting out when there's only an inch or two of snow, but when there is a lot....that lean-to isn't doing the job, Gen. But *this* will.

"Follow along, Genesis, my girl," he grins wider, turning as if painting a picture before us with his hands. "Let's pretend we're in the tunnel of the bunker here. Right in front of us is the door.

"Now, we already have the lean-to that we put out in winter. That keeps the door from getting blocked, but it only helps for a foot or so. After that, we're still faced with whatever amount of snow has fallen overnight or during the day. We can scale the snow bank and climb out in some cases, but let's be honest here...some days it's hard to even get the door open in the first place, despite the lean-to."

He acts out trying to force the tunnel door open, going as far as to pretend to slam his shoulder into the imaginary door and bouncing off of it. I catch him in my arms.

"My hero," he leers at me before closing his eyes and

puckering his lips for a kiss. I roll my eyes and kiss him, barely pulling away before he springs back into action, pushing out of my arms.

"But this little beauty could change all that. We have all that extra netting we made for the crops from awhile back," he says, referring to the material we made out of cattail leaves a few months ago to cover our crops in the cooler seasons to help protect them a bit. "We need to take one of the long ones—we can stitch two together if we need to— and run it from the top of the door over the lean-to out as far as it will go."

I hesitate, wondering where he's going with this but he doesn't notice as he runs several feet away.

"Now, obviously this isn't to scale, so don't judge by the distance here, Genesis, but let's pretend I'm as far away as the netting goes." He turns, motioning to either side of him. "If we put two poles up, one here and one here, we can then run a rope from the bunker, to the poles, and then to the edge of the netting by the door.

"I understand this will take a bit of work, but stay with me here." Jack becomes increasingly animated as he talks. "What we will do is have the netting up against the top of the door. We'll leave the lean-to there in case the netting fails, but every hour or so, we'll need four of us to go to the tunnel door and work the machine."

"That's a lot of people to go every hour, Jack."

"You'll see why in a minute," he ignores my protest,

pointing to his invention. "If we attach two of these devices on the walls inside the tunnel, we can let the ropes rest over the door when it's closed. And yes, before you point out that the door might not shut, I've already thought of that and have a plan. Even if mine fails, you know Nathaniel will come up with something."

If Jack was going to let Nathaniel take some credit in getting this to work, Jack must be really serious about this plan.

"So, we attach two of these to the inside walls, one on either side. Once we open the door, two of us will turn the cranks and because the ropes are run first to the poles, then back to the top of the netting, it should start to pull the netting away from the bunker, until it reaches the poles. If we do it right, minimal snow will fall into the path and we should have a nice walk way.

"Obviously," he continues, running back toward me only to start to walk backward, hands high in the air as he demonstrates where the netting will move, "we'll need to move it all the way to the poles and keep the ropes taut or it could collapse and then we'd have to set it back manually, which might mean digging part of it out.

"This is where the third and fourth person comes in, because I already know you're about to ask how we get it back."

"I was," I affirm.

"We're going to attach two other ropes. These will run

through loops above our heads on the outside of the tunnel door. Once the netting has reached the poles at the far end, the third and fourth person will pull in the ropes, bringing the now-much-lighter-due-to-lack-of-snow netting back toward the bunker, eventually coming to rest above the lean-to. We'll tie it off and be good to go."

"Leaving us with a clear path," I pick up, "more room to function, and a better chance of not getting trapped inside by the heavy snow. It's brilliant, Jack. I don't know how you come up with these things."

"As long as we take care of it every hour or two when the snow gets bad, we're going to save ourselves a lot of work and get rid of the risk of being trapped inside for days."

"We certainly don't need a repeat of those couple of times," I agree.

"Which brings me to the reason you're here," Jack says, "I need you to find my flaws and fix them."

"You talk too much," I instantly reply. "Your hair is too shiny. And for the sake of the entire snow globe, you need to stop that electrical spark that shoots from your eyes every single time you look at someone. And the dimple— that's got to go."

Jack stares at me for a moment, shocked that I was so quick to reply, before breaking into his perfect laugh.

"Thanks, Genesis. I will try to be less pretty for you,"

he shakes his head, giving me a *you're-crazy* look. "How about we focus on shredding apart the soul of the snow removal machine and rip apart *those* flaws so we don't hit any snags along the way."

"How are you planning to handle the netting?" I ask, walking around the device thoughtfully.

"I was just going to use them?" he responded as if it was a question. He always did that when second-guessing himself.

"What if we add a pole to the top part near the bunker. That way it won't sag should people not move their sides at the same speed when moving it in or out."

"That's good. What else?" Jack asks, falling into step behind me as we walk in circles around the machine on the ground.

We've always worked out thought-intensive problems while in motion. The movement helps us to think, even if it's just pacing.

Together, we work out a few improvements and gather up some supplies we need to make the real version of his cranks. If we have Eliza take a look at the netting over the next few days and make sure it's strong enough, and have some of the boys work on creating the cranks, we should be ready to set it up by the time Fall hits.

"Hey, Gen?" Jack says abruptly on the walk back to the bunker, device in tow. "How do I remove the electrical spark in my eyes? That might actually help us to be able to do more than run the purifier and the lights."

"Save the comedy for tonight, sir. We've got a long couple of hours ahead of us." I reply as the sun fades behind the mountains, blinding us as the orange rays glare right at us like knives to the face.

CHAPTER 5

Crickets chirp loudly as we cut down branches. They don't even seem to mind the loud chopping sounds of the ax as Nathaniel and Adam split the wood.

"This was not what I had in mind," Azra grimaces as we saw off another thick branch.

"Nope," I agree, annoyed that we got stuck on firewood duty.

We have an entire area in the storage room designated for firewood to let it dry before we can use it. We have enough to last for months, but we still have to collect it every chance we get in case we are unable to at some point.

"Tomorrow, I'm going to have the kids pick dandelions," Eliza says, dragging her hand across her forehead to brush back a few stray hairs.

"Thank goodness," Azra moans as if it's been ages since she had the coffee we make from them. "Make sure they pick them *all*. We are *not* running out like we did last Winter."

"You're addicted." Eliza shakes her head as if our friend is hopeless. "Oh, look alive. Here comes Red."

Azra's eyes grow wide as she quickly straightens. She arranges her face into a soft smile and waits for Red to approach.

"Ladies," he says smoothly. His chestnut hair shines in the moonlight. "I've finished hunting for the night, but I thought I might come help you all. Genesis, Adam said something about having you test the river. I think he's nervous after yesterday. He said to take Jack and make sure everything is good."

He reaches for my saw. I allow him to slip in where I was standing across from Azra. Eliza tries to smother her beaming grin, ducking her head to hide behind her dark curls.

"Did you catch anything?" Azra asks calmly as I walk away. She's incredible at not giving anything away.

"Jack," I call out as I walk up behind the guys cutting down thick branches to use for logs. He pauses before turning around. "Adam is sending us on a river check. Let's go."

His face twitches in the moonlight before turning to walk with me. Under the night sky, his hair takes on a silver look, almost like ice on the river when it freezes over.

"Maybe we should start measuring and tracking the water levels," Jack suggests as we walk. "It's always been pretty dependable until now—*I think*—but maybe changes in the water level could give us some indication of what's going on if the weather patterns really *are* changing."

"Not a bad idea. It would be easy enough to make a marker. We should also mark where the water reaches on the banks at different times."

"That's a good idea," he says, wrapping a warm arm around me. He squeezes my hip. "We'll pick up some branches and mark them along the way."

My hand gravitates to my hip, patting my knife.

"While we're out, we could look for a branch that's strong enough to hold the netting up with all that snow on it."

"Good idea."

I try to stifle a yawn, only to succeed in making myself look ridiculous. Jack snorts at me, pausing to flip me around to face him.

"You know, there's a solution to that..."

"Oh, and what is that?"

His lips are as searing as the sun will be tomorrow while we're out working. My cheek tingles as his fingers brush against it before moving my hair back. I'm suddenly quite awake.

Jack purrs against my skin, a rumble coming from deep within his chest. His lips against my collarbone make me quietly gasp. I wrap my fingers in his hair, setting off a quiet chuckle before he raises his mouth back up to mine. Not even men from the storybooks we read the children could kiss as well as Jack could.

"We should go," he says finally.

"We should go," I repeat as neither of us move.

"Are you trying to make this difficult?" His smirk is intoxicating.

When I don't answer, he finally pulls away, dragging me with him.

"Come on, we can make time for this later." We walk a few steps before he adds, "Are you awake now?"

"Honestly, after that, I'm not sure if I'm conscious at all."

"Ah, lack of oxygen?" he jokes.

"Well, I was *going* to go with a *you-being-a-dream* comment, but if you want to blame it on the lack of air, feel free."

"No, no. You're right," he says as he runs his tongue over his upper lip quickly, "it's because I'm so good to you, it's like a dream you never want to wake up from."

"Even dreams turn into nightmares, Jack, and your excessive use of words here is pushing it dangerously close to that line."

"Speaking of lines, we need to start collecting some branches. We're almost at the river. Which, just to point out, we can't hear, which is probably a good sign."

"I'd certainly say so." I grab my knife from my hip and flip it open.

"I'll climb. You carve," Jack says, giving me a small smile. "The last thing I need is for you to get up there and fall out of the tree because you dozed off."

"Very funny."

"I'm hilarious, Genesis, it's why you and Shanna love me so much."

"She finds you funnier than I do," I comment, giving him a boost into the tree.

"I'm aware of that," Jack calls down from several branches up. "Good thing my ego isn't taking a hit on that one."

"Does your ego ever take a hit on *anything,* darling?" I shout innocently.

"Nope. Heads up," he replies as he drops the first branch down into my waiting hands. I quickly strip off the bark and make notches in it.

By the time Jack has climbed down, we have two poles for the water and several markers for the shore. He helps me strip the last two and we set off toward the river.

THE CRACK of thunder makes me jump so high that I nearly toppled over in the water. Jack quickly scoops up the pole I dropped out of the water and jams it into the riverbed.

The bolt of lightning that lit up the entire area prompts us to rush out of the water.

"Where did that come from?" Jack asks indignantly.

"Does it matter? We've got to go."

Back on the bank, we quickly mark where the waterline sits in several locations and take off running back toward the bunker. There will be no more work tonight if it's storming.

The sky opens up, dousing us with more water than the river contains. We slow our pace, trying not to slip in the wet grass. Jack's bangs drip against his forehead, plastered to his skin, sending tiny streams of water trickling down his nose.

"I guess we'll get to try our markers sooner than we thought," Jack yells above the roar of the rain.

Our clothes are soaked through, leaving the fabric clinging to our bodies. Jack's abs are outlined with dark shadows against his navy shirt, stopping me short. I suck in a deep breath and pretend not to notice.

"You okay?" Jack asks. "Sorry I don't have anything to cover you with."

It's adorable how he apologizes for things he can't control.

"It wouldn't matter even if you did." I yelp when another bolt of lightning streaks across the sky.

"We should walk faster," Jack tries to keep his voice even but I can tell he's nervous about the storm. "We shouldn't be out here in this."

Thankfully, we're the furthest ones away from the bunker. We don't need to worry about the others being caught out in this storm.

The wind picks up, flinging flowers around in a tethered whirlwind. The bushes start to bend over, the leaves turning up to gather as much water as possible.

"What is going on here?" It's hard to hear myself over the wind.

Jack protectively wraps both arms around me and increases our speed. We're risking falling on the wet grass over being out in this storm any longer than necessary.

We run for another minute before we realize something is off. Jack's grip tightens around me accidentally. He looks in shock. I stop running, bringing us both to a halt.

I stare ahead.

After a moment, I turn behind me where rain is still crashing down on the grass.

A wall of rain separates us from the storm. As if it were a barrier, the rain has formed a straight wall dividing the area. There is no water where we stand, not even the slightest hint of moisture.

The storm rages a foot away from us, but *our* side is

peaceful. There is a distinct noise level difference between the dry area and the storm zone.

"Jack?"

"I don't know," he answers quickly. He takes my hand lightly as if my presence is tethering him to the moment.

"You *are* seeing that, right?" I blink, making sure something isn't wrong with my vision.

"Yes," he says cautiously. He watches me from the corner of his eye but I can't tear my gaze away from the wall of rain.

I inhale sharply, breath suddenly filling my lungs. It brings me back to my senses.

Jack's brow is furrowed as he stares into the wall of rain. The look of confusion he wears would be adorable if it weren't so terrifying in light of our current circumstances. He continues to stare ahead.

"We need to tell Adam." I pull away, running toward the bunker.

"Wait, Genesis," Jack calls after me, coming back to life. "If it's not storming over here, they're probably not at the bunker."

He makes a good point.

I turn back to him. With the wall of rain behind him illuminated by the silvery moonlight, he looks like he's standing in front of a sparkly dew-covered spider web, a life-sized fairy from one of his many tales for the children.

His background inspires me.

"You're right. And we also can't just go running off. We need information."

Horror washes over his face right before I turn away, marching over a bush. I rip a twig off and stomp back over to the wall of rain. He watches as I push the twig into the ground, marking where the wall of rain ends.

Spinning, I walk a few feet away and take a seat on the ground.

"What's happening?" he asks, moving closer to me.

"Sit, Jack." I pat the ground next to me. "We're seeing if it moves."

"You think it will move?"

I turn to face him, propped up on my elbows as I lay on my back.

"In all the time that we've been here, never once has the weather not affected the entire snow globe. It's all or nothing. If it rains, it rains everywhere.

"Suddenly we have a *wall* of rain? This doesn't fly, Jack. Things are changing and we need to know why."

"So you're waiting to see what direction it will go in." Jack leans back next to me, nodding in approval.

"Or if it will stay."

Out of the corner of my eye, I see Jack swallow. His collarbone rises with the motion, looking so sharp it could be glass.

"Well, if we're just sitting around," he teases, "maybe we could find a way to pass the time."

He quickly sits up, balancing himself on one hip, legs trailing behind him. I watch him quietly for a moment, intentionally forcing myself not to stare at his abs.

When I sit up to mirror him, he grins and tangles his hands in my hair.

Kissing is a delightful way to pass the time.

When our lips are swollen and I'm dizzy from lack of air, we walk up to the wall of rain.

It hasn't moved in the slightest.

Thoughts race through my head as quickly as Azra does anything athletic.

The weather is changing.

Things are happening in certain areas that aren't happening in others.

We need to work harder and gather faster, because Summer may not last as long as we think.

Adam needs to know what's going on.

If the weather patterns are changing and things are becoming location-based here...

I force myself to stop thinking.

"We have to go! Now!" I shout as I summon every ounce of the training Azra has put me through and drag Jack behind me toward the team, insanity taking over.

CHAPTER 6

"Adam!" I shriek as I race into the woods.

Everyone jumps, turning to face us as I crash through the brush. They pull their weapons, searching behind us for whatever must be chasing us.

"There's a wall," I gasp, wishing I had regulated my breathing better. "At the river....it started to rain."

Nope. Speaking takes a back seat to breathing. I point toward the direction of the river.

"It what?" Adam asks, confusion darkening his brow.

"It rained," Jack supplies, placing a hand on my back as I lean forward to catch my breath. I hadn't slowed the entire run and Jack had trouble keeping up with me, so whatever had possessed me to run that fast had certainly done its job.

I notice the burning sensation in my lungs as I take a deep gulp of air. Mistake.

"It was raining at the river." I straighten, forcing myself to speak. "It rained and we ran because it was storming so badly. Thunder. Lightning. Wind. It was crazy.

"But while we were running," I continue, "It suddenly stopped. I don't mean that the rain itself stopped. I mean that if we stood here, it was raining, and if we stood there, it wasn't."

I hip-check Jack, forcing him to take a step to the left to illustrate my point.

"We marked it and it didn't move. It was like an actual wall of rain," I exclaim, as animated as Jack was earlier today when he was explaining his device to me.

"You should come see it for yourselves," Jack says. He quickly tells them the location and Adam and a few others run ahead.

"A wall of rain?" Azra comments, sidling up next to me. She cringes when she touches me. "*Oh.*"

She glances down at my clothing, stiff from the dried rain.

"How is that possible?" Eliza murmurs as we walk.

I shake my head, still trying to work it out. I'm lost deep in thought when we arrive back at the location of my marker.

There is no rain.

Adam looks pale.

"You have to believe me, Adam, there was rain."

"I know," Adam stares at me as if he were looking through me instead of at me. "It...stopped."

I'm not sure I hear him correctly.

"It was like someone just flipped a switch and turned it off," Red adds, equally as distant.

"The entire storm just stopped at once," Nathaniel supplies, acting far more practical. "It was raining as we approached and then it just cut off. We actually saw the last drops fall in unison as if it were a lid being placed over the earth to hold the water in. It just sliced through the air and that was the end of it."

"I think it's safe to say," Jack interjects, "that things are changing. I'm no longer convinced Summer is going to last and I don't think any of you are either. We need to get back to the bunker and rest for the next few hours, because tomorrow, we have to handle *everything*. We can't afford to waste time."

He turns to look at Adam and Red.

"We need to go back now. We can talk this through in the morning."

"It *is* morning," Nathaniel mumbles under his breath.

Adam, though less than a decade older than us, suddenly looks beyond his years. I imagine in all of his time here, he also hadn't seen anything like this.

"Time to go," I raise my voice, directing everyone toward the bunker.

We walk in relative silence back to the bunker. The handful of people we had left behind at the work site would meet us there, having cleaned up and moved our work to where we could easily have the younger teens run it back to the bunker in the morning.

It feels colder inside the bunker, but that may just be the chill running through my blood after tonight's discovery. I lay down on my blanket—much harder than I had anticipated—and force my eyes shut.

THREE HOURS of sleep did little for any of us. Perrin had shaken us awake, fighting off our angry mumbles. The group stumbled around in a fog for a few minutes before fully waking up and getting to work.

We hurry as quickly as we can, taking care of everything from the night before and collecting as many resources as we can. Getting in a day and a half worth of work before dinner was worth waiting to have the meeting.

"Are the children inside?" Adam asks.

"I think Eliza brought them all in," I nod as I speak. "They worked hard today. I'm sure they'll sleep well."

"What's on the agenda for tonight?" Adam asks, turning to Jack.

"I think we need a bigger focus on finding food tonight," Jack says practically. "Even if something should happen, the trees aren't going anywhere. We can gather more wood in the snow, but we can't find food as easily."

"I think that's wise," Adam agrees.

The blue light flickers in the hallway, changing the tone of the room for a moment. We all glance toward the door briefly.

"Adam, I have an idea," I say, preparing myself for his reaction. He waits for me to go on. "Well, in light of last night, I think we need to discuss some things.

"If the weather is now being isolated to one area and not another, maybe it's time we take a few risks."

"What do you mean?" Jack asks thoughtfully, hearing my plan for the first time.

"If it's snowing here, maybe it isn't snowing somewhere else. How do we know? We never travel more than a day away. What's beyond the mountains? Is there a safer place to live? A food source?

"Now that we know it's not harsh weather *everywhere* maybe it's time we find out what else is out there," I explain.

We have no idea what we might find. Our salvation could be only a few days' walk away.

"Not everyone, of course," I add hurriedly. "Just an exploration party. We could be back in a few days...before Summer ends. Maybe we'll even find that Summer doesn't end at all over the mountain."

"She has a point," Jack intervenes before Adam can kill the idea. "If we take a trained group of people out, at least we'd know. If we find something, we can plan how to move everyone."

"What if you die in the process?" Adam counters.

"We won't," Jack says bluntly.

"We can't risk that."

"Can we risk staying *here*?" Nathaniel backs us up.

"If we go now, we can get over the mountain and back before the end of Fall," I suggest, hoping the group will listen.

Jack takes up my crusade, looking warmly at me. Sometimes I'm overwhelmed by the way that man adores me.

"It's a solid plan. Even if the weather *does* shift, it can't be *that* bad. Even if Winter comes early, it's mild for the first few days. We can make this work. The worst case is that we find more of what we already know and we come back, but at least we know," Jack pushes for approval. "But I think we should wait until tomorrow to go. We should rest tonight so we have enough strength to get there and back quickly. We can leave first thing in the morning."

"I'll go," Red volunteers.

"I'm in," Nathaniel adds.

Several others all nod in agreement, volunteering to run the mission with us. Azra looks at me for a moment to make sure we're on the same page and then she volunteers.

"We can't risk losing everyone," Adam announces.

"Not everyone is going," Jack says. "We'll take....ten of us. Is that fair?"

"I suppose," Adam agrees.

"We need people who will form the best team to work together to get over there and back," Jack decides.

We spend the next hour planning the trip as we finish our food before setting up Jack's snow removal machine so it's ready before we leave.

"GENESIS," Jack yelps in surprise, nearly crashing into me as he walks into the room. A dark coat slips off of his arm, resting in his hand. The bottom of it sags onto the floor. He smiles at me. "What are you doing up so early?"

He leans forward, touching my elbow with his free hand, to give me a quick kiss.

I offer him a confused smile in return.

"I'm getting ready to go. What are you doing?" I glance down at the coat.

Jack pauses.

"Gen, we're not going." He frowns.

"What? Of course we are." I push past him into the hallway.

"We can't, Gen," he catches my elbow, slowing me. "Something happened."

I stop dead in my tracks before whipping back to him.

"What happened?" I ask, desperate for information.

"No one is hurt," he calms me. My shoulders sag in relief. "But, Genesis, we're snowed in."

"Wait, what?" I gasp. "It's Summer...what are you talking about?"

"It switched, Gen."

"To Winter? We didn't even have Fall?"

"I don't know, Genesis. Maybe Fall happened last night?" His voice raises in pitch at the suggestion, hoping it satisfies me. "I couldn't tell you, but when I went to leave just now, I found all of the snow."

I glance down at his boots, covered in frosty crystals.

"I tried moving some of it," he says, explaining why he stepped out into the snow. A chunk of it quietly slides off his boot onto the tunnel floor.

I look back up to meet his gaze.

"If we can get a few people, we can go test the machine," he shrugs sadly.

"But what are we going to do? We can't stay here, especially if we're only going to have two days of Summer."

"Genesis, be practical. We can't go out in Winter," he says protectively. "We're not canceling the trip...just postponing it until it's safe to be out. The entire point is that we need to make it back *alive* to tell them what we find and potentially take them somewhere new. We can't do that if we freeze to death out there because we got caught in a snow drift."

"Oh good, I caught you." Perrin smiles as he rounds the corner. "I have a few things for you to take along with you."

He extends his hands, a pouch containing bottles and medical supplies stretched out to us.

"Bad news, my friend, we got hit with Winter," Jack's eyes go dim.

"What?" Perrin asks curtly. He glances quickly to the door.

"Come look," Jack responds, waving him forward. "We need a hand testing the snow removal machine anyway.

"Need another hand?" Kai asks, slipping out of the sleeping quarters.

"Actually, yes. Come on," Jack smiles. "Did you hear all that?"

"I was standing by the door. I didn't want to interrupt." Kai admits.

"So you just eavesdropped instead," I tease, messing up his hair. "*Nice.*"

"I wouldn't have stuck around if you were making out and being all gross or something," he wrinkles his nose as I give him a wide-eyed look.

I would need to be far more careful where I was kissing my boyfriend in the bunker from now on.

The world is covered in crystal white. It sparkles in the rising sun, glinting orange as it comes up over the horizon. It leaves a pink tinge to the snow, reminding me of the Summer flowers that were here only a few hours earlier.

"Oh," I gasp as the wind hits me. "*This* was a bad choice."

Jack hands me his jacket and I greedily slip my arms through it, zipping it up. I shiver when a second blast of air hits my face, whipping my hair back. I tuck it behind my ear only long enough to realize that that too is a bad idea.

"Kai, you're with me on the cranks. Perrin, you help Genesis pull it back. Here goes," Jack directs.

The cranks turn slowly at first, creaking as they move.

"Gen, hold the lean-to, please," he adds, realizing we needed to be paying attention to more than just his new play toy.

I reach out and grab the sides of the lean-to to stabilize it, assuring that it won't fall and let the snow in. Perrin starts to shake next to me in his Summer clothing.

A piece of snow falls, brushing the back of my right hand like a fish in the river might. I cringe but maintain my grip.

The fabric lifts away from its position, slowly moving the snow.

It's working.

"What—" Nathaniel yelps behind us, obviously seeing the snow.

"We know," I say glumly.

"I don't...I...what?" he stammers. "How did this happen?"

"The Snow Prince showed up and left us a gift last night, Nate, what do you think?" Jack snipped.

Nathaniel sighs, defeated by the snow.

"Can we at least get out?" he inquires.

"Mostly," I reply, peering around the lean-to.

"I'll go get the snowshoes and coats," Nathaniel turns, dragging his feet for a few steps. "I cannot believe this..."

When the netting reaches the end of the rope at the poles, Perrin and I haul it back gently, making sure it unfolds properly as we move it. Nathaniel reappears with proper gear for each of us. Zach follows behind, carrying what didn't fit in Nathaniel's arms.

I slip my thinner coat on, zipping it up to the high collar that covers my neck. I add an extra pair of pants and socks before stepping into my boots. My scarf already feels wet from where I exhale into it as I loop it around the back of my neck and tie it. It's going to be frigid out there. Finally, I add my warmer coat on top of everything else.

I place the band Eliza made me around my ears, praying between that and the hat and hood, my ears wouldn't fall off in the cold. Tucking my hair under the hat, I secure it in place. With my hood adjusted, I pick up my shovel and rest it against my knee as I strap on the snowshoes.

Outside, the world opens up into pure gold sparkling off of the snow. I hate it.

"Well, it's not as bad as it looks," Nathaniel says as Zach pulls his arm out of the snow bank a dozen yards from the bunker entrance. "Looks like it was worse directly over the bunker."

He turns and stares at the snow-covered mound that is our home.

"What should we do?"

"I don't think there is much that we *can* do today," Jack sighs. "Everything is buried. The most we can do is purify some snow so we have more water."

We use the Winter days to collect snow so we don't have to haul as much water from the river during Spring, Summer, and Fall. It's an easy task for the younger teens to do while the older members are out hunting.

"Adam is going to be furious," Zach says, sounding like he's looking forward to the show.

"He'll be fine," Jack shuts him down. "It's just another thing to deal with. Let's go back inside."

We all trek toward the bunker, ducking under the netting. Jack pulls the door open, holding it for us to slip back inside.

"How bad?" Adam greets us, having heard the news.

"A foot and a half. It's not terrible," Jack tries to play it off.

"We haven't gathered enough supplies. If Winter holds, we could be in trouble."

"We'll get to that when we get to that," Jack responds. Over the years, he's learned how to manage Adam's emotional reactions. "It will be okay. We always make it work. I have faith in us."

He sets his hand on Adam's shoulder as he passes, patting it.

"You're right," Adam admits. "I'm just so worried."

"And you should be, Adam," I add. "You're responsible for all these people. It's your job to worry for them and our job to find a way around all this. We'll figure this out."

"I'm sorry, did I hear that there is *snow* out there?" Azra wanders up behind us.

"Yep," I rush forward, grabbing her elbow and spinning her. "The boys are going to work on a solution for finding more food.

I glance over my shoulder.

"Maybe you guys should go hunting or something, I'm sure all the creatures are out of sorts with this—and you're going to help me with a little project." I turn back to face my friend. "Bye, boys."

We sprint down the tunnel, around the corner, and hide in a room down the hall from Perrin's office.

"You want to explain that to me?" Azra asks as I peel off my layers.

"Azra, there is over a foot of snow out there. It's the middle of Summer," I say, unwrapping my scarf. "It's also the day we were supposed to leave. Does that sound odd to you?"

"*You* sound odd to me," she replies.

"You don't think something is going on here?"

"What are you suggesting?" she asks, leaning her hip against the table.

I toss my winter gear over the back of a folding chair.

"Azra, something is happening and we need to get to the bottom of it. I don't think this is some kind of natural phenomenon, do you?"

"What other explanation is there?"

"That's what we need to find out. I think you and I need to do a little explorative work when no one is looking."

"*Okay*, what's going on?" Eliza asks from her place in the doorway. "We don't keep secrets."

She points to the three of us.

"Not a *secret*, Eliza," I respond, waving her in. "We just didn't want to pull you away from the kids. I also figured if I walked in there, I'd have at least two of them attached to my legs right now."

"Good point," she brushes her curly hair back. "So what are we talking about?"

"Jack and I are going out to investigate. I need you two to cover for us."

"You're going out *now*?"

"We are at some point, and when we do, I need you two to distract people for us."

"And where precisely are you going when you get out there? What are you looking for?" Eliza critiques my plan.

"I'm not sure, I have to talk it over with Jack—he doesn't know we're going yet—but maybe back to the river? That's where things started to get weird."

"Didn't things start to get weird....here? Last Summer?" Azra reminds me.

"You know what I mean. That was the first really big thing aside from a missing day of a season," I reply, pushing off of the table. I moved toward the door. "Honestly, I don't know where else to look, but it's a start. We need to measure the water anyway...assuming it's not completely frozen over."

"It usually takes a day or two," Azra offers.

"So we'll go there and see what we can find." I shrug, hoping my plan will work out. All I know is that I need to do *something*.

I turn away from the girls to face the exit and nearly collide with a tall body.

"I'd ask if you think Jack will really go along with this, but we all know he will," Nes says, standing in the doorway. "Tell me what you need."

Of course *he was listening.*

"You're going to help?"

"Gen, I just lost my fingers to whatever is out there. If something is going on out there, I want to know about it."

I nod. It makes sense that Nes would want answers, especially if something had led to his accident.

"We need to get out of the bunker without being noticed and then I need you guys to cover for us."

"And what if you don't come back? When do we send out the search party?" Nes asks.

"Give us a few hours once we get out the door. If we aren't back in four hours, then come looking. If you can't find us within an hour, I want you all to come back to the bunker. *Promise me.* I don't want you all out there in this weather."

"It's no different than normal Winter, Genesis," Azra walks toward me, followed by Eliza. "There's not even that much snow."

"Things are different now. We don't understand this yet," I remind her.

"We'll back you, Gen," Eliza answers. Her glance prompts Azra to nod.

"Just be careful," Nes says, backing up. He steps out of the door. "Stay here. I'll go get him."

They wait until he's gone to turn to me.

"Don't do anything stupid," Eliza lectures.

"I'll get your coat." Azra slips out the door leaving

Eliza to preemptively scold me, barely making a sound as she sprints down the hall.

"We won't do anything stupid," I promise as Eliza squeezes my hand.

"Good." She adds extra pressure to her grip. "Now, how do we get you out of here?"

CHAPTER 7

"You have lost your mind, woman," Jack says as the snow crunches under our feet.

"Don't be a jerk, Jack," I watch my breath crystallize in the air in front of me. "You want to know what's going on just as much as I do."

"I admit, the river is a good place to start." A puff of white streams out in front of him, wrapping around his face as we move forward. Even our scarves don't help to take the bitter edge out of the air.

"Nes did a good job of sneaking us out," Jack comments, looking up at the sun. "You really couldn't have waited another day for it to not be so cold?"

"It could be worse tomorrow for all we know. The river's not that far away." Each step grinding into the snow grates on my ears. I *hate* the snow. "We'll just go check it out and hit a few more spots."

"*A few more spots?*" Jack gasps. "Genesis, you realize the last time it was this cold, Nes came home a few fingers short."

"Technically he brought them home," I cringe even saying the words. "Oh look, there's the hill."

"Well, this will be fun," Jack mutters as he leans forward to balance himself during the climb.

By the time we reach the top, I feel like I've run the length of the forest. My cheeks sting against the wind, snowflakes catching on my eyelashes.

On the far side of the hill, we find the water has frozen. The waterfall looks like a million fragments of ice piled on top of each other in shards of sharp glass, daring people and beasts to approach.

"So much for that," Jack's shoulders sag with defeat.

"Well, I'm still going to look around," I announce, moving toward the smaller of the falls.

"Sure," Jack replies, moving into step behind me.

Up close, the jagged edges of the ice look even more vicious. The water froze mid-fall down the center of the drop in an icy sheet. I imagine if we stepped back far enough, the frozen water cascading over both sides of the falls mixed with the sheet of ice that dropped straight down would look like a giant throne from a book.

"I don't suppose any of these are actually hidden levers that control the weather, do you?" I ask reluctantly.

"I imagine it would be less of a lever, more of a wheel." Jack joked. "Silver with a black top and little indentations so your hands don't slip when you turn it. And probably a few buttons."

He holds my hand as I climb off of the ledge.

"Careful," I point to a spot on the rock that looks especially slippery. When we step off of the rock, I add, "Do you think we can cross the river?"

"I think it's thick enough to cross, yes, but I don't think we should," Jack raises his voice to accommodate the howling wind. "With the way things have been changing so quickly, I think we need to stay safely on this side."

"Okay, where else should we look?"

"The woods?" he offers, more a question than a comment.

"Let's go," I nod, preparing to leave the ice sculptures behind.

The wind rushing against my ears is deafening. My scarf catches on the breeze, but unable to escape, it flaps against the side of my face, adding to the chaotic noise.

Snow pelts against my back, pinging off of my jacket. The wind pushes against my back, making me walk faster than my legs are willing to move in their frozen state.

"Gen," Jack's voice drops to a frightening pitch. "Genesis, I need you to get down. *Now*."

When I shift so I can see him around my hood, his face is pale and turned away from me. Something behind us has his full attention.

"Gen, I mean it, get down." He pushes at me harshly, forcing me to my knees.

Whipping my head around, I finally see what Jack

sees—a massive white cloud is racing toward us, looming high over our heads.

"What is that?" I yelp. It looks like a bank of fog rolling in, but clearly it isn't.

"We have to get covered. Cover your face with your arms so you aren't in the snow," Jack instructs, whipping his backpack off.

He pulls something out and tosses it around his shoulders—a blanket. Jack waits for me to flop all the way into the snow, protecting my face with my arms, before he crawls on top of me, covering me with his body. He pulls the blanket over his head, concealing us with the little protection that we have.

"Just stay still," Jack shouts into my ear. "It will be okay."

Twice, Jack stirs, flipping the snow off of the blanket just like we did with his snow removal device earlier. Each time he moves, the sting of snow mixed with ice and wind slams into my body.

"You okay?" he asks both times. I always mumble a response, hoping he can hear me around the heavy fabric of my hood.

After only a few minutes, the wind dies down.

"I think we're clear," Jack says into my hood. "I'm going to check."

He lifts his body off of mine, eventually kneeling beside me.

"Are you okay?" he asks again, using his gloved hands to dig some of the snow away from my face before I move.

"I'm fine. Are *you* okay?"

"The blanket did its job. Sure glad I packed that thing."

"Me too. Azra didn't think to pack anything like that for me."

"Azra is a runner, Gen, not a packer. She only thinks about which route to take, not what it will take to get through that route."

"I'll remember that for next time."

"I think there's something else you need to remember too," Jack says slyly.

"Oh? And what is that?"

"Thank you, Jack," he says in a high pitched voice that is supposed to sound like me. "You saved my life. You're so brave!"

I pause for a moment to give him a look, fully intending on thanking him...then he continued.

"You're *so* brave, and strong, and *handsome*, Jack." He pauses to give a girly giggle. "I'd be lost without you, Jack. I don't know what I'd do. You're my hero!"

"You're my blanket."

He freezes. When he speaks again, he drops his fake voice.

"Really?" He looks at me incredulously. "I save your life and all I get is that I'm a *blanket*?"

"I had every intention of thanking you properly, sir," I lean in, frozen lips an inch from his. "But you ruined it—so no kissing for you. Thanks for the help...moving on."

He stands gaping at me like a fish, mouth opening and closing.

I spin around, walking toward the forest, trying not to laugh. While we set a course for the woods, I attempt to work out how it was possible for the water to freeze so quickly. Moving water takes time to freeze, much longer than stagnant waters like a pond. It is cold out, but not nearly *that* cold.

"Which area do you want to check, Genesis?" Jack asks as the trees loom ahead. He bends down to scoop up a snowball and tosses it at me. It hits my arm before falling to the ground.

I take a deep breath to steady myself. He's not going to like what I have to say. Maybe if I hit him in the face with a snowball, it will distract him long enough to agree.

"I think we should go to Sector Nine."

"No," Jack says definitively. "I did not sign up to take you into forbidden territory. You know it's dangerous out there."

"What if we just go to the edge and see what we can see? It won't hurt to look from a distance."

"I think this is a bad idea," Jack protests.

"Just from the outside, Jack. Please?"

I wrap myself in his arms. Our crystallized breath

clouds the air between us. He stares into my eyes, pleading with me to change my mind. When I don't, he gives in.

"Just to the edge," he relents. "At then we go right back to the bunker."

He looks worried as he pulls me into his arms. I rub his arms tenderly, knowing I would have the same reaction if he suggested that he wanted to put himself in harm's way.

"Thank you, Jack. I think it's important."

"And *I* think it's important that we get inside. It's far too cold out here."

My lashes feel frozen by the time we reach the tree line dividing the sectors. Much like the wall of rain, the trees end in a harsh line, opening up to a foreboding looking swamp. Rocks etch high into the skyline, though I imagine they're only really around my height. I'm tall for an eighteen-year-old girl, but the rocks still looked like they could swallow me whole.

We stand in the trees. There's a noticeable difference in the height of the snow between the open area and the woods where the trees have caught some of the snow high above our heads.

Surveying the area, I see large piles of snow. Parts of the rocks peek out of the tops of some of the clusters of rocks, making it look a bit like the distant mountains. The land dips in a few places, but it's hard to tell with the snow covering it. Usually it is safer to see the pitfalls one might encounter in the land, but not today. Today it is deceptively gentle.

Somewhere in my mind, I trick myself into thinking it's safe. I pull my hands off of the tree trunks where they rest and take a step into the swamp.

"Don't you dare," Jack warns, lashing out to catch me. "You've seen this place without snow. You are not going out there. You know what happened to Lewis out here."

"What is that?" I ask, pointing as something catches my eye.

"I don't see anything," Jack reports, squinting into the snow-covered space.

"Look, there."

I point to the left. Something moves in the wind—a tarp of some kind?

As the wind picks up, it moves harder, furiously beating back and forth. When it doesn't blow away, I assume it must be anchored down.

"If *we* don't come out here, then what is that covering?"

Jack continues to squint. Whatever it is, it quickly unveils something metallic for an instant before covering it back up.

I can tell the moment Jack sees it too.

"If we didn't do that, then who did and what is it?

Something sparkles to the right. I quickly turn to

catch it but determine that it was just the sunlight off of the snow. When I turn back, the wind has died down and the tarp has stopped moving.

"Where did it go?" I murmur.

"I'm not sure," Jack admits.

The wind gusts, licking at the snow banks. It picks up a massive cloud of snow—eerily reminding me of the storm we had just survived—and coats the area with a new layer of white as if it had snowed another inch.

Knowing better, I try again to step out. Jack stops me.

"Genesis, you listen to me." He spins me to face him, nearly causing me to get tangled in my snowshoes. "Lewis came out here and he didn't come back."

"I know, he got sucked into whatever swampy holes are out here and he drowned. We all know what happened to him. We never should have let him wander after the accident." I point between us. "But *we're* paying attention."

"He was out here in Summer, Gen, when he could see everything and he's still gone. Our memories are good, but when was the last time we were out here?"

In truth, it had been years. Jack and I hadn't been this close to the swamp since we were precocious children trying to see if the horror stories were true.

"The snow is covering everything. If the river is frozen, don't you think the swamp would be as well?"

"I'm not willing to risk that. I will never risk your

safety, Gen. If I didn't care for you so much, do you really think I'd do so much to make sure you weren't uncomfortable?" He finally grins at me. "Besides, do you really think I gave up all that bread for you *just* to let you be sucked into a swamp? I get that I like to tell stories, but even for *me* that one seems a little ridiculous."

I shouldn't have tried to avoid laughing because my snort comes out as less than lady-like. Jack chuckles.

"Please, can we go back now? I'm pretty sure your hair is starting to freeze."

He wraps himself around me, feeling far warmer than he should. I assume it's his natural radiance punching through his winter coat to fold around me. He guides me away quietly, but I look over my shoulder one more time, hoping for answers.

Jack stays close the entire walk back to the bunker.

***

MY BODY IS SHIVERING SO hard as we stand outside the bunker, waiting for Azra to give us the all-clear sign. Before we left, we decided it would be best if we made it look like we had been out with her all day so no one could question us. We'd walk back in with her. I can't force my legs to stop shaking no matter how much I try to tighten my muscles.

Jack gives me a concerned look when he notices my

teeth chattering. I know my head is violently bobbling back and forth in the cold, but I can't stop it even as I grit my teeth together.

I've been colder than this before, but my body has had enough.

"We're going in," Jack proclaims. "We're not waiting."

He starts to push me toward the door when I see Azra.

"You have been gone for hours," she hisses as she bounds up to us. "I have been out here twice to let you back in. What happened?"

"We need to get her inside." Jack's concern prompts Azra into action. She wheels around, marching toward the bunker door.

"We're going in. Come get us if you need anything," she shouts to Red as we rush by him as he walks around the building.

"Okay, warm up for the both of us," Red calls, waving over his shoulder.

We duck inside without anyone asking questions. Jack points us toward the main room and sets me in front of the fire. The children swarm around me, leaning against me to add their warmth to my frozen body. It was a mistake to stay out for so long.

After a while, Jack takes his gloves off and unzips his jacket. I leave mine on. The fire is mesmerizing as it crackles in deep orange and gold.

The color I saw in the swamp under the tarp wasn't golden; it was silver. I study the fire to make sure.

Something metallic was out there. It was so far away that I couldn't tell what it was, even if it *had* been uncovered. I had only been to the edge of Sector Nine once—Jack and I had snuck out when we were thirteen—but I think the landscaping had been a bit different. The rocks in front of what I saw hid the area better. Perhaps the swamp had shifted recently. It is the only conclusion I can come up with if that silver thing was meant to be hidden. Based on the tarp, I assumed it was supposed to be a secret.

I needed to find a way back when it wasn't snowing.

"Here," Eliza interrupts my thoughts. She drops hot rocks from the fireplace wrapped in a bag into my gloved hands. It takes a moment, but the heat works its way down to my palms. It sends a spike of electric energy racing down my spine. "You need anything, Jack?"

"I'm okay, actually." He slips off his outer coat, leaving only his lighter weight one on. "Here, babe."

Jack wraps it around me, but I know I should start peeling off my own layers as well. Instead, I accept a few extra moments of wearing layers.

"I have a few things to take care of," he says, standing. "Eliza, sit with her?"

She uses a towel to wipe off the seat before taking his place.

"I've got her," she scoops Lilly up into her lap. "Right, Lilly?"

Lilly nods, tossing her curls. Nicholas sulks at my feet until I scoop him up. A few of the children wrapped around me scamper off, taking it as their cue to go play. I miss them as the chill of no longer having bodies against me announces its presence.

"I'll see you two later," Jack gives me a soft smile before walking away. I have no idea how his limbs thawed out enough to move like that, but I am incredibly jealous.

"Here, Gen," Kai joins us, sitting on the floor in front of me. He scoots a few of the kids with his foot before handing me a mug. "The kids picked dandelions yesterday, so I thought you might like some tea."

"Yes, thank you."

I pull my gloves off to take the mug. Eliza sets them in her lap, resting her elbow on her knees around Lilly.

"So what's going on?" Kai asks bluntly. We set the kids down and send them to play.

"I'm drinking tea."

"Genesis, you left here at some point today with dark brown hair and returned with nearly white hair. You either magically aged to several decades older than *anyone* around here, or you were outside for much longer than you let on, so what's the deal."

"Oh, look who thinks he's a detective all of a sudden," I chide.

"There's nothing else to do around here when we aren't working, Genesis, and in case you haven't noticed, none of the girls my age are interested in spending time with me, so don't make fun of my choice of books. There are only so many in the bunker, you know."

"I'm aware, Kai, go on."

"Whatever you're doing, I want in."

I hand him my cup. His eyes narrow when I smile.

You asked what I was doing. I'm drinking tea.

"Fine, don't tell me. I'll figure it out."

"Guys," Zach calls from the doorway. He motions us over.

In the hallway, he nods toward the door and I'm suddenly grateful I still have the coat on. I hand Jack's coat to Eliza.

"It's melting."

"Define *melting*," Eliza says, slipping into the coat.

Zach nods to the boys at the door. We're immediately confronted by Red as he tries stepping inside. He looks like he had taken a swim in the pond the way water covered the sides of his coat.

"What happened to *you*?" I examined him.

"The temperature shot up after you went inside, half the snow is gone." He pulls his gloves off with his teeth.

I peer around him. The difference in brightness adds a temporary haze of green to my sight, but I focus on the snow banks, now drastically reduced. They look slushy as they melt.

"Convinced now, Jack?" Adam walks up behind us, Jack to his left.

"Yes," Jack admits. "Something is definitely changing around here. We're going to need a better plan."

"What does this mean?" Eliza asks. "Will it be a short Winter?"

"I don't know, but I think if we're collecting snow, now is the time." Red answers.

Collecting and purifying as much snow as possible needs to be priority right now.

"Let's get to work," I say.

"Why is it so hot?" Nicholas asks.

Eliza's guess was right, we did have a short Winter. It was so short, that it jumped straight to summer. A bird cries loudly, as if lecturing the small boy for asking such a silly question.

"I'm sorry, buddy," I nearly bend down to scoop him up but it's too hot to touch anyone. "Why don't you go take a break inside?"

I set a basket of fish down next to me as I crouch on the grass. I smile at him until he gives up pouting and grins back.

"That's better." I hold up my hand for a high five. "Can you take these to Eliza?"

He nods and scampers off with the basket of fish.

Flowers litter the yard. For a moment, I think back to the time Azra, Eliza and I made daisy chains when we were younger. We wore them inside hoping the boys would notice, but all they cared about was how the older boys had taught them to fish that day.

Jack noticed though. He made sure to tell each one of us how nice they looked with our hair.

The breeze is noticeably missing as the heat swelters around us. Sweat bubbles at my temples, but I still prefer it over the cold.

"I'm still impressed that I got more fish than you," Kai says proudly as we walk inside the bunker, the blue lights nearly drowned out by the Summer sun filtering into the tunnel.

"I'm sure you are," I comment. "And in case you haven't noticed, I think you've been hanging around with Jack too much. You're starting to sound like him. Maybe try spending some time with Perrin this week."

"Everyone loves Jack, why shouldn't I hang out with him?" Kai counters.

"Yes, but Jack's a bit too sure of himself for his own good." I wink at him. "You'd do well to be like Jack, but tone down the teasing. *Only Jack* can pull that off."

"True," Kai admits, holding up his hands in defeat.

"Speaking of Jack, we should see if he's back yet."

"Hey, Kris," Kai locates the older boy down the hall. "You're back so I'm assuming Jack is too?"

"Yeah, we got back an hour and a half ago. Surprisingly, we got a lot more than we had planned."

My guess is that it's because everything is disturbed and doesn't know what to do at this point. At least it is working to our advantage a little.

"He should be around here somewhere." Kris shrugs. Looking me up and down, he frowns. "Did you catch anything?"

"Yeah, I had Nicholas take it to Eliza for me."

"Ah." His face brightens. "At least we'll have a little food, anyway. I'd check the storeroom. He was mumbling something about supplies the last time I saw him."

I'm looking forward to having a conversation with Jack after last night.

"You're not going to believe what *I* found," Zach sings from the tunnel entrance. It feels like every time I make it twenty feet into the tunnel, I get called back.

The bright outside light outlines him, making his figure dark against the light. He holds something on his hip.

"I was out in the woods foraging and I found *this* little one."

He waited for us to come take the little girl from him.

"She was helping me out today, weren't you?" he tries

to speak softly to her. "I found her a little bit ago but I figured I should get the supplies that I could while I was still out there and she was doing fine hanging out."

I pull the little girl into my arms. She clings to my neck.

"Hi sweetie, I'm Genesis. What's your name?" When she doesn't answer, I look to Zach. "Where did you find her?"

"I was in the grove and she came wandering up. She's been quiet all day, but I got her to shake her head a few times, didn't I?" He leans in and nods to her, trying to get her to mimic him. "I've been calling her Daisy. She had one in her hand when I found her."

"Oh, is your name Daisy, sweetie?" I feel her lips twitch against my collarbone where her face is buried. I rush to keep her from crying. "Oh, hey, do you want to do see the other kids? There's lots of kids here."

I spin on my heels and quickly walk toward the main room where the kids are playing.

"Where did you come from, sweetie?" I ask, hoping to finally have an answer. She's young though so I don't hold out much hope.

Every so often, we discover a child roaming around outside. We don't know where they come from, but thankfully it's always in the warmer seasons, never in Winter—or maybe they *do* come in Winter and just don't make it to us. It's a terrifying thought, but we haven't discovered any bodies recently, so I push it aside.

I was a bit older when I arrived at the bunker, but I don't remember anything about it. This is always just what I knew. Nothing before. Many of the people who took me in are gone now, but people like Adam still vividly stick out in my mind from my younger years.

"We have a new friend," I announce, walking into the room.

When I set her down, she toddles to Zach, latching onto his leg.

"Well, I guess you have a new buddy," I laugh. I motion Azra over to talk to Zack. "I'll be back later, sweetie."

"Are we really going to call her Daisy?" Kai asks, following on my heels.

"It's as good a name as any," I shrug. "I doubt she's going to tell us anything."

"Just once, I'd like someone to arrive, tell us what's going on, and where they wander in from."

"I know," I sigh. "Why don't you go see if you can help with dinner? I'm going to look for Jack."

"I'll help you look for Jack," he says, trying to get out of dinner preparations. He follows closely behind me. I'd have to get rid of him if I wanted to talk to my boyfriend.

Jack isn't in the storeroom when we check, nor is he in the boiler room. Perrin's office is empty, as are the other rooms in the wing. Once we've checked the entire floor, I swing toward the basement.

"Why would he be in the basement?"

"I don't know," I offer, "it's cool down here? Does it matter? It's the only place we haven't checked."

Kai takes the stairs with me, matching my strides. He pushes the door open for me, allowing me to step inside first.

"Jack?" My eyes sweep across the tables and broken pieces of furniture. For a moment, I hold my breath in case the rat is back.

"Nope," Kai sighs, glaring at the empty room.

"Jack?" I call one more time.

Suddenly, Jack pops up from behind the broken counter, scaring us.

Kai clutches his chest, looking as wild-eyed as I feel. He composes himself quickly, glancing out of the corner of his eye to see if I noticed his reaction.

"What are you doing down here?" I demand, rather annoyed at my heart attack.

"I was looking for something," Jack grins slyly as he strides over to us.

"Did you find this *something*?"

"Not yet, but I will." He spins Kai around. "Gen and I need to talk. Get lost, kid."

Jack's playfulness is adorable.

"That sounds like a terrible idea," Kai protests, not wanting to leave.

"Trust me, you want to get out of here if you want to avoid a relationship talk," Jack warns him.

"On second thought, I'll go help with dinner." Kai bounds up the steps. The door slams behind him.

As soon as it closes, Jack turns to me. "Time to talk."

CHAPTER 8

"What's this talk about?" I eye him.

"Less talking, more kissing," he shrugs, fixing his eyes on me.

"Ah, a continuation of yesterday when we snuck off. I can live with that."

He takes my hand and guides me to a desk covered in scratch marks. At some point, someone had taken a knife to its surface and carved names and words all along the wood. I feel the raises and dips under my hands as I sit on it.

"What *were* you doing out last night, Jack?" I ask as he leans forward.

"I think I said less talking and more kissing, didn't I?" he croons, hovering next to my lips.

"For someone who is so talkative—" Jack's lips cut me off. I don't mind.

My feet dangle around his knee. I use my toes to gently touch the back of his leg making him unlock his knee as it pops toward the desk. He catches himself on my shoulders with his forearms, his hands busy as they are tangled in my hair.

"Don't get me wrong, Jack," I whisper as he kisses my jaw. "I loved kissing you last night, but we didn't get to talk much."

I swallow hard as he moves to my shoulder, brushing my hair behind me. My fingers curl, catching a fistful of his shirt in my hand. Jack responds by grabbing my hip, dragging me closer to the edge of the desk.

After a moment, he pulls back to speak, but I return the favor and cut him off with my lips. He grins as I tug on his bottom lip.

"If you must know, I was on a mission to handle the weather last night and you caught me just as I was slipping back in," he teases.

"But you were sitting in the doorway," I remind him.

"Oh, yeah." He kisses me again. "I was in the doorway. Well, there you have it."

"That wasn't an answer," I sing, leaning in to quietly run my lips over the soft skin behind his ear. He shivers, making me laugh. I like when I get reactions out of him.

"I was working out how to handle today, that's all. Yesterday really threw me. Then again," he sighs, "I wasn't expecting *today* either."

"Today was full of surprises," I mumble incoherently while his hand runs up my leg. "Oh!"

He pulls back quickly as I remember I have news.

"There's a new girl."

"A new girl?" Jack looks shocked. "Thank goodness the weather changed in that case. If she had been out there, she would have frozen to death had it stayed Winter.

"She's young, Jack."

"Aren't they all?" he mumbles, leaning into me. I've always kept my bangs long so I could pin them back making Jack's bangs brushing against my forehead a new sensation each time it happens. "We just have to make sure they grow up the best we can."

"You're starting to sound like the parents in all those books you read to the kids, talking about taking care of them and watching them grow."

"Aren't we though? At least a little?" he counters.

"I guess we are," I shrug. "Are you sad we won't be around to see them grow up?"

"We don't know that." He looks at me.

"You're so sure of everything around here, you always follow the data, but you choose *that* one not to believe in?"

Most people inside the snow globe were younger, closer to our age. There are a number of people in their twenties and even thirties, but nothing beyond that. People die young here. They make bad choices, go into restricted areas in search of food for the group, or get caught in the elements.

"Adam has been here longer than most. We have at least another decade before anything happens." Jack tries to assure me.

"That's assuming we don't all die in the next month because of whatever is going on."

"We're going to find a way to make it, Genesis. Not everyone gets lost while they're out working."

He tucks my hair behind my ear, a dark contrast to his hair. His eyes are intent as he watches me, waiting for my response.

"No, some of them just die."

"Not everyone dies, Gen," his voice is whinier than he means it to be, prompting a look of disgust at himself. "Listen, all I mean is that we are advancing. Look at us. We've figured out how to distribute the power we have so that it's survivable in the bunker year round. We've figured out how to hunt and trap more efficiently. We've even come up with a snow removal system, all while you and I have been living here.

"And if I'd have known you'd be joining us, I would have started working harder before you got here and surprised you with that knife sharpener much earlier." His eyes spark with pride at the first invention he ever showed me. Granted, he showed it to *everyone* our age and I just happened to be in the crowd, but he likes to claim he was showing off for me even when we were little.

"I'm sure you would have, baby." I slip my hand onto his cheek. He turns and kisses it before looking back to me.

"The point is, Gen, that we don't know what's coming. Everything is changing. Maybe it doesn't have to be the same. Maybe we can survive this and get out."

"Out where?"

"Out of the snow globe. Don't you want to see what else is out there?" He looks like a cornered animal, bits of fear and desperation mixed into the blue of his eyes.

"I thought you didn't want to go. You said we shouldn't go to the mountains or swamp."

"That was conditional and you know it," he says, looking hurt.

"Just how do you plan on getting us all out of here?" I question.

"I don't know yet, but one way or another, I'll find a way to get you out. Promise."

I tip his chin, giving me a better angle at his lips. "I know you will, but please don't do anything foolish because you're rushing."

"I promise to be as careful as I can," he assures me.

I lean back before he can kiss me.

"So what exactly were you looking for down here?"

I leap off the desk, knocking his arm away in the process. He follows quickly behind me. Nothing appears out of the ordinary.

"I was just looking for that rat you thought you heard. I figured if we bring the kids down here, we didn't need it scaring them."

"Really, you were looking for a rat?"

"I was and I didn't know how long Summer would be or how hot it would get so I was trying to be a nice guy about it. Now, should we go upstairs?"

"THAT'S HER. WITH SHANNA." I point toward Daisy. Her hair is long and dark, much as I imagine mine was when I joined the bunker.

"Hi, Daisy," I wave from a few feet away. Shanna beams when she sees Jack.

Daisy eyes Jack, looking him up and down several times. Jack lowers himself to the floor, quietly waiting for her to make up her mind. The little girl walks over to him, taking his offered hand.

He talks softly to her. She doesn't seem as nervous as she did before. When Todd joins us, it's a different story. She quickly moves into Jacks' arms, taking refuge with him.

"And here I thought she was warming up," I comment.

"She actually isn't," Eliza remarks, tucking her hair

back. "She's ignored everyone but Zach, me, and now Jack."

"How is it," I cross my arms, "that *that man* has such a way with the children here? It's like they just *know.*"

"Got me." She purses her lips. "But if he's got her, I'm taking a break. Jack, see if you can feed her."

"On it, boss," Jack answers playfully. "Want some dinner, little one?"

He moves her over to the corner of the room where Azra is handing out food.

"Careful, that little one might just steal your man," Eliza bumps her hip into mine before walking away. Shanna smirks from the floor.

If I kick her from this height...

Suddenly, her face morphs into a look of bewilderment.

"What the—"

I turn to find Red standing in the doorway, making a beeline for me. I fight the urge to tell Shanna to shoo.

"This would be child number two," he says, thrusting a little boy at me. He's nearly Nicholas' size. I blink a few times before I can talk. Jack and the entire room are trained on me.

"Hi," I address the boy. His curly blond hair covers his eyes. "What's your name? I'm Genesis."

"Cody," the boy answers, sounding like he was ready to burst into tears.

"He told me that too," Red says as my jaw drops.

"He has a name?" Shanna says, louder than she should have.

Jack starts to move to us but quickly realizes that he has a little girl attached to him and he can't leave. His eyes beg me to walk over.

"Where did you find him?" I demand to know.

"He was outside. I was doing a perimeter check and found him in some bushes. I thought it was an animal at first. I actually walked all the way around and was doing a second loop when I realized he was still in here."

"Jared," I refer to Red by his formal name, "We need to talk in a few minutes. Meet me in the hallway?"

He nods. I blink a few times, staring at nothing before I turn back to the child.

"Well, hi, Cody. What are you doing here?"

"I don't know." His voice is quiet.

"Do you know where you came from?"

He shifts in my arms so I put him down. Bending down, I wait for an answer. When I get none, I try a different question.

"Where are your parents?"

"I don't know." Cody pulls at the hem of his shirt.

"That's okay. Are you hungry?" I'll try for more information later. He nods so I take his hand and bring him to Azra.

"This is Cody," I introduce them loudly enough for the

other grown-ups to hear. "He's a little hungry. Can we share our dinner with him?"

Azra hands him bread and meat, just enough to hold in his hands. He takes a bite, chewing slowly.

"Cody, this is Daisy. She arrived here today too. Maybe you could be friends." I hope the encouragement works enough to bring Daisy out of her shell.

We spend the rest of the night trying to get the two children acclimated to their new environment, fishing for whatever information we can get.

THE NEXT DAY, Fall arrives, tearing the leaves from the trees and exposing everything the foliage once covered. We work quickly to gather apples and nuts to use, assuming Winter will follow. The new children adjust to the bunker but still require space.

"Do you ever get tired of climbing trees, Azra?" I shout through the branches.

I stand in the middle of the split trunk of an apple tree, leaning out onto a thick branch, reaching for a piece of fruit. My arm isn't long enough, though my fingertips brush the red skin. I look down, preparing to adjust my stance. My foot doesn't cooperate, sliding on the rough bark. Carefully, I shift my weight to my arm on the branch, wedging my backside against the trunk behind me. Wedged between the parts of the tree, I lift my foot, moving it along the trunk until I find a place to jam it between the split pieces, my toe and heel taking the pressure of supporting my body weight.

It's easier to haul myself up, moving along the branch until I clutch the apple between my fingers. My apple sack slides along my hip, pulled by gravity as it crashes into the trunk beneath me. I cringe, hoping the apples don't bruise.

"Do you ever get tired of spending time with Jack?" Azra counters.

I drop the apple into the bag with the others.

"You're comparing my boyfriend to climbing a tree?"

"You're right, it's not the same. I have more freedom with this than you do." She smiles triumphantly as she drops two apples into her bag.

"You wouldn't be saying that if you had a certain someone to spend time with," I carefully avoid saying Red's name so no one overhears us.

"And yet, here I am, free as a bird, and about to climb higher than you."

"That's because you're tinier and more athletic than me," I counter, reaching up to grab another branch. If I can bend it, I won't have to climb higher.

"Yeah, yeah," she mutters as she climbs into a tall tree next to the one she was picking apples in, trying to reach the top of the apple tree where there were no sturdy branches to stand on.

She leans over and plucks as many as she can reach from the twigs at the top. I grumble, reaching for a branch that is probably too far away to be reaching for.

"We need to come up with a better way of doing this."

"Jack came up with that apple picker. *You* just had to go and give away the only ones to the younger kids so *they* didn't have to climb up here." Azra lectures me good-naturedly.

"You really want to see what would happen if we let Maggie climb up in a tree for this?"

"Good point," Azra laughs. "Are you about done?"

"Yeah, I think I got all I can reach. You want to come check this one, Queen of Trees?"

"Sure," Azra laughs at her new nickname. Turning, she starts to climb back down the tree.

I'm nearly at the bottom of the tree when she screams. I drop several feet, knees bending until my hand hits the ground and I bounce back up to run to her tree.

I duck under the apple tree branches that claw at my eye. My hair flies over my face when I lift my head back up, forcing me to use the entire length of my arm to dip under my hair and lift it up, flipping it obnoxiously over my head.

Azra is on the ground, a giant cut across her stomach from her hip to halfway up her ribcage. Her shirt is missing. She sits in shock as tears pool in her eyes from the pain.

Her shirt isn't on the ground. Looking up, I see it dangling from the tree. I look to my friend to see if I should inspect her injury or get her clothing first. Her eyes dart up and I scramble to the tree trunk as I hear voices in the distance.

I assumed I would find a twig the culprit. Instead, a door has opened in the trunk—a panel that had covered something—disguised as part of the tree.

Azra gulps loudly, trying to control her reaction. She hisses when the wave of pain hits her. I glance down and see her pulling her hand away from the scrape.

I give the panel one more look. If I leave, I risk it shutting.

"Azra, something is up here. Heads up."

I drop her shirt down and she catches it before it hits the ground. Her cut is starting to bubble with blood. She flings it over her head, pulling it on enough to cover her chest but leave the wound exposed until I can examine it.

"There's a panel up here, Az," I narrate for her. "I'm going to block it open so we can check it."

"Okay." Her voice is laced with pain.

I scramble to find a branch, snapping it off. Shoving it between the hinges, I reach for a second branch for good measure. I wedge this one between the tree and the door, so even if it *does* close, it should block it from clicking shut.

Leaves crackle under my feet as I hit the ground. I kneel next to my friend, looking at the mark on her skin.

"I think it's just a scrape," she says, wincing when my fingers get to close to it.

"It looks like it," I confirm, noting the jagged, peeled skin that runs the length of the injury. "Here, let me clean it up."

I quickly pull some bandages out of my pack that I had left on the ground before picking apples.

"Clean it up while I look for some sap," I instruct, leaving a container of water next to her.

My eyes run the length of the pine tree, looking for a bump I can tap in hopes of extracting enough sap to cover Azra's cut. Perrin had taught me how to dress a wound while out in the woods when we were younger, even before he took over for all of the medical procedures in the bunker.

When I returned, Azra was picking the last few pieces of debris from the bark out of her shattered skin. She leans back on her elbows, stretching her skin smooth for me.

"I have the antiseptic." I kneel down next to her and apply the sap to her cut.

"What is going on here?" Shanna asks, Maggie at her side. They both carry bags of apples. Maggie holds the apple picker in her hand—a long pole with a metal basket at the end.

"I'm okay," Azra says. She waits for me to place the bandage over her skin.

"She slipped out of the tree. There's something weird up there," I say absentmindedly as I finish taking care of her. I straighten when I finish.

Azra pulls her shirt down and sits up.

"There's a door up there?" Azra asks, finally registering my words.

"A door?" Shanna scoffs.

"A panel of some kind. I blocked it open. I'm going back up to look. Maggie, would you sit with Azra for a few minutes?

"I'm fine," Azra protested until she realizes *she* was really the one on babysitting duty.

Shanna follows me to the tree.

"Oh," she sounds surprised when she sees the panel protruding from the trunk above us. "What is that?"

"I don't know." I grab a branch. "We're about to find out."

Instead of waiting, Shanna follows me up, climbing the other side of the tree.

Great.

I scoot out on the thick branch near the panel, forcing myself to lean out over the open space to see inside. There's a branch directly under me that is practically perfect to rest my feet on, as if the entire tree had been planned for someone to perch on it and open this panel.

Once Shanna settles into place, I direct her to hold the door open.

"How did she get this open?" Shanna asks, examining the door as I try to open the second panel that it covered. "There's no latch."

"Maybe it's a latch somewhere else on the tree. Her foot could have hit something." I suggest.

Shanna starts examining the area around the door.

"Nothing here, but maybe on your side."

"We'll check before we go back down."

My fingers work along the panel, looking for a place to open it.

"Can you get it open?"

I only purse my lips in response. She peeks around the door, rapping on the panel with her knuckles. It sounds hollow.

"Well, something is back there, that's for sure."

Eventually, I discover that it slides. I push it back into the tree, revealing a hole. It's dark inside, but I can see the outline of an object.

"There's a really good chance that this place is guarded by a rabid squirrel, so after you, Genesis." Shanna stares at me.

"Gee, thanks."

I wrap my left hand around the trunk of the tree just

in case I slip and slowly reach into the secret panel. For a moment, I panic, thinking the sliding panel might slip back into place, directly through my wrist. I laugh at the thought, prompting a look from my companion.

"A report might be nice," Azra shouts up. When I don't respond, Shanna yells down, telling the girls what I'm doing.

I pull a rectangle out of the tree. The shiny end glares when the light touches it. *Glass?* The other side is metallic. My fingers run over it, feeling the texture in the metal.

I hug it to my chest, returning my hand to the darkness to see what else might be hidden. I pull a few pieces of food out, wrapped to keep them fresh.

"This is the strangest thing I've ever seen."

My final find is two rock-like items. Each has a tiny black lever on it. I flip them and it does nothing. Back and forth, I try to see what they accomplish, but nothing happens.

"You take these," I say, handing Shanna the rocks and food. "I'll carry this down."

I shift on the branch, getting ready to climb down.

"We should mark the tree and leave the door propped open."

"Who do these belong to?" she asks.

"I don't know, but maybe someone at the bunker will have a better understanding of these things." I turn to yell down to the ground. "Hey, Maggie, get us some fabric to tie in the tree to mark it."

We slide down, careful to protect the objects when we jump to the dying grass. The wind kicks up, scattering dead leaves around our feet.

I hand the rectangle to Azra and take the fabric from Maggie to attach to the tree.

"Ow," Shanna shrieks as I finish tying on the piece of material. She drops the rocks and food to the ground.

"Shanna!" I lecture, throwing myself to the ground to scoop up what she threw. "Oh."

The rocks are warm enough to shock my system. I recoil, processing what I felt.

"They're hot." I look at Shanna. She looks vindicated. "So...whatever that is, it heats things?"

It comes out as a question because I have absolutely no idea what to make of it.

"Well, if it heats things, that could be beneficial to us," Azra suggestions. "But I think we need to get this back and have Perrin and Nes take a look at this."

"Agreed, let's go."

Maggie scoops up her apple picker and we set out toward the bunker, arriving much later than we should have been back.

CHAPTER 9

"Do you want to break it open?" Todd asks.

"Yes, that sounds like a great idea, Todd," Nes quips. "Let's smash open the only one we have and just *see* if that's the solution. Sounds like a great plan."

"*Sorry*," Todd backs off, holding up his hands. "It was just a suggestion."

"It's fine, Todd. We don't know what it is yet, so it's possible there is something inside, although, it *is* rather thin," Adam stops the argument. "Maybe we should try not to mess with it. We might not want to know what that really is."

Adam, Nes, and Perrin lean over the workbench, propped up on their elbows as they lean in to peer at the rectangle. Perrin flips it over in his hands, examining the edge. Eliza rests an arm over Nes' shoulder as she leans toward Perrin. Her brother flips it over again.

"Are you supposed to look in it like a mirror?" Zach asks as he hovers behind the group.

Several of us stand opposite them against the back

wall, watching the spectacle. We face the door, making us the first to see Kris and Jack walk in.

"Guys, come look what the girls found." Kai waves frantically as they approach.

"What did you find?" Jack says excitedly, flinging his arms over Perrin and Nes' shoulders. He leans over them to inspect the device.

Everyone's faces fall at the same time.

"How did you do that?" Nes gasps.

"Perrin, what did you do?" Adam turns to him, demanding an answer. He looks worried.

Perrin sits in shock. When he finally shakes his head, I notice a blue light glowing off of his skin. They're all covered in the soft glow of light from the device.

I push off the wall and run around the workbench, fighting for a space between Jack and Adam. The rectangle is lit up—numbers and words glowing on it like paper.

"It's a tablet," Perrin finally says.

"A what?" Jack swallows hard.

"It was a device people used to use for communication back in the day," Perrin informs us. "These haven't existed... Well, they're not in any of the journals from the bunker so I don't think we've ever had any of these here before."

"What are those numbers?" I point, touching the light.

It shifts, changing pictures. We all gasp.

"Don't touch the screen," Perrin instructs, "it changes things."

"How is this possible?" Adam leans forward, studying the words on the screen. His head blocks my view.

"This is *us*." Perrin murmurs.

Adam sits back in shock, giving me the opportunity to lean forward to inspect the screen.

Data fills the light space. Perrin scrolls through it revealing dates, weather information, temperatures, and logs. It's everything we've gone through for the last two months and information for the next two weeks.

"Winter comes tomorrow?" Perrin questions. "We're getting Winter again? Not even more than one day of Fall?"

"How did they get this data?" Nes asks. "How do they know this?"

"How could anyone predict what season we're getting?" Jack asks, joining the conversation. His eyes finally shrink to their normal size. "*We* can't even predict what is coming next at this rate. How is any of this possible?"

"Well, first we need to see if it's actually *correct*," Adam pulls us all back together. "And then we need to figure out who this belongs to, how they have access to a device like this, and why they hid it out in the woods."

"Whoever it is has answers for us," Azra adds. "We need to find this person."

"Where did you find this again?" Adam asks. His voice is dark and hollow.

We quickly explain what had happened, describing where and how we found the device. Nes picks up the rocks that we had turned off.

"Those get hot," Azra warns him. Eliza takes the other one sitting on the table and examines it, flipping the switch back and forth.

Nathaniel enters the room, sauntering up next to Adam. He leans his hands on the table, transferring his weight to the workbench. For a moment, he just stares at the tablet.

"Kai just filled me in," he announces to the group. "What are we looking at here?"

Perrin flips the device around to show Nathaniel the screen.

"It's data. It looks like it has the next two weeks predicted on here too."

"Predicted?"

We look uneasily at him, wondering what he's getting at. He stares, waiting for us to get it. We don't.

"What if it's not a prediction? What if it's a plan?" Nathaniel poses. "What if the wall of rain, the changed seasons, all of the insanity we've been going through *isn't* just a coincidence? What if it's someone's plan?"

"Who would plan something like this?" Red criticizes. "None of us even know how to use this type of technology, much less have access to it."

"Maybe it's not one of us," Kalley adds. She looks up at the group. "Before any of you joined us, back when we were kids, someone had suggested that we might not be as in control of things as we thought we were. They noticed things back then, but I don't remember what."

She places her knuckles on her temples and squeezes her eyes shut as she wills the memory to return to her. She rocks forward softly, trying to think back from her corner of the room.

Adam stares at her nervously. He looks like he's ready to rush to her but he holds himself in place.

"Would it be in the journals, Adam?" I ask, fully willing to run to get them.

"No, it wouldn't," he sighs. "The next week he and another man fell through the ice and drown. We focused on safety for two months after that and his thoughts became unimportant."

There is a certain sharpness to his words. He was friends with the people that died. I put my hand on his shoulder.

"It makes sense that someone is controlling all this," Jack interrupts. "They obviously have access to technology that is far superior to our lights and water purifier machinery. It makes sense that someone is doing this to us.

"The only question is who," Jack summarizes, "and where."

"Beyond the mountain?" Kai offers. "You were going to go into the mountains when Winter hit. Do you think they knew?"

"It's possible," Jack muses. "I don't know."

"How are we supposed to find these people?" Perrin asks.

At the same time, the entire group takes a step back, no longer crowding around the screen.

"Perrin, you and Nes study the data. Jack, you too since you're such a data fan," Adam directs. "If there really *is* someone out there, and if they actually knew we were going on an expedition by some miracle, then there has to be some way they found out about that."

"Are you saying one of us is a spy?" Azra asks, hand resting over her stomach where the cut is.

"I doubt that," Adam clarifies, looking to Jack. "If they have all this technology from before we ended up like this, then there is probably a way for them to listen to us."

"Let's remember, that tablet is actually a working device," Nathaniel reminds us. "If they really are from over the mountain, maybe there's more of it there."

"At this point, we need to see if Winter arrives tomorrow and then if the rest of these predictions happen," Adam concludes. "We need to analyze the data on this tablet and then we need to figure out how to get ourselves over the mountains to see what—*or who*—is over there."

We nod at Adam's words.

"I'll go look at the tree where the girls found the tablet," Nathaniel announces.

"I'll go," Jack jumps in.

"You need to help analyze *that* thing," I remind him, pointing to the device.

He looks torn, but finally glances at the tablet with a nod.

"Just be careful," he replies, giving me a pointed look.

"Take me to the tree," Nathaniel says.

"You fell out of the tree?" Red sounds shocked.

"At least I made a life-altering discovery," Azra replies, brushing it off.

"All for the price of what will *likely* be a lovely scar," I remind her. Red's eyes widen as he ducks to look at her.

"It's fine," she rolls her eyes at him. He gives her a look.

"That one," I point ahead at the tree with the fabric attached to it. "Up there."

Nathaniel nods, taking stock of the pine tree. After a

moment, he scales the tree as I had an hour and a half ago. He stands on the branch, peering into the recess.

"How did you get this open?"

"No clue," Azra yells up. "I was busy with the whole falling thing."

"I wasn't here," I add before he can ask.

Something tickles at the back of my mind urging me to remember why we are here. I slowly let my eyes drift, casually turning to take in my surroundings. If we really do have someone here that isn't from the bunker, we need to start taking extra precautions.

When I find nothing out of the ordinary, I lean against the tree, trying to look indifferent. When Azra and I connect, I dart my eyes around, trying to communicate my message to her. It takes a pair of squinted eyes, but she catches on, taking a position against the apple tree trunk. She crosses her arms and tips her head up to talk to Nathaniel but keeps her eyes trained on the ground, searching with me.

"How do you think they found us?" Red asks, making conversation as Nathaniel mumbles to himself above our heads.

"Are we really sure it's not one of us?" Azra jokes. "I mean, Nathaniel has always been pretty shady, haven't you, buddy?"

She yells the last part for him to hear.

"What?"

"Nothing," she sings. "How is it going?"

"I think I found the latch that opens it," he replies, tipping his head to get a look under it.

"Oh good, do me a favor and punch it for me," Azra says snarkily.

"And get on its bad side *too*? No thanks, Az. You're on your own here. If you want to break it, you come up here and do it yourself."

"I'm good." She makes a face, shaking her head. Red and I smirk.

"How about you, Red? Want to go kick it for our girl?" I quip. "Chivalry points if you do."

He grins but doesn't answer.

"Yep, definitely found the button to open this thing," Nathaniel calls down, interrupting.

"Do you think there are more of these around the forest?" I ask, suddenly realizing if there is one, there's probably more.

"If there are, they probably aren't this close together," Red comments. "It sounds like this is somewhere they store things, or maybe even communicate. Practically speaking, if this were me, I'd space them out in different areas.

"We *may* actually want to check for them the next time it's not Winter." He shrugs.

"Coming down," Nathaniel announces, giving me enough time to move before he drops out of the tree.

"Find anything interesting?" I inquire.

"Just what we expected." He looks annoyed.

"Looking for one of the portals the books told us about when we were kids?" Azra teases. He rolls his eyes.

"I think we need to watch this in case they come back," he redirects. "We only have one chance. Once they figure out that we've found them out, it's all over."

"That could be a good thing," I offer hopefully, "Especially if they really *are* controlling the weather around here. Maybe they'll just…leave."

"You think people that are monitoring us and controlling our lives are just going to pack up and leave, Genesis? You've been hanging around your dreamer boyfriend too long. We need to get you around some normal people."

"*You're* his best friend…look who's talking."

"But *I* know where to draw the line."

"He also doesn't make out with him." Azra slings her arm around my shoulder. "That might have something to do with it."

"Ew—" Red gags.

"Ugh, don't remind us."

"Oh, don't be jealous, boys," Azra grins at them. "We can't all be so lucky."

"Come, on, let's get back." I give her an exaggerated smile, eyes wild and huge.

"See, boys?" she presses. "You're missing so much! It could be *you* running back to your kissing-partner."

My threatening look silences her as I quietly promise to shove her at Red if she doesn't stop speaking. Her fingers drum over my shoulder, reminding me how much she adores me, even when I threaten her.

———

"WE'RE BACK," Azra announces, dropping her pack on the workbench.

Nes spins around in the chair.

"Great, because we're locked out." He looks tired.

"We explored a lot of it and thankfully we wrote as much of it down as we could, but it definitely locked about forty minutes after you guys left," Perrin informs us, holding up the dark tablet.

"Hey, babe," Jack leans forward, propping one hip against the corner of the workbench as he stretches to me for a kiss.

I put my hand on his shoulder and lean into the opposite corner of the table, kissing him for a moment.

"Really?" Perrin finally asks.

"You two are disgusting," Nes adds playfully.

I close my eyes, scrunching my nose as I shake my head at him. When I turn back, I notice something different about Jack.

"You took your necklace off?" I ask.

"Oh, yeah. I was pulling one of my shirts off and I

broke the rope. I put it with my stuff. I'll have to get a replacement when we're done."

He smiles and leans in for another kiss.

Seeing him without his pendant was as strange as seeing Nes without his fingers. I'd have to look for a rope to put it on for him later.

"How did we get locked out?" Nathaniel asks.

"We got distracted while talking about the notes and it went to sleep. We haven't been able to get it to open back up since," Nes describes their early evening to us.

I move around to stand by Jack, wrapping his arms around me as I step backward against his chest. He's warm and comforting.

"The kids are fed," Eliza walks into the room. "What have we learned?"

"That if the entire world were run by you, it would be a much more efficient place," I smile from Jack's arms.

"You two make me sick," she jokes, wrapping her arms around Nes' chest from behind him. She drapes herself over him, pretending to judge *us*. Nes grins superiorly at us, aiding his girlfriend's attempt at a joke.

"Maybe it's time for a break," Perrin announces, pretending to heave at the sight of his sister and her boyfriend.

"There are apples down the hall if you all want one. We're trying to conserve food until we see what's going on tomorrow," Eliza announces as her brother brushes past her.

Everyone files out of the room, leaving the device sitting on the workbench. Jack lingers, slowing so that we fall behind the others.

"Want to eat outside with me? Might be the last time for a while if Winter is hitting."

"Sure," I pause, letting him slip into the room to grab some apples for us.

Outside, the evening air is cool. Leaves bounce around the ground, scraping over the grass. Jack sweeps his arm to the side, offering me a seat on the bench we have outside the door for Eliza and the others to sit while watching the children in the yard.

My fingers wrap tighter around my mug of dandelion tea, its warmth empowering me to withstand the slight wind that hits my ear just enough to be annoying. The apple is tart and tangy and absolutely perfect. I should have had one earlier while I was out picking too, but I had been so distracted with my work that I hadn't thought about it.

"How was your day?" I ask. "I mean, aside from all this drama tonight."

His smile is gentle and thoughtful. He gives a little laugh that is more sad than amused before speaking. Jack sets his mug down on the bench and reaches for my hand.

"It was okay. We caught a few things in the traps today, and I managed to get some fish."

"That's great, Jack." I lean my head on his shoulder as I take another bite of my apple. It squirts juice toward Jack, making him grin for real as he ducks.

"How was *your* day, babe?" He turns toward me just enough to brush my hair to the side as his cheek rubs against my head.

"Well, I collected quite a few bags of apples. I'm actually a little sore from the climbing. Honestly, it's fun for awhile, but I really had to wedge myself in some of those trees. I have a feeling that I'm going to pay for this tomorrow."

"Oh. Well," he puts on a smarmy voice, "if you need help working out some of those muscles, I can give you a hand."

He looks me up and down grinning viciously.

"I'm sure you would," my eyes snap, only encouraging him.

Jack scoops up his mug and sets it on the ground so he can spin on the bench. His leg rests between us, foot hanging off the seat. I follow him, placing my drink on the ground where I won't kick it. Unlike him, I pull both legs up onto the bench and lean forward with my elbows on my knees.

I flirtatiously take another bite of my apple.

"You're tempting me, woman," Jack proclaims.

"Am I?"

"You are," he leans forward.

"What are you going to do about it?" I challenge him. For added emphasis, I lean back.

"The better question is, what are *you*?" he torments me, daring me to make the first move.

His hair catches my attention, darling blond bangs falling over his eye. I can't help myself as I reach forward to brush them back. Jack grabs my wrist, turning it to kiss it.

"Mmm," he murmurs into my skin. And he thought *I* was cruel.

I catch Jack's gaze and he lifts his face toward me. I meet him halfway, tossing my apple core to the ground so I can bury my slightly sticky hands in his hair. He doesn't seem to mind.

"We've been together for a very long time, Genesis, and I can't believe you aren't sick of me yet," he murmurs between kisses.

"Two years is a long time?" I ask, trailing my lips up his cheekbone. His eyelids flutter as my nose touches the outside corner of his eye.

"We've been official for two years," he reminds me, voice slightly higher than normal. "But let's be honest, it's been you and me since the beginning. I knew I wanted you the moment you walked into the bunker."

"You remember that?"

"I remember seeing you for the first time, but nothing else. We *were* really young, mind you. But I was older than you anyway, so I don't expect you to remember. I worked really hard over the years to get your attention."

"So you've said." I scoot closer so our knees are touching uncomfortably. Neither of us care. "Fourteen years is a long time."

"It is, but I wouldn't trade any of this if it meant I didn't have you," he croons. At least two of my organs jump inside me.

When I can't breathe, I pull back. His lips are as swollen as mine feel. Jack stares for a moment before dipping down.

"Tea?" he purrs, handing me my mug. It's cold, but it doesn't matter as long as it helps the dehydration.

"Jack, I was thinking," I start, knowing I'm about to ruin the mood. "If there was one hiding place in the woods, don't you think there would be more?"

"It's a logical assumption. We'll have to look into that. *Maybe*," he eyes sparkle mischievously, "we could go on a special little trip to see what we can find out in the woods...*all alone*."

I push his shoulder as he leans toward me. His laugh is perfect.

"We *will* look though," he grows serious. "There was a lot of data on that tablet, Gen. I think they've been watching us for a while now. They have a lot of information on us. I wouldn't be surprised if they've been taking notes on *us personally* too."

"What do you mean?"

"Best guess? They've been studying us."

"But why?"

He shakes his head.

"No matter what, Genesis, I promise I'll take care of you. You will always be safe."

"I know and I adore you for that." My eyes are focused on his lips again. "You're a good man, Jack. And for the record, I'll take care of you too."

I look out at the yard, beyond it to the hills, and out toward the distant mountains. Our home has never been safe, but now it was downright terrifying.

Jack sees my apprehension and pulls me forward, erasing my fear with his eager kisses.

CHAPTER 10

As anticipated, Winter barrels in the following day, leaving Jack's snow removal device covered in a blanket of white fluff. We gear up early in the morning to go out in search of food.

"Have everything?" Jack asks as we reach the point where we will separate.

"*Now* is a great time to ask that, babe," I tease. "Good call."

He branches off with Adam, waving his hand, as Azra and I head toward the pond in the woods. We usually do well ice fishing there.

"Oh no," I yelp as I realize my mistake. "Jack has my seat. I forgot he put it in his pack to carry for me."

"Better go get it," Azra replies. "You don't want to be sitting on that ice without it."

"I'll catch up with you."

When I turn, Jack and Adam are out of sight. Jack walks quickly when he's not slowing down for me.

I follow their boot prints in the snow, knowing I'll eventually catch up to them. The first set of prints walks into the woods, pauses, and then turns around, coming back to follow the second set of prints. Both sets continue on for a while until the second set goes into the woods a sector later, leaving the first set to continue on alone.

I pause for a moment to puzzle out why one of the men walked into the woods and then turned around. They didn't go to the same location. I keep walking to see where the first set of prints leads.

Then I reach a point where I start to worry. The tracks are getting farther away than we normally go in this area. There's no reason for them to be going so far.

A few sector dividers away, I run out of marks in the snow. Unexplainably, they just stop in the middle of nowhere. There are no trees to climb, no alternative paths to take. It is as if a giant had reached down, picked him up, and moved him without leaving a trace.

My eyes check left, then sweep right. Tightness grips my chest and my heart beats faster than it ever has before.

"Jack?" I shout, listening for a reply. "Adam, please answer me!"

"What's going on, Gen?"

I scream at the unexpected voice behind me.

"Gen, what is going on?" Nathaniel repeats.

"I forgot something with Jack so I was following him to get it but his tracks just...end."

"You assume those are Jack's prints?"

"Well, it *could* be Adam. They were out here together. But one of them branched off and then came back out of the woods. They only went in far enough to walk a few feet before turning around."

"So you're guessing that the sketchy prints are from Jack? Why would you think that?"

Because Jack and I were just at the swamp.

"I...don't know, I just assumed," I stammer.

"I know your boyfriend is weird, but let's be logical here, Gen. Of the two, who has been acting stranger lately?"

I blink, thinking over his words.

"You saw how Adam has reacted to everything that's been happening recently. You saw how panicked he looked when we found the tablet. He's been off lately."

"And you're just bringing this up *now*?" I ask. I'm a little shocked. I'd noticed Adam acting weird, but I didn't realize others had too.

Adam was always secretly pulling Jack off to the side lately. I haven't asked Jack what it's been about—I assumed it was bunker stuff—but what if he's really connected to all this? Jack could be in danger.

"You don't honestly think Adam has anything to do with this, do you?" I ask pointedly.

"I think we need to be mindful of him, Genesis. Something's off here. He's the one that pointed out that one of us could be involved. What if it's to throw us off?

"Adam is the only one who can do sketchy things and get away with it," he continues. "He can also point us in the wrong direction without us questioning him because he's in charge."

"He *has* been here the longest," I murmur.

"I'm not saying it's him, but out of everyone at the bunker, he's the one who has been acting strange lately. I know you've noticed it too."

"I have."

"So let's go check this out. If it's Jack, no big deal—it's Jack being weird. But if Adam really *is* up to something, we might get some answers. But Jack is pretty straight-laced. He's on a mission today and nothing is going to tear him away from it. It's the way he is."

"Good point," I nod. Jack always stays on task, even if he has a little fun while doing it. "So what happened to these prints?"

I point out at the snow where his prints are carefully being filled in with snowflakes pushed by the wind in front of our eyes.

"Maybe the wind covered them up?" he suggests.

"The wind covered all of those, but barely touched these?" I look at him like he's insane. In truth, *I'm* the one who is probably a little crazy right now. "Don't you think it would be more gradual? Some of these would be filled in a bit if that's what had happened, right?"

"Usually, but if you'll recall, we're still technically

supposed to be in the middle of Summer from two Summers ago," he reminds me, holding up his fingers. "Do you still think this is Jack and not Adam?"

"Does it make a difference? *One* of them just disappeared. I thought it was Jack, but now I'm not so sure."

He doesn't look convinced.

"Come on, I'll help you look for him. Don't need either one of you getting lost out here, that's for sure."

I start walking forward, but Nathaniel's hand stops me.

"You probably don't realize where we are right now, Gen, since you were so intent on following the tracks, but *that*," he points, "leads to the swamp. It's much more likely that he went this way."

He tries to guide me back toward the woods.

"No, I think he went this way. Call it intuition."

If it was Adam, he was probably going for that shiny thing I saw last time I was there. He's been here longer than any of us and would easily know where to hide things.

Nathaniel reluctantly follows me. I look for anything to show me that I'm headed to the right place. Not that it matters...if Adam is working against us, he could be anywhere.

We stop at the tree line, looking out at the swamp. I expect a lecture about the dangers of the area, but it never comes.

"Careful where you walk," Nathaniel warns me as he steps out of the trees.

"What are you doing?" I gasp, channeling Jack's feeling the last time we were here.

"Investigating," he turns around and frowns. "Isn't that what we're here to do?"

I launch myself forward, partly afraid that he will change his mind and definitely afraid that *I* might change *mine*. The first step feels dangerous. The second step feels rebellious. The third step feels...incredibly slow, so I pick up my pace and catch up to Nathaniel.

I search for the place I saw the shiny thing last time I was near the swamp. I spot some rocks covered in snow in the distance.

"Let's look over there," I try to say casually. He doesn't need to know that I know exactly where we need to be looking.

He eyes me but says nothing as he lets me take the lead.

As we draw near, something moves, catching my attention.

"Let's go," Nathaniel says as he sees it too, widening his steps to cover more ground to reach it faster.

The closer we get, the easier it is to hear the sound of a rope pulling against something. Over and over it sounds, pulling back and releasing. A loud roar fills the air. It's so loud I think we're going to die.

Nathaniel and I both hit the ground, covering our heads to protect ourselves from whatever explosion we just heard. The roar thrums a few times before a silver contraption shoots out from behind the rock.

The noise fades away as Adam rides off, blond hair flashing in the sunlight.

"Adam?" I ask.

"What just happened?" Nathaniel asks. "And what *was* that thing."

"It was a vehicle. Like the kind from the books."

"But we don't have those here. Those haven't existed in decades and no one here has the ability to build one of those."

"*Someone* must have built one."

I continue to stare at the place where Adam disappeared. He left tracks in the snow, but there's no way we could catch him in time.

Nathaniel tears his gaze away from where Adam rode off and marches toward the rocks.

"Time to find some answers."

THE TARP SITS EXPOSED behind the rock. It was definitely the one I saw while I was here with Jack.

"How did you know about this?" Nathaniel demands, wheeling around to face me.

"I don't know about *anything*. I just saw the tarp last time and—"

He takes a dangerous step toward me.

"You were here?"

Oops. I wasn't supposed to mention that.

"Yes," I say, trying not to sound guilty. "When Winter hit unexpectedly last time, Jack and I snuck out to search for some answers since we couldn't go on our trip to see what was beyond the mountains. We ended up coming out here because we already know what's in the areas that we're free to go in. We stayed in the tree line though."

"And you saw this thing before?" he tries to clarify.

"I saw the tarp flapping in the wind and the sun glinted off of that...thing." I pause. "What are you going to do?"

I don't know what I want him to do.

"What do you *want* me to do?" he read my mind. Nathaniel has always been good at getting into other people's brains. It's how he could so easily get under Jack's skin all the time.

"I don't know," I admit.

He places his hands on my elbows, forcing me to look at him.

"You know Jack better than any of us, Genesis. Do you think he knew about this?"

"No!" I yelp. I can't believe he thinks Jack could be involved.

"Adam mentors him. We don't know what's been going on."

"I can't believe he would keep secrets from me," I protest.

"Jack's never been the best at keeping secrets. I don't think he knows about this," Nathaniel offers. "I don't think we should tell Jack. We don't want him giving anything away to Adam."

More than that, I'm worried about what will happen to Jack. He's always been close to Adam and learning that his mentor might be behind everything that's been happening to us could crush him.

"We could be putting Jack in danger if we tell him. We don't know what Adam's doing yet."

"I agree," Nathaniel confirms. "We don't have all of the facts yet. We can't *follow the data,*' as Jack says. We need to know what is going on first. That means we need to get answers before we tell everyone."

He didn't want to sell his friend out too early either.

"We can either get them from Adam or we can find them out ourselves. Honestly, I think we should watch him for a bit." Nathaniel gives his opinion. "We need to watch Jack too. He might be involved without knowing it."

"How do we watch him?"

"We'll take turns. Whenever we see him go somewhere or do something, one of us will follow him. We'll figure out what's going on."

"What do you think we're going to find?"

"I have no idea, Genesis. Truthfully, I hope we find nothing. I hope Adam is investigating this on his own without telling the group and came out here and found that thing and figured out how to work it and he will bring it back to the bunker. I hope it's new technology—"

"It's *old* technology."

"—that we can figure out how to use to our advantage. You saw the way that thing moved over the snow. If we had that, we *could* go over the mountains. Maybe we could even build more of them."

"And if he doesn't?"

"We follow him, and when it comes time, we ask questions. He will answer them, like it or not."

"What do we do *now*?" I finally ask after an uncomfortable amount of silence.

"We wait a few minutes to see if he comes back. If not, we go about our business and you and I meet as soon as we get back to the bunker. You're going to have to start ditching Jack for a while, I think. He can't know about this."

I want to keep Jack as far removed from this as possible, so if that means doing things behind his back, so be it.

"I guess I'll have to stand while I fish." I squish my lips

to one side at the prospect of standing in the cold, hunched over a hole in the ice all day.

"You can take my seat," Nathaniel says, "I was going to roam around today anyway."

His words leave no room for argument. Jack would do the same thing.

I graciously thank him as he pulls it from his pack and hands it to me. I unzip my coat and tuck it inside to keep it warm against my stomach.

"I think we've waited long enough. Go fishing and come find me as soon as you can once we get back to the bunker. And Gen, if he *doesn't* bring it back, we're going to need to look up what that thing was."

"I'll look into it. Maybe I can enlist Nes or Perrin to help without tipping them off."

"Good luck there. You know those two ask too many questions," he smirks.

As I turn to leave, I notice another mound of snow. Nothing peeks out of it like on the other rocks. I glance at Nathaniel. He raises an eyebrow but waits for me.

I drop my forearm onto the snow and brush it away. A few bits of ice slip inside my glove, coming in contact with my skin. I jump at the icy talons.

"*You okay?*" Nathaniel steps quickly toward me.

"Snow in my glove," I yelp, still shocked form the pain of the cold slush.

"Ah," he relaxes, helping me brush the snow off.

It takes a moment, but we brush off the layers of snow until Nathaniel hits something.

"Ow."

We work quicker to uncover another tarp. Underneath it sits a black motorcycle just like the ones I'd seen in the books at the bunker.

"A motorcycle," I breathe.

"A what?"

"It's another vehicle. Usually vehicles have four wheels, but this one only has two. The books said it's pretty dangerous, but also an easy way to get around back in the day. It's not for snow though."

"So one vehicle for snow and one for...Spring, Summer, and Fall?" He puts one hand on his hip. "Gen, this is starting to sound worse and worse. Whoever put these here has them here for a reason. There is some kind of plan for these things."

"I'm starting to see that."

I thoroughly regret coming here.

"When we get back, talk to Jack and see what he knows without giving away that we know anything. You need to be careful with the questions you ask. If he thinks you're looking for something, he's going to want to get involved."

I don't want Jack involved. If Adam really is the enemy, Jack could be an easy target for him.

"We need to cover our tracks," Nathaniel says.

Which is probably what Adam did too.

"Back the same way, please."

I trace my steps, trying to place my feet exactly where they had been before. Nathaniel uses a branch to swish the snow over our tracks, letting the wind do the rest of the work. We covered everything all the way to the woods where I ran into Nathaniel.

"Just make it look like you walked out of the woods, and it should be fine by the time he comes back through," he instructs. "I want you to know, Gen, that I trust Jack. I'm sure he doesn't know anything about all this. We're just being cautious."

I purse my lips and nod.

"It will be okay, Genesis. We'll figure it out. And as soon as Spring hits, I'm coming back and moving that thing. We need every advantage we can get."

He nods before turning back into the woods. I wrap my arms around the seat pad under my coat and walk back toward the pond.

AZRA ASSUMES Jack and I spent a little extra time together and didn't question why I had been gone so long. We fish for a few hours before returning to the bunker. I rush off to find the books to research the vehicle we had found.

The pages turn quietly as I flip through them. No one

has bothered me while I work so far—they're probably busy working with the tablet. Eventually, I find an entry about the device—a thing called a snowmobile. I learn enough to know that it hasn't been sitting there for decades, waiting to be discovered. Someone has been using it for it to be in working condition like that.

"What did you find?"

I jump at Nathaniel's voice. Before the seasons shifted out of synch, I never jumped at anything. Now I was jumping at everything. I need to pull it together before I get myself caught.

"I found it." I point to the book.

"That was convenient."

In the fourteen years I've been at the bunker, never once have I found anything this easily.

Footsteps sound outside and I quickly mark the page with a scrap of paper. I slide it across the table toward Nathaniel and flip another open as Adam steps in.

"Should I even ask?"

"Just doing a little research," Nathaniel comments casually.

"If you're looking to see when the last time this season swap happened was, check journal twenty-eight. If you're looking for more information on how to get the tablet to work, you're too late. Perrin pulled all those this morning. I'm on my way to see him, actually if you want to join."

He offers a tight smile before wandering down the

hallway. He looks tired. I can't blame him. He's been living this life longer than any of us. We're all pretty surprised he's still here—most people die young around here. There are far too many accidents. It's a dangerous world and the older people take on far too many risks. Even Jack and I are starting to do it.

Then again, if he's been working against us, I shouldn't be surprised that he's tired from all of the extra running around, nor should I be surprised that he's still here when most people his age aren't.

"Time to go," Nathaniel says, scooping up the book. He tucks it inside his deep pocket. "We need to see if Jack's back yet anyway."

We make our way to the main room, looking to see if the hunting party is back yet. When we don't find Jack, we help Shanna and Zach with the snow removal device.

I glare at the snow before we shut the door. If I could eliminate a season, it would be Winter.

I take my coat off as soon as I walk into the main room. The kids do their job, swarming me with their warmth. Lilly attaches herself to my side, Nicholas taking the other. He plays with my hair, running his fingers through my straight strands.

Cody walks over, his hair flopping in his face. It might be time for his first bunker haircut. He watches me for a moment.

"Hi, Cody. Do you remember me? My name is Genesis."

The boy nods. Feeling threatened, Nicholas leans in and wraps his arms around my neck, pulling so tightly that my entire body shifts toward him, knocking Lilly off balance.

"How are you doing here?" I ask him.

"I'm fine, how are you?" he replies in a gentle voice.

Where did this child come from?

"Cody, do you know where you came from?"

He shrugs. I wonder if we could get something out of him if we worked with him.

"How is Daisy?"

Cody points across the room to where Daisy is sitting at the table with Eliza. I hope she's making headway with the little girl.

"Come on, Cody," Maggie says, stepping into my view. She reaches down and takes the little boy's hand, clearly pleased to have someone to focus on.

"Bye, Cody," I call as she leads him over to the table with Eliza and Daisy.

"*Don't* tell me I'm being *replaced*."

Jack appears behind me, resting his hands on my shoulder.

"I don't think it's *that* one that you need to worry about," I laugh, looking at Nicholas.

Jack pries his hands off my neck.

"I need to borrow her, buddy. You can have her back later."

He reaches down for my hand and pulls me up. I wink at Nicholas and Lilly before leaving.

Moment of truth—what would he tell me about how much he knows?

CHAPTER 11

othing.

He says absolutely nothing.

Jack goes about our daily business, never once mentioning anything that could be helpful.

"Hey, I found your seat in my pack today, I'm sorry, babe."

"Don't worry about it. I ran into Nathaniel and he lent me his."

"That was kind of him," Jack says, tipping the bucket of snow into the purifier.

"Yeah, he said he was going to be walking around today so he didn't need it."

"Still, it was nice."

"We take care of each other around here," I reply, handing him the next bucket of snow. "It's a shame you didn't get anything today."

"I'm sure tomorrow will be better for hunting," he offers me a smile as our hands brush while transferring the next bucket. "You better stop sulking, Genesis, or I'm going to have to use one of these buckets to start a snow-ball fight. You don't want to find out what it feels like when you have an entire bucket of snow down your back."

"You wouldn't dare." I roll my eyes at him.

"Wouldn't I?" he grabs my waist and pulls me close, nearly tripping me. His scent is overwhelmingly comforting. "I think we've established that I'm willing to do a lot of things, Gen."

I lean out of his embrace to pick up another bucket of snow, holding it to the side of our hug. When he reluctantly takes it from me, I reach into the bucket, pick up a handful of snow, and throw it at him before running into the hallway.

"Gen!" he yells. I hear him brushing the snow off. It hits the floor with a crunch. "It's a good thing I love you!"

Nathaniel appears, handing me another bucket of snow. He leaves one on the ground outside the door.

"Anything?" he mouths. I shake my head.

Nathaniel glances at the door before retreating to bring more snow in. Kris and Zach follow behind him, each carting buckets of snow.

I walk back into the room, prepared for an attack. Instead, he gently takes the bucket from me, dumping it into the purifier. I step outside, continuing the cycle of bringing in more snow.

"Do you really think it's going to be Summer tomorrow, Jack?"

"The tablet has been right so far."

"It's been one day and we assumed Winter would come after Fall. This skips an entire season."

"That's true," he says, lifting another bucket. His muscles pull against his shirt, making me pause to stare at his arms. "I suppose if it *does* jump, we'll have to watch for things."

"Like what?"

"I don't know, extra mud? Extreme heat? Some weird storm because of the drastic switch."

"Oh gosh, not another rain wall."

"Let's hope not. That was freaky," Jack shakes his head.

"What's freaky? The fact that you two are still madly in love with each other?" Azra asks, struggling under the weight of the bucket of snow. "I agree. It's freaky."

"Really, Az? You know Red is going to walk around that corner any minute," Jack teases her.

"Did I hear my name?" Red calls from right outside the door.

Azra looks ready to murder Jack. I elbow him hard enough to knock the wind out of him.

"Hey, did you need me?" Red asks.

"Yes," I cover, "could you please move a few of those buckets in here? My arms are getting tired."

"Sure, Gen." He ducks into the hallway and starts moving buckets two at a time in front of the purifier.

"Hey, guys, Adam called a meeting in half an hour," Azra finally says. "Time to wrap this up."

I grab a bucket and lift it. If Red moves them all inside, Jack and I can quickly put them through the purifier. We work quietly next to each other as Azra goes to tell the others to pause on bringing in more buckets.

***

"ACCORDING TO THE TABLET, tomorrow will be Summer," Adam informs the fifty-some people in the room. "We need to be prepared if that's the case. We also need to be prepared if it isn't.

"Our goal is to gather as much food as we can if Summer decides to grace us with its presence tomorrow," Jack adds.

"We're going to break you all into teams. Some of the younger teens are coming out with us tomorrow. If you're in charge, you need to watch over them, but you also need to be sure to instruct them." Jack says, looking around. "If things even out, we'll have more time to test them before sending them out on their own, but for now, we need all hands on deck."

Jack is animated as he speaks, hands moving with

every word. I notice his necklace still hasn't been fixed. I'll take care of it after the meeting.

"Keep your eyes open for anything unusual," Jack instructs the group. "We don't know what we might find out there. The animals are being disrupted by all of this, the river might not unfreeze completely, and you never know if a new child might wander in."

"Under no circumstances should you be with a group of less than three people," Adam instructs, making eye contact with as many people as possible. "If we really *are* being observed, we don't want to be caught alone. If they've figured out that we found their hiding place, we don't know how that will change the game. They've never approached us before, but this might make things different for them now. Be prepared to defend yourselves and each other at all times."

Adam really knows how to play the part. It makes me question just how deep his involvement is.

"In your groups, keep at least one person on look out at all times," Jack adds. "One person should be vigilant and paying attention at all times. Take turns, but make sure one person is focused on your surroundings and not just finding food. Food does us no good if you're all hurt or dead."

The frightening thought has a ripple effect on the room as faces pale. Jack looks pleased with the reaction to his point. I could smack him for that.

"We're assigning groups tonight so we don't waste time tomorrow," Jack continues. "If anything looks strange tomorrow or feels off, we want you to return to the bunker. Until we can gauge what will happen now that we've discovered their little toy, we have to be careful."

"Questions?" Adam asks, looking around the room. Everyone stays silent. "Good. Now, go get ready. We'll be around with assignments in a bit. And Red, take a few of the boys and go handle the snow removal."

Red nods, snagging Kris and two of the other guys. The four of them jog down the hallway to the tunnel door.

"Have you taken another look at that tablet," I ask Adam as we walk.

"No, haven't touched it. Why, did you want to play with it?"

"Oh, I—"

"Why don't you grab something to eat and come take a look," he pats my shoulder with his open hand. "Bring Jack along. Maybe you two can discover something the rest of us haven't."

Jack managed to get quite a bit ahead of us while we walked, putting him out of hearing range, but Nathaniel catches Adam's conversation. He quietly keeps us in his peripheral vision until Adam splits off from me.

"He wants me to look at the tablet," I mumble, trying not to move my lips.

"Do it. Just don't go alone."

"He told me to bring Jack." I reach up placing my hand on the back of my neck to work out a kink. It's a sneaky move that allows me to better see Nathaniel out of the corner of my eye without my hair falling in the way.

"Get to it," he replies, branching off.

I make a quick stop to pick up some rope and Jack's pendant so I can fix his necklace. Maybe he won't ask many questions if I can distract him with my gift.

In the main room, we quickly eat before I pull Jack back into the hallway.

"I have a gift for you" I inform him. "And Adam sent us on a mission."

"Sounds interesting," he grins. "Tell me more."

I pull the pendant out of my pocket, clearly surprising him.

"Well, would you look at that? Thanks, babe."

He kisses my cheek as I drop the necklace into his palm.

"You're the best," he reminds me as he fixes it around his neck. "Now what's this mission?"

I pull him through the doorway to the workroom and have my hand on the tablet on the workbench before he realizes what's happening. I have little hope that we can unlock the tablet, but at least we'll be able to say we tried.

"Adam asked us to look at it."

He stares at me as I touch a button on the locked device.

When his face is suddenly illuminated in a blue glow, I whip back around.

It's on.

CHAPTER 12

"Where have you been?" I hiss at Nathaniel the next morning.

"I went out and moved the motor-thing," he hisses back. "By the way, it really *is* Summer out there. I nearly drowned in my own sweat."

"You moved the motorcycle?" I question.

"Yeah, that way he can't use it. You can't use what you can't find," he snips. "Well, *one* of our people will probably find it—it's not like I could move it very far—but I got it a few sectors away and covered it up. We can get at it if we figure out how to use it and need it."

"Did you drive it?"

"Does it look like I'm stupid enough to get on a piece of machinery that I don't know how to use?" He glares at me. "What happened last night? *Oh*, hey, Todd."

I look up as he quickly changes the subject.

"Hey, man. Did you hear? It's Summer," Todd salutes as he walks by us.

"Yeah, I heard. See you out there?"

"Hope not," Todd grins. "We're in two different areas today."

"Good point," Nathaniel chuckles until Todd is out of sight. He drops his voice so we aren't overheard. "What happened last night?"

"I touched the tablet and it turned on. There was new information. We now have the weather for an additional three days."

"So they haven't figured us out yet," he stares at a spot on the ground as he processes what this means. "It can't last much longer, but at least we still have the upper hand."

Jack bounds up to me, possessively wrapping an arm around my waist.

"Morning, babe." He kisses my temple, never taking his eyes off Nathaniel. Whatever he's trying to prove, I'm getting a little annoyed with it. "I hear you two are hunting together today."

"That's what I hear," Nathaniel responds. "We can head out whenever Azra is ready."

"You're going out with Kris and Zach, right?" I double check. At least I know he'll be responsible with Zach's oversight.

"Indeed, I am. I have a feeling you three will make it back before we do." He shakes his head jokingly.

"Aww, am I missing the sob-fest between our two lovers?" Azra wraps her arm around me as she approaches, pulling me out of Jack's embrace. "Too bad, she's mine today, *pretty boy*. You can have her back tonight."

"Now, now, you two, play nice," I mock them.

"Fine, but just remember, Azra, I saw her first," Jack says playfully, waving me off.

"Yeah, but I was her best friend first, pretty boy." She winks at me before sidling up to Nathaniel. "And then there is this one. You kids ready to get going?"

We say goodbye to Jack and walk out of the bunker before the other teams are ready. Nathaniel is right—it's incredibly warm out.

"Even the mud has dried up," Azra complains as we walk toward the sector of the woods we're supposed to be trapping in.

Nathaniel sets a quick pace, pushing us to not fall behind. Keeping up with him is one thing in the open areas, but once we reach the tree line, ducking under branches and jumping over roots makes it harder.

"I know you're eager to see what this weird Summer has brought us, Nate, but slow down, would you? I'm short, remember?" Azra calls.

"Hate to break it to you, Azra, but we're not hunting today." He glances over his shoulder at me. "Tell her."

"Tell me?" Azra's voice raises several pitches as she excitedly turns to me, walking sideways. "Tell me what?"

"I don't know what he's talking about," I reply, "What are you talking about?"

"We're not going hunting today, but we need everyone to think we are. We have another mission to run."

I suddenly realize we're headed toward the swamp. Then again, this path could take us to several sectors, but I have a feeling I know where Nathaniel is going.

"Tell her," he insists again.

"You can't tell anyone, Az. Not even Jack knows."

"You didn't tell your *boyfriend* about this?" Her eyes widen in concern. "What's happening?"

"We think we know how the people who are watching us know so much about us."

"How?" she demands to know, latching on to my arm.

The sun dances on the back of my neck, creating shadows of warmth against my skin. My body tingles making me stretch up to catch more of the rays. I almost want to chirp for joy like one of the birds in the trees after having suffered through Winter yesterday.

"We think it might be Adam," I admit. "He's been here longer than any of us, he knows all sorts of things we don't know."

"*Because* he's been here longer than us," she protests, using my words against me.

"He was surprised about the tablet," I point out.

"Weren't we all?" Convincing her isn't as easy as Nathaniel thought.

"But did you see his face when everyone saw it, Azra? Something was off." I explain, hoping she remembers.

"Get to the point," Nathaniel criticizes.

"We saw him, Azra. Last Winter when you and I were fishing and I went to get my seat from Jack. I didn't find Jack. I found footprints that stopped in the middle of nowhere. I ran into Nathaniel—which is where I got the seat from—and we went searching for the missing person and ended up at the swamp.

"Honestly, I thought it was Jack and he was going to investigate because he and I went out there a few days earlier and we saw something—" I say as she cuts me off.

"You were in the swamp? Lewis *died* in that swamp, Gen, have you lost your mind?"

"We didn't go in," I try to calm her. "Well, *Jack and I* didn't anyway. When Nathaniel and I went, it was all covered in snow and safe, so when we walked in to investigate what I had seen before, we found Adam on a snowmobile."

"A *what*?" Her voice is growing grumpier by the second.

I point to a branch, reminding her to duck. She slips under it without poking her eye out.

"It's like a sled but it has a motor on it so it goes really fast. I'll show you a picture in a book later." I didn't expect to find it back in the swamp. "The point is that Adam was hiding a snowmobile and a motorcycle—that's another type of vehicle but for times when there *isn't* snow— in the swamp and has been using them to get around," I add before she can ask. "We're guessing he's working with the owners of that tablet."

"So what are *we* doing about it and why doesn't *Jack* know?" Her hands find their way to her hips, making her look like an annoyed pixie from one of the bunker storybooks.

"We're watching the site where the snowmobile and motorcycle are," Nathaniel finally reenters the conversation. "I hid the motorcycle early this morning before the bunker woke up, and he can't use the snowmobile without snow.

Oh, so he *did* return it to the swamp.

"Jack doesn't know because we don't have any evidence yet and if we're wrong, Adam is his mentor. That would break Jack, and their relationship would never be the same, even if we prove him innocent."

"He's not going to like that when he finds out," she scolds.

"I know." I sound like I'm whining.

"Sorry, I'm Team Jack on this one." She shakes her head at me.

"Azra," I protest, "If he *isn't* innocent, that means Jack could be in danger."

She gives me a look that says *I-get-that-but-he-still-needs-to-know.* Her older sister techniques would have been amazing outside of the bunker. Good thing we're the same age and she can't hold it over my head.

"I'll tell him. Later." I promise. It isn't fair to keep this from him.

"I don't like this," Azra says, realizing we're closing in on the swamp.

"You don't have to go into the swamp, Azra," Nathaniel chides. "You can stay in the trees."

"Actually, you know what? That's just our training kicking in. *I'm* the daring one in this little group, not the dark-haired raven. Let's do this." She puffs out here chest and takes longer strides. I stifle my laugh at her change in demeanor.

"Here we are," Nathaniel announces. "We'll watch from over here. One of us can watch where the motor-cycle should be, one will watch the path, and the other can look from something to take back so we don't look like we did nothing all day."

I'm glad Nathaniel is on our side for this little show-down. I hadn't even thought to spy today.

We show Azra where everything is. Her eyes grow wide when she sees the snowmobile. The group hurries back to our positions, hiding among the trees far enough back that even if Adam *does* enter through the woods the way we normally come, he shouldn't be able to see us.

Painstakingly, we wait.

"Pst," I make a noise, alerting Nathaniel. He passes it along to Azra who is further in the woods, watching for game. She slowly makes her way toward us, careful not to be seen.

Someone approaches, but I can't see his face yet. I feel Nathaniel behind me. He gently places his hand on my shoulder to let me know he's watching.

We see it at the same time.

The man walks into the swamp like he owns the place. I supposed he *does*. Without a care in the world, he moves behind the large rocks, looking for the motorcycle.

His cry when he discovers it is missing confirms what I swore my eyes lied to me about.

He moves quickly around the area, looking for his lost mode of transportation but it's nowhere to be found thanks to Nathaniel.

He looks angry, stomping off in the opposite direction —the "fast" way toward the bunker—avoiding walking back through the woods.

"We have to go after him," Nathaniel whispers harshly in my ear.

We wait until Jack is far enough away and then we follow him.

CHAPTER 13

M y head is reeling.

It wasn't Adam after all. It was Jack.

My boyfriend was the one behind all of this.

"Maybe it's not as bad as it looks," Azra whispers. "Maybe he's doing the same thing we are, only he's a few steps ahead of us. You said he probably came out here to investigate what you saw, so maybe he did and he already knows something we don't."

"It's possible he's going back to the bunker to tell everyone. Or confront Adam." I try to convince myself. "He spends a ton of time with Adam so maybe he pieced it together before we did."

"Stay quiet. We'll find out soon enough," Nathaniel lectures.

We follow Jack, turning long before we come to the bunker, dismantling the idea that perhaps he really wasn't a traitor.

He must assume no one knows where he is because he never turns back to check if he is being followed. The moment he turns into a restricted area, I feel the temperature drop. Not just my body, but the temperature of the air actually adjusts to be more comfortable.

"It's cooler, right? Somebody tell me they noticed that too." Azra looks around, eyes squinted.

"Definitely noticed it," I respond, trying to take in my surroundings.

"Yep, I noticed," Nathaniel replies in a whisper. "I think we need to get a little closer. We don't know this area and if we lose him, we'll never find him."

We gain a few yards, still staying far enough back to avoid being spotted easily. Jack's figure is small on the horizon ahead of us, but I can still see him.

We walk for half an hour. We're several miles into the off-limits zone outside of the bunker. I wonder if this is where Jack was always slipping off to at night. It's close enough to the bunker that he could come and go without it being too troublesome, but far enough away that no one would think to look here—especially with the dangers I assume we passed.

The building is taller than anything I've ever seen. The sun reflects off of it, sending a menacing shadow out behind Jack as he sprints toward the structure.

He walks inside without hesitation.

"*That's* bad," Azra says what we're all thinking.

"What is he doing here?" I switch my concerned girlfriend button on like I had turned on the heat button on the rocks we found the other day.

"Wait," I say, the thought triggering another. "The tablet isn't Adam's, is it?"

"Probably not," Nathaniel confirms. "But that doesn't matter now. We need to get inside."

"*Excuse me*?" Azra yelps. "We're not going in there. What if we never come out?"

"I'll go," I say, overcome with a moment of crystal clear rationality. "If Jack is involved, he won't let them hurt me, and if I don't come back out, or if he leaves without me, you'll be able to launch a rescue mission."

"No way—" Azra points her finger at me.

"Azra, you go back to the bunker and find some help," Nathaniel instructs.

"Not a chance, hot shot. You're forgetting that we still don't know who else is involved. What if Adam *is* in on this? What if he's only sending Jack on errands? The only thing we know for sure is that the *three of us* aren't involved—or we're really good at lying."

She has a terrifying point.

"I'm going in. Stay here. If I'm not back in an hour," I pause, thinking it though. "Just...get out of here. Don't do anything stupid."

"We're coming in for you," they both say at the same time.

"And you have half an hour, so don't pull anything stupid, Genesis," Nathaniel adds.

"Be safe." Azra squeezes my hand. "And be smart. Don't do anything to get caught. Just observe if you can and then report back and we'll decide what to do together."

I nod before turning to walk up to the building. Staying behind the trees that line the path up to the metal structure, I creep quietly along. When I see no one around, I slip inside.

UNLIKE THE BUNKER, there are no blue lights in this building. Everything is brightly lit. The hallway I step into leads to another hallway. I follow along its path until I hear noises. Not knowing where else to look, I move toward the sound, hoping I find Jack here against his will.

My mind conjures up reasons for him being here. *He* was threatened. *I* was threatened. Maybe he's following Adam's orders or doesn't know what's really happening. There has to be *some* explanation.

I press my ear to the door. Someone is inside, but it sounds like they are far enough away that I might be able to crack the door open.

Risking it, I open the door just enough to peek inside. There's a pile of boxes I can hide behind if I can make it through the door. I push it open another inch, just enough to get a better picture of the room. Still nothing.

I swallow, holding my breath as I open the door just enough to slip in. I hold my chest tightly with one hand to make myself as small as possible to fit through the doorway.

I dive behind the boxes, waiting to be found. When no one comes for me, I try to locate the source of the sound. It's a thunking noise, like someone turning one of the hand crank washers at the bunker. When it feels safe, I slowly turn around, crawling to my knees.

"How could you let them find the tablet?" an angry man's voice rumbles, echoing around the large room. It sounds like a cavern. "It's not like you have a hard job. There's nothing complicated about it."

The clunking noises stop as the voice grows louder.

"You have an easy life. You're safe from all harms, you're never in any real danger, and all you have to do is help me. Is that too much to ask?"

The man pauses but not long enough for anyone to answer.

"Do they suspect you? Do they know you're involved in this? What would you have done if they had managed to get the tablet open? Just what do you plan on doing about all of this?"

I lift my head up over the top of the boxes.

"They saw the tablet," Jack grumbles, looking down at

his shoes. He stands over a giant wheel-like valve of some kind, resting his hands on it. Behind him are rows of tables and chairs in straight lines on different tiers. Lights sparkle and glitter.

Screens, much like the one on the tablet, are suspended from the ceiling, facing the rows of tables and chairs. Numbers scroll across them with weather data similar to what we found on the tablet, information, and numbers I don't understand.

Jack looks agitated, rocking back and forth on his heels. He still refuses to make eye contact with the man standing across from him.

"You need to salvage this," the white-haired man growls.

"Yes, Uncle Mory," Jack replies, eyes still trained on the ground.

What?

The man stomps away and Jack walks over to one of the seats. It swivels when he touches it and he sits. He taps something on the table and the undersides of his fingers start to glow. There must be a tablet screen embedded in the table.

He looks up at one of the screens and I scramble to duck, but he doesn't notice me. I crawl to the end of the boxes, carefully lifting one knee at a time and gently setting it back down.

Jack taps away on the screen on the table. The

numbers change on the screens facing me and I assume they must show the same things on both sides. He swipes at the tablet screen and all of the screens in the air change.

I watch as he reads the data. His lips form the words he is reading. Most of the time he types without looking back down, but occasionally, he glances at his hands with an annoyed look on his face. When he looks back to the screens above him, I assume he must have found his solutions because he looks more at ease.

He launches himself out of the chair, frightening me. I dart backward, hoping he didn't see anything. My heart is beating so fast that I can hear it over the sound of Jack's heavy footsteps.

Jack walks up to the giant valve in the middle of the room and he spins it. The turning motion causes the loud thunking sound I heard earlier.

My boyfriend pauses to watch the screen before angling the spinning valve back and forth, clicking something into place. When he gets it where he wants it, he sighs. His shoulders sag as he steps back, walking over to the desks.

"Is it done?" the white-haired man asks, walking back into the room.

"It's taken care of," Jack answers reluctantly.

Jack leans over the table. He taps a few more times on the tablet screen, pulling up maps of the snow globe covered in colors. Each is marked with a date. Yesterday, today, tomorrow.

He presses a button as the two quietly mumble and point to the screens. The map with today's date starts to shift, changing colors as it dances across the screen.

Jack is the one controlling the weather. I lurch backward, away from the man I thought I knew.

Their heads jerks toward me as my foot catches one of the boxes, sending it tumbling to the ground.

CHAPTER 14

There's a spark when we make eye contact. It's that same ever-present electric current I feel every time I look at him. Only now, it's also mixed with fear and uncertainty.

My boyfriend punches a button on his screen and leaps up, body at full attention. Horror washes over his face.

Jack nearly collides with the table as he tries to weave his way around the furniture to get to me without crashing into his uncle. I have the advantage. I'm across the room and near the door.

I no longer know this man. I can't trust him. I have to get out.

I manage to push myself up, though I'm not sure how, and I throw the door open, attempting to slam it behind me.

"Genesis!" he calls, struggling to catch up.

I veer down the hallway and barrel toward the main door. I'm actually surprised no one is guarding this building. They must have thought they'd never be found.

I expect the air to be stifling, but then I remember that the temperature is controlled here. It's more temperate and comfortable. Thinking back, even inside the building was cool and refreshing, better than anything I had ever experienced inside the walls of the bunker.

"No," Jack reaches around my waist as he catches up to me, dragging me back toward the building.

"No," I yell as he pulls me inside, hoping to warn off the others. I shake my head to emphasize that they should wait. "Stop! Not yet!"

"Inside, Gen," Jack growls viciously. Suddenly he's starting to sound like his uncle. His voice is cold when he speaks quietly into my ear, "You play along with whatever I say or I might not be able to protect you."

I catch him by surprise when I elbow him in the shoulder as he pushes me forward down the hall. He struggles to catch his breath for a moment, but Jack manages to tighten his grip on me. My arms are twisted behind my back.

"I'm trying to help you, knock it off," he hisses in my ear. "Play along, Genesis, or so help me!"

His words are clipped and increasingly frustrated with each step we take toward the door.

"You're going to get us *both* in trouble. Now smile."

Just before we reach the door, he spins me around to face him. I cringe as his lips dart out for mine, trying to convince me that nothing is wrong. He looks horrified by my reaction.

"You have to pretend you already know about this place. If he doesn't think you're going to work with us, we're in trouble," he rushes to speak. "We can talk about this after, but for the love of storybooks, Gen, please just act nice when we go in there."

He looks like he wants to drag me close to his chest and protect me from an oncoming avalanche from the mountains with his own body. He looks helpless and hurt and small.

Until a few minutes ago, that would have meant something to me.

"Please, Gen, let me protect you," he begs.

Jack tentatively holds out his hand to me.

Having no other choice, I take it.

IT TAKES Jack twenty minutes to convince his uncle that he told me about whatever operation they are running. He sets me down in a chair in the back where a big, burly man sits and stares at me so I won't run.

I try to make out what Jack and his uncle are talking about, but their short, clipped words are intentionally low so I cannot hear. I lean to the right, trying to get closer. I stop when the man glares at me.

Finally, Jack climbs the steps to me, taking my hand and pulling me out the door.

"I'm going to give her a tour," he calls to his uncle.

He forcefully guides me out the door, clamping down so hard on my hand that I think he might accidentally break it. I can't blame him for being nervous that I'd try to run again. I have every intention of doing *just that* the moment I find an opportunity. I'm worried what Nathaniel and Azra might do to attempt a rescue.

"I know this is all confusing," Jack whispers into my ear. I used to love when his breath moved my hair, tickling my ear. Now it repulses me. Unfortunately my brain forgets to tell the rest of my body and it melts under his touch. "Please just hear me out. It's not as bad as it looks."

"It looks like *you're* the traitor, *Jack*. It looks like you've been controlling the weather all these years. It looks like *you're* the one who has been starving our children and taking our fingers and toes, *Jack*. *That's* what it looks like." I can't help my anger.

I emphasize his name like it's a cuss, never to be said in front of the children.

"*Wait*," I snap.

I wheel around to face him.

"If you've been doing all this..." I pause, the gravity of the situation washing over me. "Jack, did you kill our friends? All of those people are dead because of you, *aren't they? How can you live with yourself*, Jack?"

I pull away from him, but I can't go far...I'm in a tiny hallway.

"How did you decide who lived and died, Jack? Am I alive because we were dating? Was I supposed to die at some point too?"

I must look as deranged as I feel. Jack jumps forward and clamps his hand over my mouth.

"They're okay, Gen, they're all fine." I hear his words but I don't process them. "They're all okay, I promise. Here, I can show you."

He grabs my wrist and drags me to his right, down a side hall. I'm pushed into a chair that swivels, covered in a soft cushion. Jack leans over me to push buttons that activate a screen. I jolt backward as his elbow nearly collides with my jaw.

"Here. Look." He desperately points to the screen where an image of a man in a bed pops up. "This is called a video feed. It's live footage, see? And look, look who that is."

I eye Jack warily but eventually look back to the screen. Jack hits a button and it zooms in closer.

"Lewis?" I blink back tears of confusion.

"We just made it look like he had died in the swamp, Gen. He's okay. He was cracking up in there and we couldn't let him suffer like that." He tips his head to the side. "Well, technically, Uncle Mory didn't want him to hinder the results, but I got him out because he needed to get out of there."

His expression was hopeful, though there was a touch of pride mixed in as well. *I could claw him, kiss him...one of those actions would work.*

"But see? He's fine. We're getting him the help he needs."

"Locked in a room?" My doubt hurts him and his face crumples. He swallows, unsure of himself.

"He needed help, Gen. It's a medical facility."

"Where are the others?"

He wants me to play nice? *Tough.*

"Eustace is down the hall. Once we explained everything to him, he wanted to help. You remember him, don't you?"

He was Adam's mentor during my early years at the bunker.

"Eustace did this to us?" I ask harshly. I clearly don't care about Jack's feelings here because I have no ability to reign myself in.

The room is painted in white, with soft gray accents everywhere. A board is attached to the wall with pieces of paper pinned to it. A white colored board sits next to it with notes scribbled in red and blue. For a tiny room, it looks so spacious.

"Gen," he begs.

"No, Jack. You don't get to act like this," I can feel the rage building. "You've lied to me for..."

I realize I don't actually know.

"How long, Jack?" I demand. "How long has it been?"

On the screen behind Jack, Lewis shifts in his bed, tossing the covers off of his legs. I ignore Jack as I stare. He waits for me to look back.

"Let me explain everything."

"Get to it," I snap. No mercy.

He leans against the desk, taking my hands in his. My instinct is to pull away, but if I want answers, I have to listen.

"I've always known about this. I was put in the snow globe to monitor everything. There's always been someone from Morozoko there."

"From where?" I purse my lips. I will myself to stop.

"Morozoko Industries. It's where you are now. Well, one of our locations anyway." He gives a tiny shrug. This is bigger than I thought. "It's been run by my relatives for decades. Gen, there's a whole world outside of the Globe."

He ducks his head, looking out from under his bangs. I will not give in to him, despite his little tricks.

"In the outside world, there's a war raging. Things are changing and it's dangerous out there. It was so dangerous that my own parents sent me to my great uncle, Mory, to be protected. That's why I'm here.

"Mory took me in and put me to work in the Globe.

There's always been at least one of our people in the Globe at all times."

Apparently, I've discovered where he got his cutesy little name for our snow globe of a home and it's no coincidence.

"Which is why you're basically second in command." I glare at him.

His finger thrums over the soft spot on my hand. He means to distract me and soften his words.

"So Adam is in on this little game too?" I press.

"No." Jack looks shocked. "Adam has nothing to do with it."

"Than why was he behaving so strangely?" I ask pointedly.

"You see, Gen, whenever people start asking questions, or they get to close, or they get to the point where they compromise the study, we removed them from the Globe. Adam started asking questions and I intervened before things were noticed. He knows I'm somehow connected to all this, and he understands that if he asks questions, he'll end up like Lewis and Eustace." So Adam kept quiet to save his own skin. "He doesn't know they are safe though."

"And why would you do that? If being here is so great and you have people like Eustace walking out of the bunker and into a job with you, why did you stop Adam from being pulled out too?"

Jack takes a steadying breath before answering.

"It's safer inside, Genesis. As hard as it is, it's safer there. And Kalley, of course. I didn't want to risk separating them."

"Why are we in there, Jack?"

"Like I said, Gen, outside of these walls there is a war going on. Bombs are being dropped, toxins and viruses are being released. Scary things are happening. One of the scariest things is a type of bomb that will have such an impact on the world that it will alter things like the weather. We've already seen it on a small scale, but the people building it are creating a larger version faster than we can create something to stop it or counter its effects.

"We've known about this for a long time. We've seen it in action since before you and I were ever born." This sounds rehearsed, like he's told this story before. "A few years before the Globe started, my uncle witnessed the aftermath of one of the trials runs. His family's company has always been working in this general area, but he saw a need. The government granted him money to start a research project to help us adapt to whatever we might face."

"So we're a test?"

He pauses, trying to find the words that wouldn't set me off.

"In a manner of speaking," he says softly. "We've been working to study the way people adapt. We need to know what changes they can survive and learn how they do it. We need to know what we need to do to prepare people to withstand—"

"Do you even *hear* yourself?" I explode. So much for holding it in. "You *experimented* on us."

"I was in there too, Genesis," he offers quietly.

He sucks in a gasp when I slap him.

"You were in there to monitor and report on us," I correct.

"Gen," he begs again.

"Let me go, Jack. If you care for me one bit, you will let me out of here right now."

"I can't do that, Gen. You don't understand yet."

"I'm not staying here, Jack. Nathaniel and Azra know I'm here. They'll get everyone in the bunker and they'll all show up here."

"How do they know about this place, Gen?" Suddenly he's concerned. "Are they here, Genesis?"

I refuse to answer.

"Gen, where are they? We can't let them find them. We have to get them out of here."

Again, I say nothing. I have no intention of making this easy.

"Stay here," he instructs, rushing to the door. I try to follow him, but he slams the door so quickly that he nearly catches my fingers.

I tug on the doorknob, but it's stuck.

"Jack!" I yell, pounding on the door.

"I'll be right back, Gen," he calls through the door.

When I finally get it open, the big man is standing in front of it, leering down at me. I back up and allow him to close the door.

Lewis is still on the screen so I sit to watch. Jack had used the buttons to operate the screen. Maybe I could too.

I tap on the buttons, waiting after each one to see what would happen. Eventually, I find arrow buttons and the screen engages. I flip through several video feeds, watching different people.

If Jack could watch people like Lewis, was he also watching people inside the bunker? Is that how he always knew so much about me?

I turn as Jack walks back in.

"I sent them back to the bunker," he says, closing the door behind him.

"Where are they?" My voice sounds more desperate than I want it to. "Are they okay?"

My face feels strained, like I'm holding back tears. Maybe I am.

"I wouldn't hurt them, Genesis. Who do you think I am?" He looks so betrayed. "Gen, you know me."

Unexpectedly, he sinks to his knees.

"Gen, please, *you know me.*"

"You're watching Lewis...were you watching us in the

bunker too?" I look straight ahead, refusing to make eye contact with him where he kneels on the floor. He clings to my wrists.

"No, there's not enough power in there. We only pump in enough for the lights. Uncle Mory didn't want to risk anyone tapping into it. We had to make it the most basic conditions possible to get the best results."

At least Mory and his friends haven't been sitting around watching me kiss his nephew.

"Where are Nathaniel and Azra?" I ask again.

Jack bows his head in defeat. Ordinarily, I'd comfort him, but I couldn't bring myself to give him even the smallest mercy.

"I went outside and I found them hiding. I waved them over and explained that something was going on and that you were safe. I told them that you and I would be out in a few hours and if we weren't back at the bunker by night, they could come storm the castle."

He glances up hopefully.

"This hardly looks like a castle," I finally make eye contact. "It's more like the evil villain's lair."

"Where do you think I got the description for those stories Lilly likes?" He laughs pitifully at his own joke.

I roll my eyes, trying not to grin at the look on his face. He takes it as a sign that I might be relenting because he jumps to his feet and wraps his arms around me protectively.

"We're going to go back to the bunker tonight, but I have to be sure you're going to keep this between us. I know we have a lot to talk about, but just give me a few days to explain it all to you before you make any decisions."

He leans closer, trying to touch my forehead with his. I stiffen and he holds off his advance.

"What happens if I don't buy all this? Do I disappear?"

"I told you, I love you. Nothing is going to happen to you. Now that you know, you can help me. I've been trying to keep people as safe as possible without damaging the study, but with *two* of us, we can prevent more incidents like Nes'. I've wanted to bring you on for years."

"*Oh*, you think I'm *joining* this little cabal. No, thank you. Take me back to the bunker."

"I will. I promise."

"Now."

"I can't do that yet. You still have to be introduced to Mory."

"Parading the test subjects around? Suddenly I'm your little prize?"

"Genesis," Jack snaps at me. "You are being difficult just to be difficult. Knock it off."

I bite the tip of my tongue, jutting my jaw out to challenge him.

"I'm sorry." He's annoyed, but he throws his shoulders back, resigned to continue to try to convince me to be nice. "We're going to meet Mory now. Make him think you're not going to be a problem, say yes to everything I say, and we'll leave for the bunker right after. We can talk on the way back."

"Fine," I reply. If this is what it takes to get out, I'll do it. I'm positive Nathaniel and Azra are still waiting for me outside.

He takes my hand, folding his fingers between mine.

"We're going to be okay," he promises me.

I close my eyes, trying to think back to this morning when I felt on top of the world while holding his hand. I let him guide me out the door before I open my eyes again.

Instead of returning to what Jack informed me was called the Control Center, he leads me down the hall to an office area.

"This one is mine." His finger brushes against a door, but we bypass it.

My eyes stay glued to the light brown door as he continues walking. I bend around, looking over my shoulder until I can no longer physically arch far enough to see it.

Jack has a whole other world that doesn't include me.

"Here we are." He pauses before knocking. "Ready?"

I nod, giving him permission to knock.

Jack opens the door to a shiny office. The walls are cement, much like the rest of the building. Shiny trinkets sit on shelves lined with books. Several screens rest on a desk, Mory sitting behind them.

"So you're Genesis," the old man leans forward, resting his elbows on his desk, fingers entwined. "I've heard quite a bit about you over the years."

I smile, biting my tongue to hold in my snappy response. When Mory continues, Jack squeezes my hand.

"I hear you'll be joining us. I wasn't impressed with the idea at first," he admits, "but Jack could use help around that place."

"I showed her around a bit, but we need to get back before people notice we're gone."

"Very well," Mory says, eyeing me. "There are some supplies for you outside. You'll be back soon?"

"Yes, Uncle."

"Young lady, I know my nephew has been speaking out of turn about all of this to you, but please remember, you're actions now fall on him. If you mess up, he will pay the price for it."

Funny enough, we were here because Jack *hadn't* spoken out of turn.

"Yes, sir," I reply, speaking for the first time.

"Ah, she speaks. Very good," Mory looks amused. "Jack, I noticed you turned the machine off earlier. Make sure you turn it back on before you go."

"Of course," Jack nods. He tugs on my hand so that I will step back.

I lead the way out the door, Jack following so closely that he steps on the back of my foot twice. I barely keep from stumbling.

"Sorry," he mumbles.

Jack leads me back to the Control Center. He leaves me inside the door and hurries down the stairs. Once he reaches the platform—what he informed me they called the main floor of the room—he trots over to the center station with the valve.

Adjusting the wheel, he clicks it into place and moves over to one of the screens on the table where he hits a few buttons. He places his thumb on it and waits.

After a moment, he nods and sprints back up the steps to me.

"Let's go," he places a hand on my back and puts slight pressure on me. "We have to beat the storm back."

CHAPTER 15

"You can come out," I call as I march away from Jack, now far enough away from the building that we can't be seen.

Azra darts out of the tree, taking a place by my side. She keeps her eyes trained on Jack, but her hand around my wrist suggests that she wants information and she's willing to squeeze it out of me.

Nathaniel takes a different approach.

He knocks Jack off his feet in one swift move, hand around his throat by the time he hits the ground. Nathaniel pins Jack, threatening to punch.

The good girlfriend in me shrieks, worried for his safety. I instinctively reach for Nathaniel's hand to pull him back. The second I lurch forward, I realize what I'm doing.

When I pull back, Azra's eyes fly open and she lunges at Jack too, getting in his face. Her verbal assault is more powerful than any physical damage she could have done.

"Enough," I finally force them to back off. "All I know is that he works for the enemy."

"I'll explain, but we have to start moving," Jack insists, still on the ground under Nathaniel's grip.

"Why?" Nathaniel asks, still fully prepared to hit his friend.

"It's about to snow. We need to beat it back. It's going to be a rough one," he informs us.

"Is *that* what you were doing? Initiating a snow storm?" I gape at him.

"Yes," he replies, sitting up as Nathaniel backs off.

"*Initiated*?" Azra squeals. "What is going on here?"

"They really do control our weather in there," I offer the simplest explanation I can find. She pales.

"We need to get back," Jack insists. Nathaniel allows him to stand.

As Jack maneuvers himself to stand by me, Nathaniel wedges himself between us, wrapping an arm around my waist.

Jack looks like I slapped him again.

"You lost this privilege, buddy." Nathaniel pulls me away, walking ahead of them.

If looks could kill, Nathaniel's body would be crumpled on the floor in pieces, and unlike Lewis and Eustace, he wouldn't be coming back.

Nathaniel turns us to walk away. He's awfully trusting that Jack won't do something while our backs are turned.

"Oh, I don't think so," Azra says from behind us. "Get

up there. From this moment on, you will always be in one of our sights. Move."

She forces Jack to walk alone ahead of us. He must feel ridiculous, but he accommodates her demand.

Things are different now. He's not one of us.

"So, I take it you three are the ones that moved my motorcycle this morning?" Jack muses, trying to make conversation.

"Well, we couldn't have you running off to who-knows-where," Nathaniel grumbles. "Where were you going anyway?"

"I had a mission to run today. We've also been testing the environment to see how *it* adapts to the weather changes."

"I thought you manipulated things," Nathaniel objects.

"We do, but we're testing to see how the earth reacts to certain situations. Surprisingly, it's adapted better than we thought it would. We've been testing areas in and beyond the mountains, so I was supposed to go out there today and record everything."

"Instead, you went to see your uncle," I supply.

"That...was unfortunate. Because I was there, he moved the timeline up. We'll be okay though." Jack glances back over his shoulder to a trio of unwelcoming faces.

"What exactly are we walking into here?" Nathaniel asks unnecessarily.

We step out of the tree line that marks the zones we aren't supposed to enter and the temperature instantly drops.

"It's going to snow. We're not dressed for this, so we'd better pick up the pace. The others will know to come back." Jack sounds so sure of himself.

"Jack, how did you ditch Red and Zach? You're supposed to be with them and after a speech like last night..."

"Jared is an understanding guy," Jack pauses, turning to look at me. "I told him I thought I had a lead on what was happening and the only way we could make this work was if he watched Zach while I looked for answers."

He turns back, continuing to walk through the increasingly colder weather. He's willing to play along for the moment and do as we ask.

"Well, *trusting* you won't be an issue for much longer," Nathaniel replies.

"You can't tell them," Jack halts, flying around to face us. His voice is so calm and cool. "Nathaniel, they can't know about this. It will compromise the study. If we compromise it, they'll pull every last person out of here and put you all back in the real world, and trust me, you don't want to be out there. You're safer here. I know it's hard to believe, but it's much safer here.

"Tell them, Genesis," he begs me.

"I have nothing to tell them, Jack. I've never seen this outside world."

"But I told you that my parents sent me here to protect me," he steps toward me and scoops up my hand. Nathaniel backhands him across the chest, pushing him back as he lets go of my waist.

"You do not ever touch her again," Nathaniel threatens.

"She's *my* girlfriend, Nathaniel, back off," Jack shouts, no longer willing to be pushed around for his sins.

"Oh? Is she?" Azra decides to get in on the conversation, stepping up to him with a puffed up chest. "Seems to me that boyfriends don't treat their girlfriends like this. Frankly, I think you're lucky she's still speaking to you at all."

"Genesis," Jack ignores them, directing the conversation to me alone. "No sane person would send their only son into a snow globe without good reason. They wouldn't ship him off to a distant relative unless that relative could protect them. Please, you have to at least see the logic in that."

I step forward, taking his hand in mine. Nathaniel looks ready to throttle me, every muscle in his face tightening.

"Listen to me carefully," I say with measured words. "I don't care about you or your parents or what is out there in the world. What I care about right now is the people in the bunker. We have close to two hundred people in that bunker and right now you're telling me that if we reveal your secret, your uncle will hurt them."

"He won't *hurt* them," he says, but he nods. His uncle would hurt them.

"Okay, so we are going back," I look up as the snow starts to fall, "and we won't share your secret until we've had some time to talk about this. By that, I mean the *three* of us—*you* will not be a part of this conversation.

"You will be watched closely and you are not to leave our sight. You're going to show us how to open the tablet and then you're going to teach us how to read the information you pretended not to understand when we found it."

"More than that, your double agent act just got expanded, Jack," Nathaniel jumps into my list of demands. "You're now acting as a triple agent—congratulations. You're going to work with us to figure out how to stop all this and get out of here without your uncle coming after us."

"And if you argue, we'll expose you right here and now, take everyone back to Mori-whatever Industries, and we're going to tear that place down," I add.

"Morozoko," he corrects me. "And there are enough people and enough technology in that building to end whatever battle you want to bring before it even starts, so please don't do anything irrational."

He actually sounds concerned that we might get hurt if we try to take his uncle on. *How sweet.*

"*Irrational* is locking people in a snow globe and running experiments on them." The snow is falling faster now. I shiver in my short sleeves. "*Irrational* is having all that technology and not using it to help people. *Irrational* is *still* talking to you after having found out you lied to me and used me for *fourteen* years. *Irrational* is everything about this situation," I challenge him.

Irrational is wanting desperately to fling myself into his arms and let him comfort me about all of this.

"*Irrational* is snow in the middle of a Summer day. *Irrational* is being willing to make it look like nothing is wrong even when everything is wrong, but we're going to do it anyway, *so let's go.*"

I stomp around him, waiting for the rest of them to follow me. They quickly do and we all fold our arms, fighting off the cold. Azra and Nathaniel sidle up next to me. I let Azra take the middle because she's tiny and needs more warmth as we press our arms together for the heat contact.

Jack reaches for me but I pull away.

"You can take my hand when we get back, but that's it. I'll play along for tonight, but tomorrow we will have a whole new set of rules."

"You could publicly break up if you need to," Azra suggests. "That would explain away any weirdness we're *all* going to have to deal with now."

"Good call," I say, making Jack shrink back. "Right now, we just have to worry about getting back. I think it's time to start running."

We take off, trying to stay close to each other even though it doesn't help. Jack runs far on the outside of the group, as he should.

***

"Where have you been?" Red accosts us as we walk into the tunnel. He has been waiting for us.

"I'm here, just go with it," Jack replies. He slips into an easy smile and waves at the people further down the tunnel. "Hey, guys. We're back."

Red slips into place behind us, Zach on his trail. Zach looks nervous, but he doesn't say anything. After a moment of watching Jack casually interact with people, he relaxes.

"Can you believe it's snowing?" Shanna muscles her way toward us. "It's the middle of Summer and suddenly it's snowing."

"Yeah, who saw this coming?" Jack asks.

Dang, he's good.

We walk to our bags and pull out warmer clothes to

change into. The main room already has a fire lit and the children are gathered around it, warming themselves and waiting for a story.

"Oh, good, you're back," Eliza calls as she sees us. "The kids want a story, do you mind, Jack?"

"Of course not, Eliza, happy to oblige." Jack picks his way around children, making a path to sit by the fire.

"After you," Nathaniel mumbles, waving his hand toward the spectacle. "I'll be back."

He slips off as Azra and I take a seat on the floor, watching Jack closely.

"I don't like him near the kids," Azra complains. "He shouldn't be near them."

I don't blame her for being protective of the children. She works with them more than I do, and *I'm* terrified for them, so I can only imagine what she must be feeling.

Lilly crawls over to Jack and wraps herself around his arm. Nicholas, thankfully, comes to me.

"Come here, Lilly, let's give him some space," Azra tries to call the little girl, holding out her open arms as an alternative. Lilly shakes her head and looks up adoringly at Jack.

"Once upon a time," Jack starts, glancing at me, "there was a brave princess who discovered a secret."

"Was she a fairy?" Lilly asks.

"No, she wasn't a fairy. Just a normal princess, but the most beautiful princess in all the land." He picks up the pace, his voice rising and falling with each sentence. "She lived in a land full of snow and secrets."

"Gag me," Azra mutters under her breath. Nicholas looks over at her, quickly forcing her to smile and wave her fingers at him to cover for her outburst.

Jack spins a clever little tale featuring me as the princess who discovers a secret that she has to keep and in the end, she ends up saving her entire kingdom and all of the surrounding kingdoms. It's a sweet story, and before this, I would have thought it absolutely charming. It might have even become one of my favorites from Jack's stories. Now that I know better, I wonder how many of his other stories he based off of real-life events, or worse—maybe he just stole them from books in the outside world and claimed them as his own.

"Tell another, Jack," Lilly begs. "Please?"

"Just one tonight." He taps her on her nose with his knuckle gently.

"I'll tell one," I surprise myself when I speak. Azra and Jack swing around to me. Jack's face freezes in an unsure state, but Azra leans back, looking very amused.

"I'll help," she volunteers.

The children cheer. Azra waits for me to take the lead.

"The fire crackled, sparking and dancing during the cold, long night," I begin, watching the fire glow to Jack's left. "Orange embers tumbled out of the fireplace, dancing across the floor in the middle of the night. Only one person was awake to see them.

"He watched as the embers grew in the night, changing shape and taking on a new form—the form of a dragon king."

Azra looks impressed as I talk. I genuinely have no idea where I'm going with this, but dragons seem to be a good reference right now since Jack is about to burn us all.

"The dragon king grew so large that it broke all of the walls of the house, shattering it to pieces, before he stomped off into the night.

"The people in the town thought perhaps this dragon king could save them, or at the very least, help them, but they were wrong."

"The dragon king," Azra jumps in as all of the children swing their heads to look at her, "did not want to help. He only wanted to control the people and soon the villages realized they were in grave danger."

"Are the fairies coming to help?" Lilly shrieks, looking frightened as she curls into Jack.

"Oh, yes, Lilly," Azra says dramatically, "The fairies are coming to help."

She swings to face me, waiting for me to take over.

"The fairies, you see," I continue, "have been watching the villages from high above and they know something is wrong. For as tiny as they are, they know if they work together, they can rescue the villagers."

Ah, I see where this is going.

"Together, the fairies come up with a plan to help the villagers escape. One bold fairy flies into the village to talk to the dragon king, but he will not listen. He sees nothing wrong with what he is doing to the poor villagers."

"When the dragon king isn't looking," Azra picks up as the fire snaps, "they strike!"

The fire pops and hisses making all of the children jump.

"They use all of their magic and pixie dust to help the villagers, even though it will cost them their wings," Azra says dramatically.

"Knowing they will take the brunt of the attack, the fairies valiantly fly in, willing to risk getting hurt to protect the innocent villagers. They know it won't be an easy battle, but the dragon king cannot be left to win.

"The fairies try very hard to convince the dragon king to do the right thing, but when he won't, the fairies put their plan into action."

"Only a few fairies make it out, but they rescue the villagers and vanquish the dragon king. His fire is no longer able to hurt them," Azra concludes, lowering her voice into a soft hum.

Jack shifts uncomfortably.

"Ice now runs through the dragon king's veins and he spends the rest of his days alone and sad because he gave up his people instead of giving up power," I conclude.

The children start to chatter.

"Who's ready to eat?" Eliza asks, holding a basket of bread.

The children climb off our laps and toddle over to her. She hands them each half of a roll—their meal for the night.

"They have *you* to thank for that," I say cheerfully to Jack. Anyone who overhears will think it was simply a girlfriend praising her boyfriend for helping to take care of the children. Jack and Azra are the only ones who know I was referring to starving them.

"Time to go," Nathaniel towers over us, returning. "We have work to do."

He looks in disgust at the children's meager meals. We all wave off our bread as we leave, preferring to save it for the children.

Nathaniel guides us to the workbench, closing the door behind us. The tablet sits, waiting for us to activate it.

Jack pulls his pack off his shoulder where he had slung it when we stood up. When he opens it, he pulls out several loaves of bread. He tries to hand them to us.

"You have to eat," Jack protests.

"Now that we know what's going on, our priority is

protecting those kids. If that means I don't eat, so be it," I say confrontationally. "Give it to the kids."

"I intend to, but you also need to eat something," he insists. When I refuse, he adds, "Where do you think I got all that extra bread I slipped you before, Gen? It was good enough for you then."

"I thought you were sacrificing for me back then. I didn't realize you kept your perfect figure because you had access to whatever food you wanted."

"I always wondered how you didn't waste away with the amount of food I saw you consume," Azra muses. "Now we know...it's because you never went hungry a day in your life."

"I did what you all did, Azra," Jack tries to remain calm. "The only time I had extra was when I snuck back to report to my uncle and even then, I distributed most of it to you and the kids. Stop trying to turn me into the bad guy."

"Enough." I can't help my annoyance. "Open the tablet."

"It's unlocked," he nods to it without moving. "And please remember, I also brought game back to the bunker for us to eat."

Game that I assume his uncle's men got for him and allowed him to claim as his own.

"So much for being one of the best hunters here," Azra mutters.

I reach over and touch the button under the screen. It springs to life, painting the ceiling in a blue glow.

"How do you unlock it?" Nathaniel searches for answers.

"There is a remote key trigger."

"A what?" Nathaniel asks for clarification.

"It's a device that syncs with the tablet and gives it permission to open," Jack informs us.

We pause, waiting for him to continue. He sighs, lifting his hand to pull his necklace out from under his shirt collar. The blue pendant sparkles in the light.

"You didn't break that the other day, did you?" I accuse. "You took it off so it wouldn't open. That's why it *did* open when I surprised you...because you had it around your neck."

He nods miserably.

It must be so hard to have to live with your choices once you're caught, I think sarcastically.

"Time to explain this to us, *buddy*," Nathaniel commandeers the conversation. I sit back and watch as he swipes the tablet to life.

CHAPTER 16

"Hello, Jennifer," Mory says, glancing up momentarily from his desk.

Jack had dragged me back to Morozoko Industries through the snow. I stand in his uncle's office, bundled up in my black, fur-lined jacket. My boots surprisingly aren't dripping, but that might be because there's no snow near the building.

Jack has already stripped off his coat and slung it over his arm. He nods that I should do the same, but I like my coat and I'm keeping it on until *I'm* ready to take it off.

"Genesis," I correct his uncle.

"Apologies," he finishes typing before turning to me. "Still cold, are we?"

When I don't answer, Jack mumbles something about me being cold blooded. I feel *anything but* when his knuckle brushes against mine, sending a jolt of heat through me.

"I suppose it's time to show her what we do around here," Mory stands up. "Come along, Genesis. You saw the

Control Center before, but it was empty then. Now it's time to see what we really work on here."

The quiet of the hallway never betrays the bustling activity inside the Control Center. Screens flash like before, but this time, they are accompanied by the sounds of fifty people typing at their stations, moving from one screen to the next on the higher tiers of the platform where they had individual screens to work on instead of having to depend on the main screens on the ceiling.

Some men sit silent, while others murmur back and forth to each other. It appears that some are working in pairs, while the majority work on their own. Several people I assume are oversight walk around checking monitors and conversing with people when necessary. A few women are mixed into the group, their hair all swept back to be out of their faces as they tilt their necks down to see their keyboards and screens.

No one looks up when we walk in. Mory guides us to the lower level where we walk out on the main platform to stand near the valve Jack had been using before.

"This is where we control the weather for the Globe. We study the data feeds and analyze what we discover," Mory says, sweeping his hand to the side. "Over there, you'll find our analysts. They read the data and interpret it. Over here, we have our scientists, though most of them are in the labs down the hall. A few join us each day to get real-time information.

"But these people *here*," he points to the area Jack had been standing in yesterday when I discovered him working. "These are our Globists. They control what happens inside the Globe.

"They listen to the data and suggestions from the scientists and they put it into practice inside the Globe."

They're the ones that control our lives.

"Where does Jack fit into all of this?"

"He is a Globist, but so much more since he is also inside the bunker. He is our eyes and ears inside, telling us what we cannot see for ourselves."

"But if you have all of this equipment and technology, why not just monitor it for yourselves? I've read that cameras are small...do you honestly think we'd find them inside?" I question. "Why go through all the trouble of sending someone in, risking him potentially being discovered or even possibly ending up hurt or dead, when you could simply view it from your Control Center?"

Mory frowns. He does not like his authority being called into question, but I also see his lips tug just a little as he launches into his explanation. He's enjoying talking about his work.

"We have to respect the boundaries of the experiment. We can't risk it affecting the study, which is why we don't have things like cameras inside the Globe. We have sensors that read things like the temperature and precipitation levels, but anything more than that would require an advanced level of power that we just can't afford to offer the Globe." He clasps his hands behind his back, turning to watch his workers with pride. "I won't risk it being discovered and ruining four decades worth of research. That's why at any given time, we have one to three people in the bunker."

"How many do you have now?" I ask, shocked that there have been others I might not know about.

"Just Jack presently, but you remember Ginger from when you were young." I thought back to the lanky brunette from my youth. She seemed rather quiet but was very good at her missions. "She stayed until Jack was ready to take over. She was having some trouble adjusting to life inside the bunker after she met one of our young scientists here at Morozoko Industries. We made her stay until Jack was ready and then allowed her to join us here."

He pointed across the room to the analysts. Mixed in with the crowd was Ginger, now adorned with much shorter hair. I wouldn't have recognized her with all that makeup on.

"Before Ginger there was Jerome. He was the one that brought Jack into the bunker in the first place. He raised Jack on the inside for us, eventually bringing him to me when he was old enough to keep our secrets. Jack learned everything he knows from Jerome and me. We have *him* to thank for Jack's success inside the bunker."

Jack runs his tongue over his lips looking like he wants to say something to me. His uncle continues without noticing, though I don't think Jack would have said anything in front of the man.

"Sadly, Jerome was nearly discovered and we had to pull him sooner than anticipated, which is why it was such a good thing that we also had Ginger inside. Unlike Jerome, she kept her distance, just making sure Jack was in the right places at the right time."

"Ginger was never talkative except when we got back here," Jack mumbled.

"Where is Jerome now?" I distinctly remember Jerome's face and scan the crowd looking for him.

"He's no longer with us," Mory informs me. "He had trouble adjusting to life outside the Globe. He works in one of the other facilities now."

I glance at Jack for further explanation but he shakes his head.

"Show her, Jack." Mory waves at the Globist seats, changing the conversation.

Jack takes my hand and leads me to the first two seats. Mory takes up a position behind us, one hand on the backs of each of our swiveling seats. He leans heavily on them, making them bend backward. I scoot to the front of my seat, feeling like I'm about to tip over.

"Right now, it's snowing outside," Jack says pointing at a column of numbers on the right of the small screen in front of him. I lean over to examine it. "We can tell how much is falling *here*, and the locations *here*."

He points to a set of coordinates that correspond to a map on the screen. The different amounts of snow are represented by different colors.

He glances up at Mory. I turn just in time to see him nod.

"We're at the stage of the study where we're varying what the Globe is used to. We do this every so often to test the reactions. You and I haven't seen much of this until recently," Jack explains, his fingers hovering over the keyboard. "That's what the wall of rain was and that's why the seasons were mixed up."

"Jack is about to strengthen the snowfall in a certain area, making it accumulate much faster than in the rest of the Globe. Why don't you help him decide where," Mory suggests.

"What? No, I..." My protests fall flat as Mory waves his hand at me like I'm a petulant child.

"I insist. It will be your first assignment with us. Anywhere you choose inside the Globe, Genesis."

"Pick, Gen," Jack mumbles informing me that I'm not going to get off the hook with this one. "Pick or he will pick."

I study the map. I want no part in this. I don't want to

be responsible for what happens inside the bunker. But I also don't want Mory dropping a blizzard in front of the tunnel door.

The swamp is a good location. It's a restricted area, so no one will be affected.

"Not the restricted areas," Mory chides, knowing where I'm thinking of directing it. That, or perhaps he watched where my eyes were focusing.

"Near the mountains," I say, knowing we rarely get close to them.

Jack nods, pressing a few buttons. The map rotates on the screen, zooming in on the area near the mountains.

"I'm altering the precipitation levels here and here," he touches the screen for me to see. "We'll be dropping a significant amount of snow, but it will only last for a few hours."

He programs something into the system.

"Let her hit the button," Mory orders. Jack doesn't even hesitate when he reaches forward and taps the buttons.

"Oh, sorry. Next time." He glances back at Mory innocently. Mory expresses his distaste for Jack's actions with his face but doesn't say anything. Jack turns back. "Now watch here."

The map slowly begins to shift as the area by the base of the mountains decreases in temperature. Projections for the accumulation levels show a drastic rise in precipitation.

"Over the next hour or so, three inches of snow will fall. After that, there will be up to seven feet of snow during the course of today," Jack concludes, pointing out the data.

"Now, from here, our analysts will watch the data and handle soil samples and measure things like the depth of the river. We'll also be watching for how this affects crops and the wildlife," Mory sounds delighted.

"And people. You'll have Jack spy on the people," I add, wondering if Mory will catch on.

"And you too, Genesis. Now that you're helping Jack, your job will be to report back to us too."

"Sir, you might want to look at this," one of the scientists calls from across the room.

"Excuse me," Mory slides away from the table and walks gracefully across the Control Center.

"Play along," Jack sings under his breath before I can say anything. I compose myself, crossing my hands on my lap. He continues, this time loud enough for people around us to hear. "I know this is all new, but you'll figure it out soon enough, sweetie."

"Drop it in the swamp too," I challenge him.

He deftly hits a few buttons while he continues to speak.

"Now that we're testing reactions to abnormal conditions, we actually get to be a little creative with what we do," Jack grins at me. "Like this, for example."

He taps a few more keys and one small area on the map shifts, producing a warmer color. I wait for him to explain.

"Like I mentioned, we're mixing seasons now...so what would happen if one area stayed warm, while everything else was covered in snow?" Jack poses a question. "How would this affect the growth process? Would it throw off the animals? Would it change the soil? Would there still be fruit growing there in the patch of warmth, despite the snow a few feet away? These are all things we need to know. Beyond that, we need to know how long after a snow squall or storm it would take the people to find the resources. Would they find them in time to use it? Would they find it at all?"

My head is spinning from the possibilities. Had there been times that there were resources that we missed? If Jack knew about them, surly he would have found a creative way to get us to that location so we didn't miss out on food for the children.

The screen glows in warm and cool colors. Jack hits a few keys and shows me the projections for the next few hours. If I was stuck here, at least Jack was giving me the hope of doing a little good. I wonder if we could convince Mory to do it to a larger area.

"How long is this Winter going to last?" I ask, brushing my knee against Jack's. His breath catches.

"It's going to last for a while, with the exceptions of the random days we throw in there to test things. Two months or more."

"That's twice the normal length, Jack."

"They'll be fine. We'll be there to help them." He raises my hand to his lips to kiss it. "We'll take care of them."

"But, Jack…" I protest.

We're already struggling with food. We're not prepared for a normal Winter, let alone one that lasts twice as long.

"All right, everyone," Mory suddenly shouts. "Time for our meeting."

He moves to the center of the room, standing near the valve that clicks the different seasons into place at Jack's behest. He smiles, looking to the people under his employ.

We sit through several reports from the scientists and analysts. Jack and Mory have apparently been breaking things down into simple terms for me, because the words flying around the room are incredibly hard to understand.

It's the Globists who concern me though. When Mory turns to them, their faces light up like creatures ready to please their masters. The first few stand to their feet, offering suggestions of what they can do over the next week to the bunker.

As if it is a game, the men and women on the Globist team start shouting, adding creative spins to each idea until they remind me of the fish in the pond when we start throwing in pieces of bread to catch their attention so we can scoop them up in nets instead of wasting our time waiting for them to bite our hooks. They leap out of their chairs, bumping into each other like the fish do underwater, crashing into the people next to them, pushing their neighbors out of the way for a bite of food. Each time Mory calls out an affirmation, they wiggle back as if they have stolen the last crumb of bread on the surface of the pond, quite pleased with themselves, until another, larger crumb is dropped.

They suggest splitting locations with two different extreme temperatures that would act as the wall of rain had, dividing the land. One yells out an idea about rotating the extreme weathers on an hourly basis for a week to see how the people and land react. Still another talks about using temperate climates, lulling everyone into a false sense of security before hitting them with extremes for a day at a time to see if they can prepare for what won't ever actually come.

Jack remains quiet and I get the feeling he usually does in these meetings. When it quiets down, Jack speaks up, acting as the voice of reason.

For a moment, it's as if he forgets I'm there, still sitting in the chair he is standing by. He addresses them, pointing out the flaws or potential downfalls to each idea, praising the merits of the ones that seem the most rational for the testing they are trying to do. Mory watches him warily.

Jack carefully works out the rationale behind each plan, convincing the Globists to be logical. The scientists back him up, lending their expertise when needed.

Mory finally adopts a plan, heeding Jack's advice, and the Globists build off of it to form each facet of their strategy. Jack sinks down into the chair, taking a deep breath before he notices me.

"I didn't just do that for you," he huffs.

"I could tell," I assure him. Maybe he wasn't *all* bad.

Maybe I should lighten up on Jack a bit. He's obviously caught between his work here and me. Then again, he *did* lie to me. Where am I supposed to draw the line in this situation?

Before I discovered the truth about what Jack had done, this would be the part of the conversation where I assure him that everything would work out. I'd take his hand in mine and run my fingers gently over it. I'd stare at him with a ridiculous grin pulling at the corners of my lips until he finally turns to me and gives in, smiling before he kisses me. Ordinarily, this would be the part where we work out life together.

But apparently *life* has never been *ordinary*.

I need to get Jack alone. I need to get out of this suffocating room. The noise swells back up, hands flying in the air as the discussion takes a turn. The games are beginning again.

As the deliberations continue, Mory wanders over to us.

"It inspires them, you see. It's not easy working in the Control Center all day. We see bits and pieces of information and we make decisions that affect the outcome of this study, but these people so rarely see all of the pieces.

"It can be disheartening to spend so much of your life working toward a goal—especially one as life-altering as this one—only to never fully realize that dream.

"We do great things here, Genesis. We've used this study to make a difference in the world. We're nowhere near done yet, but we've taken what we have learned from you all inside the Globe and applied it to real-world situations."

I was about to learn the outcome of this little study.

"A few years ago, there was an attack," he continues. "It damaged the soil and the people couldn't handle it. Based on what we had learned over the mountains where we were testing the environment, we were able to help them get it back on track to being productive soil again. The area should be able to sustain vegetation again within the next two years and be almost as productive as it was before.

"We never would have known that had we not been able to test it and study it inside the Globe.

"So, yes, I encourage friendly debate here. I make it more fun. I let them play and experiment because when they are excited to walk into this room every day, they are more productive."

He's even testing his testers.

"We need innovative thinkers here, Genesis. Based on what Jack has told me, I think you are one of those minds. You're not required to be a Globist like Jack, of course—you can choose whatever occupation you'd like here at Morozoko Industries—but I think you'd be a great asset to the team."

When I don't respond, he squints at me. "Come with me."

Jack and I follow him back to his office. He sits at his chair.

"You don't need to scare her, Uncle Mory," Jack says softly.

"I have no intention of doing that," Mory responds gently. This is a new side of him...it makes me leery.

I stand through several videos of people talking about how Morozoko Industries has helped them. Apparently Mory wants to paint himself in a good light for me.

"This one is my favorite," Jack whispers in my ear, brushing my hair with his nose.

I turn to him slightly catching his crystal blue eyes. His closeness unnerves me. I have to force myself to remember that we are not together anymore.

When I turn back to the screen, a little boy who looks like Cody appears on the screen with his father. His parents sing the praises of Morozoko Industries. When the boy speaks, I realize that it doesn't just *look* like Cody, but actually *is* Cody.

"Right after this interview, his parents begged Mory to put Cody in the Globe. They live outside of an area that was recently attacked. They came so close to losing their son," Jack informs me. "They asked for Mory to bring him here and keep him safe. They told us that Cody was an extraordinary boy and he would be a great asset to the study.

"They sent him here not only to protect him, but also so that he could help protect others. They asked Cody before they sent him and he agreed that he wanted to help people."

"Cody's IQ is higher than most children's his age," Mory continues, adding details. "He's already developmentally further along than most of the children in the bunker. His parents believe, as do we, that Cody could be the key."

"He's a little boy," I protest, wringing my fingers.

"He is," Mory nods. "But, Genesis, he's the boy that could change the world."

"If he's so smart, why not raise him here, inside the building? Why not let him be one of your scientists?"

Cody would now be subjected to not having enough food while he grows, having to fight to survive every day of his life, and all so he could "better the world."

"We thought of that, but we think putting him into the Globe environment will teach him to be more strategic. He won't know this is an experiment until he is removed from the Globe. His only goal in there will be to survive. That will make all the difference."

Mory turns on another video, this time one where scientists announce they've lifted the ban from a certain area due to toxin restrictions. They attribute their success in returning the area to acceptable levels to Morozoko Industries.

"Sir," a voice calls at the same time we hear the knock on the door. "We're wrapping it up for today. Do you want to come dismiss the team?"

Mory stands, gliding to the door. I wait until he is gone before turning to Jack.

"Cody is a child and you have just subjected him to starvation. What happens if he ends up like Nes and loses his fingers and then he can't do whatever it is you need him to do?"

"Cody will be protected," Jack puts his hand on my

elbow. I used to love when he did that, pulling me close to him.

"How? *You?*" It's a fair question.

"Yes. I'll be looking after him. I'll be fostering his educational growth as he gets older, pushing him in the right direction. You can help me with that."

"Jack, listen to yourself. You're talking about manipulating a child. One of those sweet, innocent kids that listens to your stories in the bunker."

"Try to see it from my perspective," he begs. "We're doing so much good here."

"We're having the same conversation again, Jack. We keep going around and around." My hands find their way to my hips.

"Gen, I wouldn't have brought Cody into the Globe if I didn't think it was the right call."

"Wait, *you* brought him in?"

"Yes, I've brought most of the children in. That's why they were all found so easily. I planted Daisy near Zach the other day—by the way, that really is her name. I figured Zach would see the flower and run with it.

"And I hid Cody in the bushes when I knew Red was around. You nearly caught me as I was sneaking back in."

"What do you mean?"

"In the basement downstairs there are secret doors that let me in and out of the building. "

That explains how Jack could sneak around so easily.

"That's also how I found Lilly," he admits. "She got in there when Eliza lost her. For the record, it wasn't a rat you heard."

Oh, it was a rat.

I would have to force him to show me the other hidden locations around the bunker later.

"What would have happened to me if you hadn't vouched for me with Mory?"

"Hmm?"

"When you discovered me here yesterday…if I hadn't been your girlfriend, what would have happened to me?"

"Roughly the same thing. They would have asked you a lot of questions. There would have been an interrogation to see how you found us and why you were here, but in the end, you would have been presented with the facts and offered an opportunity to work here, just like the others who came from the bunker." He pauses, waiting for me to comment. When I don't, he continues, "They would have made it look like you had died inside the Globe so the others wouldn't come looking for you."

"What if I say no? What if I don't go along with all of this?"

"It depends on if they think you are a threat. If you just want to go on with your life in the real world, they usually let you. I'm sure it's not easy, but they must manage somehow.

"If you *are* considered someone who might challenge

the integrity of the mission here, you're handed over to the government and I don't know what happens from there," he replies candidly.

"*Jack*," I stretch his name out like the air is leaking out of my lungs. "This is bad. Why can't you see that?"

"It's not as bad as you think, Gen."

"What would your uncle do if you betrayed him?"

"You're asking a lot of questions, Gen." He steps forward and wraps his arms around me. I freeze, not responding. He sighs. "I would be kicked out and sent back to my parents."

"That's not something you want?"

"Come with me," he says, tugging me out the door.

CHAPTER 17

Jack ushers me out the door quietly.

Down the hall, he places his hand on his office door. It hasn't changed in the day since I'd been there. I'm not sure what I expect as we walk in, but I discover a brightly lit room with a chestnut desk and several chairs. Much like his uncle, he has several screens around the room.

It looks important. His office is that of an important man. It makes my heart sink a little.

"Here, you can take this chair. It's very comfortable," he offers me *his* chair as he drags one of the others over to rest next to it. I don't need another argument, so I take a seat.

He watches me for a moment, running his thumb over my hand as it sits on the armrest of the chair. Jack smiles.

"I think you'll find our research to be very interesting," his words trail off as he notices me studying the room. His gaze follows mine.

"These are my parents," he says, lifting a picture off of

his desk. He hands it to me to examine. He has his mother's eyes and his father's smile. He's only a baby in the picture, but he completes his family.

"Do you ever talk to them?" I hand the picture back to him.

"No, but Uncle Mory gives me updates once in a while. They're still alive last I heard. I'm sure they miss me, but it's for the best. They wanted to give me a chance to survive."

That brings up another question I came up with last night when I couldn't sleep.

"Jack, where do all of the people come from?"

"What do you mean?" he asks cautiously, setting the picture down where it belongs on his desk.

"Inside the snow globe...where do they all come from?"

Children show up every few months. They can't have come from nowhere. I brace myself, waiting for him to tell me they were all kidnapped or grown in test tubes.

"Their parents sent them to us, just like mine did."

My head jerks back. I wasn't expecting that.

"You're telling me that *my* parents sent me here?"

Jack turns and types something onto his screen, pulling up a file. Two sets of eyes stare back at me.

"Yes, they did." He allows me to gaze at their faces for a moment. Both have dark hair like mine, though my father's was much wavier than my mother's straight hair. I must have inherited that from her.

My father has green eyes the color of summer grass while my mother has blue eyes. Her smile is a reflection of my own.

"You have your father's eyes," Jack says tenderly. "Your parents didn't make it, Gen. There was a fire about a year after you joined us. I'm sorry."

I hadn't even had time to process that they were alive and existed in the world before they were taken away again. Maybe that will help with the loss later when I have time to think about it.

"Everyone who is a part of the Globe was sent to us by their parents out of love. They got nothing out of it other than the offer of hope for a better life for their kids.

"Funny enough, a few of the people in the snow globe are actually siblings. I try to direct them together whenever I can." His smile fades.

"Do you honestly believe you're doing the right thing here?"

"I think I'm doing the best I can with what I've been given. It's not easy keeping these secrets."

I put my left hand over his hand. It still rests on my right one.

"Why can't Morozoko Industries take volunteers for this study?"

"They *are* volunteers," he insists.

"No, their parents volunteered them. It's different. How many of those people do you think would choose to stay inside the Snow Globe if they knew they had an option? Don't you think you could get the same results if you worked with volunteers? Don't you think they'd work harder knowing that the fate of the world was at stake?"

I pet the top of his hand, hoping my words are getting through to him, that, somehow, my touch will force them deeper into his conscience.

"I've thought about that over the years, Gen. The truth is, I don't think that would be the case. If we put people into the Globe knowing that we were on the other side and could save them if they failed, they would have no incentive to make sure they survive."

"The kids that show up are so young, Jack."

"I know. It doesn't seem fair, but not a single one of the kids has been hurt and no one has been pulled out without good reasons."

"I need to talk to Eustace," I announce, surprising him. "You said he was here."

He blinks a few times before standing and offering me his hand.

Jack's skin feels warm against mine, just like it always has. For a few steps, I walk closely, but as we round the corner, I put a little distance between our bodies.

"This can't be her," a man looks up from the corner of

the room where he is studying some papers. He looks vaguely familiar.

"Eustace," I greet him. His dark hair is starting to lighten at the roots and his face has seen some wear.

"Little Genesis all grown up. It's so good to see you." He stands, walking over to embrace me. I'm not sure what to do so I lightly tap him on the back. "Come sit down and we'll talk."

"I'll come back in a bit," Jack says, retreating.

"Jack's been filling me in on you," Eustace says after the door closes, "but how have you been?"

"Confused."

Eustace's office is much smaller than Jack's but has the same light and airy feel to it, as if they had somehow managed to bring Summer inside. A few pictures sit on his shelves. He notices me looking.

"That's my wife and our little girl."

"How old is she?"

"She's two," he tells me, smiling at the picture of his daughter.

"What is going on, Eustace?"

He's either going to be honest with me or I'll have my proof that they've brainwashed him or forced him into this.

"It's a bit hard to take in, isn't it? Before we talk about what's going on here, can you tell me a bit about the bunker? How are Adam and Kalley? Are the others doing well? Jack gives me updates, but *Jack* is also very invested in the success of this mission."

"Jack told me Adam's been getting close...asking too many questions. He told me he's been warning him off."

"I always knew Adam would figure it out early on. I taught him too well." Eustace smiles ruefully.

"Eustace, if you're so comfortable out here, why not bring Adam out to join....all of this." I motion around the room.

"I'm sure you don't remember this, Genesis, but back while I was still in the bunker with you all, I started poking around. I had the same ideas a lot of people have inside the bunker. I ended up getting pulled out.

"I had two choices: work for Morozoko or go into a community to be studied. Morozoko wanted to look at the lasting effects of being in the bunker once subjects were removed from the environment.

"I could test or be tested. It's not an option they offer to everyone. I took their deal and I'm doing my best to help the bunker without hindering the study."

"You believe in the work here?"

"I believe it's the best place for the children. I've seen the outside a few times, Genesis. Everything they say it is is true. The last time I saw skies without toxins in the air was inside the bunker. Even here we have to use a ventilation system to purify the air."

"You said your daughter is two..." I ask the leading question.

"My wife and I have agreed that she will go into the bunker in a few years. It's safe for her there and Jack will see that she's taken care of. She'll learn to survive. The people outside haven't learned how to do that. They're soft."

"You would give up your daughter to these people."

"I would give up my daughter to give her the best chance possible."

A siren goes off in the hallway. It's so loud that I cover my ears.

"What's going on?" I shout over the noise.

"It's okay, don't be worried," Eustace shouts, covering his own ears. "Someone is trying to get into the compound, that's all."

The siren lowers but still persists in the hallway.

"The initial few blasts are loud to get attention. They lower the volume after that so it isn't as disruptive. If it gets louder again, that's when we need to worry.

"It will end once the intruder is handled. We've all learned to block it out."

"Everyone okay?" Jack opens the door and steps inside. He locks eyes with me.

"Fine," Eustace tells him. "I was explaining the alarm to Genesis."

"Who is trying to get in?"

The sharp noise in the hall makes my eye twitch every time it wails. Jack seems unaffected.

"People know it's safe inside the Globe. They want to volunteer to be involved in order to be under our protection," Jack clarifies.

"On occasion, others try to get in," Eustace adds, earning a glare from Jack.

"What others?"

Jack's lips quirk to one side as he chooses his words.

"There are people who know about this study who don't like it. These people are from the countries with the weapons that are currently and will continue to destroy our people. They're still working on perfecting their weapons, but in the meantime, they don't want us to make any leeway in learning how to survive their attacks."

"A decade ago, they found one of the Midwestern facilities and destroyed it," Eustace adds. "So far only one or two have ascertained our location here in the East, but I imagine we can only stop so many."

"Don't worry. We learned from the last attack. Security measures are in place and no one can touch the people inside the Globe," Jack assures me, petting my hand.

"If they're dropping bombs from the sky like they used to according to the books, or even if they have that old technology to fly, why can't they just buzz over our heads and wipe us out? Or at the very least, get information about out location?" I pull my hand back.

"They don't have access to the snow globe."

"But how is that possible?" I tip my head dramatically as the siren continues to sound in the hallway.

"The bunker is a man-made structure, Genesis," Eustace informs me. "Everything inside is a simulation. It mimics the real world, including landscape and weather."

"It's reinforced and hidden where people can't find it."

"How did you find an area large enough for all of this?"

My brain is having trouble figuring it all out. We're part of the world, but they can't find us or reach us?

"Gen, we're underground," Jack reveals. "It's why they can't find us from the air. We're in an underground bunker that's miles wide."

A bunker in a bunker. Brilliant.

"So how do we get out of here? Find a ladder and tunnel through the sky?"

Jack grins at me playfully.

"Did you miss the part where I told you it was a reinforced bunker?"

"The entrance is through the building here. But honestly, it's much safer down here," Eustace says lightly. "I'd just as soon block off the entrance and hunker down for the rest of eternity. We could live in a temperature controlled environment, the weather would always be perfect, we could take the toxins out of the rain—"

"The what?" I gasp. His eyes widen.

"No, no, they're not that bad," he exclaims, backtracking. "We all survived it and it's nothing compared to what's out there, anyway. It's fine. They were just building up our tolerance, that's all."

"Hey," Jack says, holding up his hands, "I was in that rain right beside you."

As if that makes it better.

I could smack them both.

I make a mental note to tell Nathaniel and Azra about the rain and to start finding more shovels and ladders.

"What about the snow? Is that toxic too?"

"The snow is fine—" Jack tries to say.

"Just made with the same water as the rain, that's all," Eustace interrupts. At least *he's* giving me information.

"We drink that," I remind Jack.

"Mory has it under control."

The shrieking in the hall suddenly stops.

"Neutralized," a loud voice says.

"That means we're all clear." Jack smiles as he takes my hand. "I can show you the toxin reports if you like. It's really not that bad, especially compared to outside."

I spend the next two hours combing through reports, trying to commit as much to memory as possible. Jack's right, the toxins don't seem to be as bad as they sound, though they certainly aren't good. He leaves me alone unless I ask questions, Eustace by his side to confirm what he's telling me.

The two work quietly at their own stations in the Control Center while I sit a few chairs away, scanning through documents on a tablet they handed me. The screens on the ceiling catch my attention from time to time as they flicker with different colored lights.

"It's getting heavier," Eustace frowns.

"Is it?" Jack asks, looking at the data. "Oh, it is."

He sits up, leaning over the table as he taps the keyboard with his fingers. It's his frown that concerns me the most. I study his movements, tight and controlled. He's upset and that makes me nervous.

"What are you going to do?" Eustace asks.

"This isn't supposed to be happening. I'm going to slow it down."

"He won't like that," Eustace counters.

Jack blatantly ignores him, but Eustace's smile tells me he already saw that coming. Jack continues to type while Eustace turns just slightly to give me a look.

Standing up, I move over to Jack's side where he sits at the end of the table. I gently touch his shoulder to let him know I'm there. The speed at which his fingers fly over the keyboard amazes me.

"What's going on?"

"This isn't right," Jack mumbles, brushing me off.

Whatever it is, I don't want to interrupt him so I turn to Eustace.

"It's snowing too much," he informs me, pointing to the screen. "If it keeps up, it could result in blizzard-like conditions. If the bunker isn't prepared, bad things could happen."

"So this is another test?"

"I assume so. I don't always get all the facts," Eustace sighs.

"Apparently neither do I," Jack grumbles, working away at the keyboard. "Eustace, go get my uncle."

Reluctantly, Eustace stands.

"He's not going to be happy," he mumbles.

"When is he ever?" Jack snaps, glancing up for just a moment before returning his gaze to the screen as he pounds away on the keyboard.

"He's only been this bold since *you* showed up, just so you know." Eustace pushes past me and takes the steps leading up to the main door.

"I know I promised you I was watching out for everyone and I am, but I'm not sure how this happened," Jack says without looking at me.

"What do you mean?"

"I'm the only one who can control the weather, Gen. It's biometric-based. Everything has to be run off of our bodies," he explains. "It's like with the remote key for the tablet, only this time it's based off of our fingerprints and DNA so that no one can fake being us."

"Why are you the only one—?"

"Because Mory no longer has finger prints. They've worn off through the years. He's done a lot of hard work and had handled a number of chemicals that have deteriorated the ridges in his fingerprints. He hasn't been able to control the system for a year and a half. He can program things, but I have to initiate the sequence. Unless he's found some way to get around that, which apparently he has."

"What is the meaning of all this?" Mory croaks as he walks in. The man who likes to hold me in rooms follows behind him along with a second man I haven't met before.

"Why did you change the plan?" Jack looks up, ready to defend me even though I have nothing to do with this conversation.

"I didn't," his uncle grumbles. A younger version of the man might have had similarities to Jack's facial structure, but the white hair and wrinkles have taken away from his lines.

"Then what is *that*?" Jack points to the screen.

Mory studies it, reacting when he notes the change in the snow.

"What did you do?" he accuses.

"I found it like this," Jack continues to implicate his uncle. "Now tell me what you did."

Mory's hand lashes out, striking Jack across the face. He stumbles backward away from the table.

"You will not speak to me that way. Your parents would never have tolerated this," he roars. "I allow you to bring that girl into *my* institute and suddenly you're behaving like those wild men we pull out of the experiments. You dare threaten me for something you don't understand? How dare you."

He takes another step toward Jack, grabbing onto his upper arms and shaking him violently. He's strong for being so old.

"Fix it," he yells.

Jack lifts his hands up, bringing them up between his uncle's so he can push them out to the sides, off of his arms. Coolly, Jack steps around him, hurrying back to the console.

"Find out how this happened," Mory instructs the two men he brought with him. They both take a seat at different consoles on the table, tapping away as they search for answers.

Eustace takes up a spot by me, watching the scene unfold.

"I can't help with this," he mutters quietly, explaining his presence.

"Sir," the tall man calls Mory over.

"If I find out you had anything to do with this," he points his finger in my face as he walks away.

"This is the first time I've ever even seen devices like this. How on earth would I be able to work them?" I shout, earning a glare. "Oh, of course, silly me. I wouldn't be able to work them *on* earth, but *under* earth, *by all means*, assume the girl is a child protégée who can learn computer science in under an hour."

Eustace smirks next to me. Jack glances up, eyes sparkling. He must have heard me too.

"There," Jack says, sinking into a chair.

I rush over to him, looking like a doting girlfriend. I'm embarrassed by my display of eagerness, but I play it off as concern for the snow globe residents.

"That breach from this morning," the tall man says, "I don't know how, sir, but I believe they compromised our system."

"What?" Mory, Jack, and Eustace all shout in shock.

"They're controlling our network, sir." The man's voice is higher than I thought it would be. From how bulky he is, I assumed he would have a naturally deep voice. I focus in on his pitch as he speaks. "They're the ones that did this."

"Do we have control back?" Mory asks, finally sounding human. His hand runs through his hair absent-mindedly like Jack sometimes does when he's trying to puzzle something out.

"I stopped the blizzard," Jack offers meekly.

"How did they get inside our system? Forty years and no one has managed to break in..." Mory rambles as the two men work on their keyboards.

"Uncle, who did you catch today?" Jack asks, hoping for more useful information.

A series of numbers appear on the screen in long chains. I don't understand any of it, but it appears to be telling a story to the two men reading it. Their heads bob back and forth as they scan the screens. The new man mouths the things he doesn't say out loud as he makes sense of the numbers.

"It was one of them," Mory admits. "He was trying to break into the building. I don't know how he found us, but we caught him in the hallway."

"He made it into the building?"

"Only a few feet...we didn't feel it was necessary to raise the alarm because we caught him so fast. We left it ringing while we escorted him to the holding cell."

"We need to talk to him," Jack announces, walking around the table. "We need to find out what he did."

His blond bangs bounce over his eyes as he walks, curling slightly to the side, just enough that he can still see out from under it. His white shirt makes his eyes pop.

"You can't right now," Mory replies.

"We have to," Jack protests, demanding to be heard.

"He's not awake right now, boy," Mory snaps. "You were so much more agreeable as a child."

Mory rolls his eyes as he walks over to where Jack had been working and rounds the tables to take a seat by his men. He starts typing away.

"Go, if you want." Jack's uncle waves us off.

"Come on." Jack leads us out of the Control Center.

He takes us through the building, winding through the halls, until we reach the main door.

"Is he here?" he asks me pointedly.

"Who?" I ask.

His look tells me everything I need to know.

"Outside," I say reluctantly.

"Take her to the cells," Jack darts out the door, calling instructions to Eustace. He follows orders, guiding me to the holding cells.

The lights are dim in the hallway, but the cell itself is covered in harsh light. I assume it's to make everyone with eyes uncomfortable.

Inside, a man sits in a chair, flopped over on the table. His wrists are bound to each corner of the table on his side. I assume he's sleeping.

"Who is he getting?" Eustace looks uncomfortable as he fidgets, rocking between his feet. Or maybe that look is one of hope.

He thinks it's the man he mentored.

His eyes widen in surprise as Jack rounds the corner with not Adam, but a grown-up Nathaniel and Azra.

"I'd recognize you two anywhere," he breathes, moving to hug them. Nathaniel looks uncomfortable, but once he moves to Azra and I catch her eye to tell her it's okay, she drops her tough girl act and shows the emotion Eustace is craving from at least one of his old friends.

Nathaniel eyes the man attached to the table.

"I guess I'm up," he says, walking toward the man. Jack follows.

"What is he doing?" Eustace asks.

"Nathaniel is incredible at getting information out of people quickly. He's even better than Jack, and you know how Jack sets people at ease," I reply.

"Nathaniel is a little brusk about it, but he definitely knows how to gather intelligence quickly," Azra adds. "The two of them together will get information out of this guy in no time.

"In the meantime," she turns to me, "who is this guy and why don't we like him?"

I quickly explain what just happened. She looks ready to punch the man as the boys wake him up and start his interrogation.

As we watch from behind the glass window, Eustace fills Azra in on his life, asking questions about hers. She cringes as she learns he's actually willing to put his daughter in the bunker with us. If we're still here in two years, we could be taking care of his little girl. We will have to decide whether to tell her about her daddy or not.

Would it be more cruel to keep it from her or to tell her?

We watch as Jack and Nathaniel try tricking the spy. We continue to look on as they move into being nice to him. Eventually, they switch to using scare tactics, but nothing breaks him. I'm about to step inside when an alarm goes off.

Azra and I grab our ears, nearly going down to the floor in shock. Nathaniel looks just as upset as we do, while Jack and Eustace remain upright, trading looks.

It's not the same alarm as before. It's very distinctly different, rising and falling in a different pattern. Jack motions Nathaniel out.

"Why is it different?" I shout over the noise.

"It's a system shut down," Jack responds. "This isn't good."

We rush back to the Control Center where Mory is in a complete panic. He's pacing around the room, shouting. All three men glance up as we enter. They eye the two new faces warily but Jack waves them off before they can attack, thinking it was the enemy. I cling to both of their arms just in case Jack's message isn't clear enough. Nathaniel and Azra get the picture and stay close.

Jack rushes to the console in the middle of the room. He spins the wheel, clicking something into place. I hadn't noticed before, but in the center of the valve, there is a tiny interface. Jack pushes buttons as he directs something within the system to bend to his will.

"They have total control," he shouts over the siren, which thankfully is quieter in the room than it was in the hallway.

"Fix it," Mory instructs him.

"I can't," Jack apologizes. "There's nothing I can do."

Mory shoves him out of the way, typing on the interface.

My breathing is heavy, like when I'm out in the woods alone and something snaps in the bushes behind me, persisting even after I speak to scare away whatever little woodland animal wants to spend time with me. It comes in slow, controlled gulps, filling my lungs and running through my blood to the tips of my fingers.

Jack places his finger on the interface several times. He adjusts the valve for his uncle while he types. They seem to understand what the other one needs without speaking. The two must have worked closely over the years, despite Mory's treatment of his great-nephew.

I hear myself audibly gasp when both of their jaws fall open.

CHAPTER 18

"They've initiated a weather meltdown," Jack says, blinking at the screen. "Everything is going to happen at different times and we have no control over it. At one point it could be a heat wave and a snow storm colliding in the middle of sector nine, and at another, it could have rain so heavy that all of the animals drown within a day. It could even flood the bunker."

Jack's body shakes, not out of anger, but out of shock. He's horrified at what is about to happen.

"No, no, no," Mory exclaims. "We can't let this happen, we've worked so hard on this for so many years, we can't let it all go."

Tears stream down his face in rage over the loss of his life's work. He looks to his nephew for help. Mory's shoulders sag.

"We'll be safe here, sir," one of the men says. The entire room glares at him.

"We can't let the people in the bunker get hurt," I object.

"We won't," Jack rushes to make me a promise he intends on keeping but has no real way of doing so. "There's only one way to stop this."

"No," Mory cries.

"It's the control program or the entire study, Uncle, which is it?" Jack shouts as he launches himself toward the interface on the valve.

Mory swallows, rocking back on his heels. After a moment of uncertainty, he nods.

"Do it."

Jack tackles the interface, typing faster than before.

"When I do this, it's going to be stuck in whatever weather pattern it's locked into. Right now, it's spinning out of control, cycling between rain, snow, and heat. I can't promise anything, but I'm going to try to stop it on tolerable weather."

"He's going to crash the system," Eustace explains. "It will be a total system crash. It will prohibit them from being able to control the system. We'll be locked into whatever it lands on."

"Then what happens?" I ask.

"Toxin levels are rising," the shorter of Mory's men shouts.

"Hurry up, Jack. Control this thing," Mory's words are short.

The drama of the siren blasting, mixed with the shouting in the room is overwhelming. Azra shifts nervously next to me, still clinging to my arm. Nathaniel hasn't let go either as he watches Jack work.

"Total system crash in ten, nine, eight..." Jack counts down as additional sirens flare up inside the room. A light flashes red, striking our eyes like lightning every time the siren goes up.

The entire building sounds like it shuts down as Jack reaches zero. It's followed by a strange noise.

"That's the backup system booting up. It will give us power again so that the lights stay on," Eustace explains.

"Jack," Mory yelps. "You have to go. You have to go fix this."

He grabs on to Jack's arm, begging him to rectify the situation.

"I will, I'll go fix it," Jack promises, shaking him off. "We have to go. Now."

He looks up to us. I pull Azra and Nathaniel backward, indicating that we should start for the door. Eustace looks more torn with each step we take.

"Come on, man," Jack says, smacking his arm as he rushes by. "Help us, or Charlene has nowhere to go."

That springs Eustace into action. He bounds up the steps behind Jack.

"Where are we going?" Nathaniel asks.

"We shut down the system, but we're locked into whatever weather pattern they had programmed in," Jack informs us. "Honestly, I'm hoping we landed on eternal summer, but I'm not holding my breath—"

We burst through the outside doors and are immediately hit with a wall of cold. Jack's breath crystallizes on his last words.

"*Of course*," Eustace growls in frustration.

"Now that the system is down, there's nothing protecting this area and keeping it controlled," Jack informs us. "Back inside, we need coats and gear."

We wheel around and rush back inside as Eustace leads us to where they keep the winter supplies. We bundle up quickly as Jack continues his explanation.

"This system is no longer operational, but the actual machines that carry out the tasks are housed in the mountains. We have to shut it off manually or it will never stop snowing. The entire area will be covered in so much snow within days that everyone will die from starvation or suffocation."

I hurry to zip my coat that's definitely too big for me. Jack shoves another, smaller coat at me to put under it to fill the space and add some warmth.

Eustace hands out the warming rocks Azra and I discovered, then he quickly explains how we have a heating system built into our outer coats. It doesn't do much, but it helps.

"We need to get to the mountains and turn the machine off immediately," Jack continues.

"Why is it so far away, Jack?" Nathaniel asks, pulling on his hat. He wraps a scarf around his throat loose enough to pull it around his chin and mouth to breathe through once the air gets icy. "If *this* is your base of operations, why is it across the entire Globe?"

"It was a central location." Jack looks guilty. "We needed it so we could test the environment on the other side."

I contain my sarcastic words, as does Azra.

"We need to get a group together from the bunker and get out there," Jack changes the subject. "We need as many hands as we can get. We might need to dig our way in."

"And we need to get to them before they're blocked in. We don't know how bad the snow is by them yet," Eustace says as we rush for the door.

Looks like we'll be running back to the bunker.

I breathe through my scarf, soaking it as I run. I'm used to breathing through material, but this is particularly bad. It must be exceptionally cold.

After awhile, I notice my throat is dry, making it hard to breathe. I try to swallow, but all of my spit is gone, transformed into the moisture that I breathed out, drenching the front of my scarf. Having no other choice, I keep running.

Soon enough, we leave the tree line dividing Morozoko Industries from the rest of the Globe. Eustace is surprisingly fast for someone who has had a desk job for all of these years.

Azra pulls ahead of us in an effort to reach the bunker before us. She's several paces in front of us when she goes crashing to the ground, toppling over another figure.

We all call her name at the same time, rushing to help her. Jack reaches her first, plucking her from the snow. Nathaniel and I grab Red's arms, lifting him upright.

"Jack?" Red gasps, seeing him first. "We've been looking all over for you!"

His gaze travels down to Azra and his eyes go wide.

"Oh, Azra, I'm so sorry! Are you okay?" He darts to her side. Red pauses to help brush the snow off her Winter gear.

Red turns back around to face Nathaniel and me only to find a strange man with us. He freezes like a cornered rabbit, looking Eustace up and down. Clearly he doesn't recognize him.

"Jared?" Eustace asks after a moment. Red looks ready to run. "It's me, Eustace. You know me—"

"Eustace? But you—" Red exclaims. He's seeing a ghost.

"We don't have time, we can do this later," Nathaniel instructs. "We have to get back and get the others."

"But how is he here?" Red questions as we all start running toward the bunker.

"Right now we just need to get help," I shout, knowing

we haven't had time to discuss how we would handle this conversation. "We have a lead on what's happening but we need to move quickly."

Red keeps glancing over his shoulder at Eustace. I can't say I blame him. I'm still shocked to see him and I've been with him for hours now.

I all but collapse when I make it to the yard outside the bunker. Half of our older people are standing around outside, studying the falling snow.

"They're back!" Zach shouts as he sees us approaching.

Everyone turns to look. I can see them counting us, noticing that the number is off. Several people squint to see who is with us.

"We know what is going on," Nathaniel shouts, rallying our team.

"We have to get to the mountains, now," Jack continues. "Get everyone geared up. We have to get out of here before we're snowed in!"

"What is going on?" Adam bellows, pushing his way through the crowd. His steps slow as he takes in the scene. Adam pulls one shoulder back, rocking onto his heel when he notices his old friend.

"It's me," Eustace smiles timidly. "We don't have time to explain right now, but trust me, we need to get to the mountains. We know how to stop this."

Adam eyes Jack but doesn't say anything.

"Please, Adam, there will be time for questions later," Jack pleads. "We need to get as many of our people as we can and get to the mountains. Trust me."

Adam waits until Nathaniel, Azra, and I nod before releasing our people to gear up for the journey. Inside, the children try to swarm us, as they're trained to do in Winter. Several of the older people pause when they see Eustace, looking to Adam for an explanation.

Instead of waiting for Jack or Nathaniel to take charge, I step into the middle of the room.

"We know what's going on. There's not much time to explain," I start as everyone quiets around me. "We were right—our weather is being controlled. We found the people who were doing it but something happened and the machine is broken.

"We're going to the mountain to turn it off and stop it from eternally snowing here."

Everyone gasps.

I bend down quickly, noticing the children's terrified looks.

"Eliza will explain it all to you later," I say to the kids, winking. "It's just like one of Jack's stories."

I straighten back up, addressing the adults in the crowd.

"We need everyone who is willing to come. A few people need to stay with the children, but we need as much help as we can get. If you're coming with us, get ready now. We leave immediately. We have no time to waste."

Everyone scrambles to get dressed. We let the people who are staying gather supplies for us. Adam follows us to the door, demanding answers.

"You did this, didn't you?" He asks Jack harshly, a look of utter betrayal on his face.

"You know I'm involved," Jack admits. His voice is dark.

"You too?" Adam wheels around to face Eustace.

"No, well, I mean, yes. I wasn't until they took me out, but now I work with them. It's not as bad as it sounds. Just let us explain after," he pleads with his old friend. "Right now we really need to shut this machine off or the bunker is going to be buried and none of us will survive."

"Are we ready?" Nes asks, rushing up to us as he slings a pack over his shoulder.

"You're not coming," Jack says.

"I'm perfectly fine, Jack, and I'll do as I please," Nes retorts.

It's only been a few days since Nes lost his fingers. That can't be healthy.

"I'm coming along too. You're going to need me out there," Perrin announces, following Nes closely.

"They're going to need you *here*, Perrin," Nathaniel insists.

"*You're* going to need me more. I have my things

packed and ready to go, now let's get the others and move out."

"He's right," I say, cutting in. We're going to need them."

The rest of the group quickly fills the tunnel, waiting for directions. Jack tells them to stick together once we're outside, informing them that we need to stop the weather machine inside the mountain.

Once outside, we discover the snow has become increasingly fluffy making visibility hard. I lift my hand up to my face to protect my eyes from the flakes gusting toward me.

Red sidles up next to me to ask what is going on.

"The people who did this developed a machine that controls our weather. They were testing our ability to adapt to different environmental situations." I realize I'm beginning to sound far too much like Jack and Eustace. "They were testing us and the machine broke. The only way to fix it is by manually disabling it."

"And Eustace is one of them?" Red pushes.

"He didn't really have much of a choice," I mumble, hoping it's enough to keep him from asking too many questions.

"Is Azra okay?" I ask, trying to distract him.

"Probably. Maybe I'll go check on her though," he replies, falling back in the ranks to find her.

"You pawned him off on Azra?" Jack says snarkily.

"The alternative was to tell him everything," I bat my frozen lashes at him cruelly.

"You know he can't resist that girl."

"Which is why I sent him over there. Maybe at least one good thing will come from this."

I tug at my scarf, grateful we had the opportunity to switch them out while we were at the bunker. Frustration sets in when I can't adjust it to where it covers my nose but also doesn't suffocate me.

"Are you okay?" Jack finally asks.

"Peachy," I snap back. I take a breath. "I'm sorry."

"Me too," he says immediately, giving me a meaningful look. I ignore it.

The hills are hard to climb, as they always are in Winter, but especially difficult today. We help each other up over the raised land, ensuring no one slips back down. Jack offers me his hand as we scale the far side of the hill near the river.

"Do we cross it or go around?" Kai asks.

It's been snowing all day and has since dropped in temperature. There's a significant amount of snow on the ground, but no telling if the ice is thick enough yet.

"I'll go," Jack says, taking a step forward.

"No," I reach out, grabbing his hand out of instinct. To cover, I whisper harshly, "You're the only one that can disable the machine. I'll go."

"Not a chance, Genesis," Nathaniel picks me up by the waist and sets me behind him. "I'll check it."

We wait as Nathaniel walks up to the river without hesitation. Carefully, he sets his foot along the edge, transferring part of his weight to the snow-covered ice.

When nothing happens, he shifts, moving his full weight onto the edge of the ice. If the edges are strong, it likely means the entire thing is thick enough.

Nathaniel slowly moves his other foot ahead of him, standing fully on the ice. He tests another step and another before bouncing up and down. The ice appears strong.

He turns, giving us a nod. So far, so good.

We know enough to wait until he has finished his test, so we stand on the shoreline, watching each painfully slow step. Bit by bit, Nathaniel makes it to the middle of the river.

I notice the waterfall has frozen, the same beautiful shards of glass protruding from the rocks as they had when Jack and I had explored. Mixed with the snowflakes, it looks like an ice palace from a story. I have no idea how those princesses tolerated living there.

"It looks good, but I think we should cross a couple of people at a time just to be safe," Nathaniel calls.

Everyone yelps as the sound of ice cracking explodes around us.

CHAPTER 19

Once, when I was little, I went through the ice. I was learning how to ice fish and we were standing on the shore listening to the person teaching us. She showed us what it looked like when the ice wasn't safe. I vividly remember stepping onto an area that looked frozen solid right along the shoreline of the pond.

My boot cracked through the ice, making me sink into the mud just enough to scare me and make my heart beat wildly. It was two months before I'd go back on the ice and Jack was by my side, helping me to be brave.

My heart is beating the same way now, thundering in my chest as if I had just fallen through the rushing river, water flying over my head as it forces its way in my ears and up my nose. I can't breathe.

"I'm okay," Nathaniel yells from the center of the river. "It was just the ice making more ice. Sometimes it cracks like that."

The crowd lets out a collective nervous giggle. Jack takes the lead, marching toward the ice. I follow.

I close my eyes, drifting back to the time I fell through the edge of the ice. Jack must know because he takes my hand, holding me as we step out onto the ice.

Nathaniel waits for us to join him and the three of us continue to the other side of the river. The rest of the group begins following us, walking across in groups of two or three.

It takes fifteen minutes for us to get the entire group over the river. I huddle against Jack, shivering in the cold. Standing still in the weather makes it seem much worse than when we're moving and keeping ourselves warm.

When we're finally on the opposite shore, we start out again, trekking over the snow. The snow falls enough that I'm not even sure we leave footprints behind us, though, to be fair, I don't waste time turning around to check.

Eustace finds his way to Adam on the outskirts of the group. They veer off so they have a buffer between them and the rest of the group. I assume Eustace is explaining everything to Adam. If Morozoko Industries continues to exist after this catastrophe, I imagine Adam will be the next member pulled out. I wouldn't even be surprised if Jack and Eustace come up with a plan to make it look like Adam died on this trip.

I hope it doesn't come to that.

Nearly one hundred of our people travel with us, crunching through the snow. In our large group, we sound incredibly loud, despite not speaking.

I tap my knife at my side, glad I have it with me for protection, though I doubt anything will try to approach us as we're traveling in numbers this large. Its presence gives me comfort.

We walk for several hours, knowing we're going to need to stop for the night soon. Even in Summer, the mountains are well over a day's walk away.

Thankfully, we know of a place we can stay. It *should* be large enough for the group. According to the journals, it is one of the original places considered for the bunker, but the location where we currently reside was already set up, not to mention, larger.

After hours of walking, we finally arrive at the cave. It's dark against the darkening sky, making it difficult to notice at first. Several of our people go in first to make sure it's clear and nothing has taken up residence there since the last time we checked.

They wave us in and we cram inside, barely leaving room to lie down. Sitting makes it easier. We build a few small fires near the entrance, knowing to keep them where the air can steal the smoke away for us.

Once settled, they turn to us for answers. I take the lead, explaining the situation without implicating Jack. If they find out he is a traitor, they won't trust him and the mission will never go forward.

I suddenly realize the position Jack has been in. He knows what he's doing isn't great, but he also knows the implications of upsetting the balance. For the first time, I sympathize with him. I still don't agree, but I understand his position.

The group goes along with it without too much fuss, though I imagine that's going to come later. We quickly pull out a small portion of the food we brought with us. A few of the men go out to hunt, returning an hour later empty-handed.

Knowing the team is watching, I shift closer to Jack. I need to protect him until we can find a proper time to tell the group about his involvement.

We sit in the back of the cave, furthest from the fires. The warmers in our coats and pockets give us an edge the others do not have.

"Getting chummy again so soon?" Azra whispers at me when no one is paying attention.

"You know why," I hiss back, hoping Jack doesn't take offense.

"Just be careful," she cautions, scooting closer to me. She rests her head on my shoulder. It would be a lot easier if we weren't wearing these puffy jackets. My sleeve makes a loud noise every time she shifts.

Eventually everyone settles down, lying down on the cave floor. A few people try to stretch out but quickly realize there isn't space for that. We all huddle together to make sure everyone has at least some semblance of a promise of space to sleep.

A few people take turns sitting in the doorway on watch duty, rotating every hour. Jack and I are scheduled for the third watch but we end up wide awake for the duration of the first watch, huddled in the back of the cave.

I lower my head to his shoulder. I know my body is tired, but my brain has not made my body aware of this yet. I can feel the ache starting to register in my muscles—they tighten as I sit.

Along the tops of my eyes I can feel the pressure building but my head screams that it's a lie and that I'm fine. I will pay for my inability to sleep tomorrow, but there's nothing I can do to tame my thoughts into calming.

After a moment, Jack leans his head on mine, taking a deep breath. I know him enough to know what he's thinking right now, that is, assuming at least some of what he said to me while we were officially together was true. He's processing every decision that brought him here, winding through each choice he made, everything his uncle said to him, and weighing in what was happening in the outside world.

He's wondering if being with me was really worth it or if he merely tricked himself into being happy all this time.

He sighs.

My eyes drift shut and I take in the sounds of the

cave. Soft snoring filters through the room over the noise of quiet breathing. The fires crackle and pop, hissing when the wind touches the flames. Jack's deep breathing is a steadying force, the constant acceptance and release of our current situation. I listen with each inhale and exhale, focusing on Jack as I try to lull my mind into a steady pattern, a sad attempt at tricking myself into sleep.

I WAKE WITH A START.

Jack's hand is on my shoulder to rouse me from my sleep. He silently takes his finger off his lips and extends his hand to me to help me up.

His hand, like always, is warmer than I expect.

Jack guides me to the mouth of the cave as we replace Red and Todd. They thank us for relieving them and head back inside to warm up.

The fire they started outside definitely helps, but the wind isn't doing us any favors. It kisses my cheeks, making me cringe.

"Here," Jack mumbles, shifting closer to me. "Stay with me."

Momentarily or beyond this?

We watch the flames together, occasionally scanning the darkness. We can't see anything beyond the snow that's lit up by the firelight. It dances orange, just out of reach.

I curl into Jack's arms, trying to stay warm while simultaneously lending him *my* body heat. The wind picks back up, shoving the snowflakes to the side as our fire licks at the white pieces.

"I know you're only trying your best, Jack," I finally give in, starting the conversation before he does. "I know you mean well and you're trying to take care of us."

"I understand that it's not fair that you and everyone else have been dropped into this life without really having a choice. I know it's not easy to sacrifice to take care of people you don't even know." Jack speaks while fixing his eyes on the flames. I focus there too.

"You're sacrificing too. I get that." I slip one finger under his hand as it rests on his knee. "It must have been so hard keeping this secret for all these years."

"I wanted to tell you so many times," Jack suddenly turns to me. "I knew if I told you when we were younger, if Mory found out, he would pull you away from me. I couldn't risk that. And then as we got older, I wasn't sure if you'd understand.

"Or maybe," he sighs, closing his eyes, "maybe I just wanted you to keep looking at me the way you always did. Guess I screwed that up pretty good, didn't I?"

I'm not sure how to answer that.

"I tried so hard not to lose you, Gen, and in the end, I

did anyway. But I'm glad we got to spend as much time as we did together.

"To be honest, I had this vision of us working together after we left the Globe. I thought we'd go on to help the country together and start our own family."

"Did you intend on putting our children in the Globe?" I turn with a start.

"No, I would never do that to you. I always thought they'd stay at Morozoko with us and grow up to take over for whatever we ended up doing together."

At least that was one thing I couldn't hold against him.

"Maybe I didn't think it all through. Maybe it was just wishful thinking, but I'm sorry I dragged you into all this, Genesis. I'm sorry I hurt you.

"I love you and you know I would never intentionally hurt you, right?" he asks quietly.

"I still love you," I admit. He looks so hopeful. "But that doesn't mean I agree with you and I think we need to take some time to figure out where we both stand on things and then decide what to do about it. I just know that I can't be with you right now."

He blinks back a tear but holds himself together.

"That's fair," he finally chokes out. "I need you to take this."

He reaches around his neck and pulls off his pendant.

"I don't want your remote key." I hold my hand up to wave it off.

"It doesn't just unlock tablets, Gen. It will keep you safe. It's connected to the sensors around the Globe. It's why I'm never caught in any of the really bad weather. I'm not supposed to get seriously hurt in here so the pendant triggers the sensors, allowing the weather machines to know when to lighten up.

"If you wear it—even if something happens to me—you can get everyone back to safety. I'll also be able to do my job knowing that *you're* going to be safe."

"But, Jack—"

"It doesn't work on everything," he cuts me off, "like the ice—there's no way to control that. But the snow won't be as bad and the rain won't be as toxic. Just put it on, Gen, please. You can stand around Azra and Nathaniel and pretend you're their personal snow removal system."

He gives me a pathetic look as he tries to joke with me, his blond bangs tumbling out from under his hat. Without thinking, I reach up and brush them out of his eye. His face is strained when I touch him.

"Thank you for respecting my decision," I whisper.

He nods, lips pursed together.

"At least nothing is out here tonight," his head swings back to the fire.

"I can't imagine any creature would be out in this

cold," I respond, turning back to the flames as well. "Hey, Jack. Why didn't we take the snowmobiles out here?"

I could slap myself for not thinking of that earlier.

"We only have a few and they're hidden around the Globe for me to use. The others can't come in aside from dropping things in the hidden tree compartments, so there's no point in having one by the building. And in case you forgot, we dumped a bunch of snow on the one in the swamp today."

"Oh." I make a face. "Yeah, we did."

Now I wish I hadn't forced him to do that, especially after Mory prevented it from happening and I did it as a dig to the two of them.

"It wouldn't have done us any good to get there before the team anyway. We're going to have to dig our way in—we dumped snow on that too."

I realized what we had done just as he said it, the thought hitting me like a lightning bolt. I feel sick.

"We couldn't have known this was going to happen." He squeezes my shoulder. "We'll make it through this. Tomorrow we'll make our way to the base of the mountain. Then we just have to locate the right one and dig our way inside."

"Do you really think we'll make it there tomorrow?"

"I'm not sure," he replies as a strong gust of wind knocks into us, nearly sending me crashing sideways into Jack. "It depends on how bad the snow is."

"Hate to interrupt...but I'm going to interrupt," Nathaniel says, exiting the cave. "Genesis, why don't you go inside and get some more rest. I want to chat with Jack for a bit."

I glance at Jack. He lowers his eyelids just slightly so that only I can tell—our universal sign for agreeing to something. I pull away from him, my entire left side suddenly feeling cold now that I'm not against his body. I give Nathaniel a short, tired nod before walking back into the cave.

I nearly scream when something attaches itself to my ankle as I pick my way through the sleeping bodies on the ground. When I look down, Adam is starting to sit up.

I clamp my hand over my mouth, willing myself not to yell at him. He nods that I should go ahead, back to my corner of the cave. He follows silently behind me.

He slides down along the cavern's wall alongside of me, taking the tiny space that had been occupied by Jack. Adam props his forearms on his knees, angling himself to look at me.

"Do you trust him?" he asks me earnestly.

"Jack?"

"Yes."

"I know he wants to protect us. He thought he was doing that before, but I think he just made some choices not all of us would agree with." I whisper, not feeling comfortable talking even though everyone was asleep. "Do you trust Eustace?"

"Eustace was like a brother to me. I don't think he would lie to me. From what I can tell, he didn't have much of a choice." Adam looks away across the sleeping team members sprawled out on the floor.

"That's what it sounded like to me. Did he tell you he has a family now?"

"Yeah, I heard about them. They sound great."

"You know, you can get out too now when this is all over. Eustace and Jack can get you out, assuming we *all* don't get out." I try to offer him a little hope. We no longer need to fear what's on the other side of our time in the Globe.

"I'm sure they could. But I don't want to abandon any of you. I can't leave you alone to handle this big secret."

"So you think we shouldn't tell them?"

Adam pauses for a long time to think. Frankly, *I* don't have an answer for that either. I'm not sure what's best for the bunker, especially if we can't get everyone out.

"I'm not sure, Gen. I think we need to protect them. I think you, Nathaniel, Azra, and I have to do what is in their best interest. Though, from what I hear, if they pull me, they might also pull you three for knowing."

The reality of that statement hits me harder than the wind blowing outside. I hadn't considered that Mory might order all four of us pulled from the Globe. After all, he doesn't know if he can trust us to stay quiet like his nephew.

"You should get some rest." Adam pats my knee before making his way back to his spot. I curl up next to Azra and try not to think.

———

When I wake up, Jack is by my side again. His head rests gently on my hip as I lay slouched over on Azra's shoulder. I'm not sure how to untangle myself without disturbing them.

The group is just starting to stir, so I take a moment of quiet while I can get it. I leave my head on Azra's arm—something she's probably going to regret later if the stiffness in my own muscles is any indication—and I lift my hand to brush back Jack's bangs. For all the times I've had to do that over the years, any sane person would have mentioned a haircut to him, but I could never bring myself to do it.

His hair is soft. In the Summer it flutters in the wind, prettier than any mane I've ever seen. If we're being honest, I'm jealous of his long eyelashes too. The darkness of those perfect lashes brings out the icy tones in his eyes.

Jack wastes no time in coming to life under my gentle touch. His eyes blink open, find focus somewhere on my face. He smiles softly as if he's forgotten the events of the last few days. His expression morphs after that one precious, fleeting moment, sending him crashing back to the reality of the cave we're sitting in.

"We need to go," he says, detangling himself. "Everybody up. Time to go. Let's move."

Adam stretches, following suit. He leads the call to move out, Nathaniel calling out as well. We douse the fires, secure the zippers and fasteners on our coats and boots, and head out of the cave.

Jack leads the way, which means I am also dragged to the front of the team. Ordinarily I'd like the view of the untouched snow covering the mountains that loom in the distance, a clean, unmarked path ahead of me, but today that means having to create the tracks for the others.

When leading, one has to take on the hardships of being the first set of tracks in the snow. It isn't easy, but each footprint carves a path for those that come behind.

My friends fill those steps, carrying on behind me as we march toward the same goal. The people closest to me stomp down the trail for the people behind them, who in turn take away more of the struggle for those that follow behind them.

I notice Jack checking on me from time to time. He glances at me from the corner of his eye. When he turns to check on the group, he always looks over his left shoulder so he can get a good look at me too.

"I'm fine," I mumble, slightly out of breath. I do worse when it's cold out.

The weight of Jack's pendent around my neck is a physical reminder of the heaviness of the secret we're keeping between us. I've also always looked good in blue, so I don't mind wearing it despite the fact that no one can actually see it.

"I know," Jack grins behind his scarf, the edges of his cheeks tweaking up enough to crinkle the corners of his eyes. "You always are."

"I'd say you're making me sick, but..." Azra chirps from behind us.

"Oh, Azra, you're just jealous," Jack winks at her. He drops his voice to a whisper. "Not everyone can be so good at faking relationships."

"Ah, I see what you did there," she bends down, scooping up a snowball that she lobs at his back. Walking only three feet behind him, she hits dead center.

"If we had the time, my dear friend, I'd shove snow down your back," Jack playfully threatens.

"Are we picking sides here, because if we are, I'd probably recommend you duck, Jack," Red shouts from a few feet away.

"Oh, suddenly we're all about cracking jokes while we're running this little mission?" I grumble, unamused. My toes are so cold that all I feel is an icy, stabbing sensation.

"You're fine," Perrin pulls out of the line behind me. "I saw you look down. You're fine. It's not frostbite...yet."

"Good to know, doctor," I chuckle.

"You'll survive, Gen," he says gently. "Whatever is going on, you'll survive it."

I turn to him, trying to see his face.

"I doubt the others can tell, but I can," he says without turning. "You've been close with my sister and I for a long, long time, Gen. I can tell when something is up."

"Well," I nod my head, trying to think of something to say. "Thanks...for...noticing, I guess."

"That's what I'm here for. I'm sure you'll figure it out," Perrin nods before leaning around me to yell, "Hey, Jack. How are you doing, buddy?"

"We're getting there," Jack waves across me like a salute.

"Glad to hear it," Perrin fades behind us, making the rounds between our team members to keep an eye out for anything we should be worried about.

"He's not the only one who noticed," Nes makes his way between Jack and I. "Granted, I've had a lot of extra time lately to study people, but let's just attribute this to my brilliant intellect. So either you two can tell me, or I'll start asking the people you've been cheating on me with."

"You mean this weather machine?" I joke. "I guess we *have* been spending some extra time with it, but if you want to challenge it for our affections, you go right ahead and get us there faster. I will happily watch you take it on for us."

Jack snorts, trying to keep from laughing. Nes follows suit.

"Well, if that's what it takes."

The sun starts rising as we head into another sector of trees. I'm hoping to find some fruit or plant life that wasn't prepared for the shock of winter to still be waiting where we can find it. I keep a sharp look out for it while we walk.

The trees ahead of us start to glow orange in the rosy early morning sunlight. It morphs into a golden color with each step we take through the crisp snow. The ground sparkles as brilliantly as the stars in the night sky. Powder blue shadows extend from each tree across the landscape, adding a stark contrast to the golden-high-lighted snow.

Something rustles off to the side, likely snow falling off a tree branch. I realize how wrong I am as the trunk of a tree uproots from the ground under the weight of the snow, snapping in half as it tumbles down onto part of our team.

CHAPTER 20

The branches shake, bouncing up and down as the tree settles on the ground. Beneath the confines of its ice-covered restraints, three of our people are trapped.

We race over to assist them. Jack and I start digging the snow out from around our people, trying to identify them. Perrin nearly collides with us, finding it hard to stop after running so hard to reach the accident. He assesses the scene and begins barking commands.

Nathaniel and Adam lead the group that is tasked with getting the tree off of what we've determined to be two of our men and one of our women. Jack and I continue to dig as Azra instructs our group on removing the snow so we can easily slide our people out once the tree has been lifted off of them enough to move them.

Perrin gets down on his hands and knees, crawling around under the scratchy branches to determine the extent of the injuries. It appears everyone is alive and capable of moving at least a little.

Azra sounds nervous as she shouts to people. She

circles the tree, calling out whenever she notices adjustments need to be made. The small girl pauses by me, leaning down.

"Kalley's hurt," she whispers. I dig faster.

The team manages to lift the tree high enough to slide people out one at a time. Eustace was smart enough to grab our supply sleds to help move the people under the tree. Several of us climb under the branches when it is lifted and moved the trapped people onto the sleds. A group of people then pull them out from under the trees.

The guys are fine, only incurring several cuts and bruised muscles. One has a nasty gash on his face, but it will heal. Kalley is pulled from the accident with an injured leg where one of the branches pushed it into a dangerous angle.

Spreading out the supplies from the sled among us, the stronger people in the group take turns pulling the sled in pairs because Kalley can no longer walk with us. Adam stays by her side when he isn't pulling her along.

We slow our pace for a while, allowing the men enough time to find their balance again after the accident. It doesn't hurt our travel dramatically, but the mental strain on having to slow down pulls at us fiercely.

After a few hours, we're shivering so badly that we make the decision to stop and find shelter for an hour in hopes of building a few fires and waking up enough to continue without risking anyone losing fingers or toes along the way.

With great difficulty, Azra climbs a tree to scout for us. She nearly slides coming back down, reminding me of the day we found Jack's tablet in the pine tree. She catches herself, but several people on the ground gasp.

Red and I wrap ourselves around her as she shivers violently from the cold.

"If we keep going, we're about to walk out of the woods," she informs us through chattering teeth.

My own body reacts the same way to the cold. Tears stream down my face, pooling in the corners of my eyes as we walk because the wind is hitting my eyes so hard. I've always hated that my eyes water so easily.

I reach up and dab a tear away from the corner of my eye before it can spill over. It absorbs into my glove, leaving a salty residue on my face. The continuous tears have been leaving their crusty aftermath on my face all day, but until I can take my hands out of my gloves to wipe it off properly, I'll continue to look and feel as though I've been sobbing all day.

"If we sit just outside of the trees, I think it will give us enough shelter to build a fire," she continues. "There's a hill on the right side and I think it might block some of the wind for us, but I'm not sure.

"It's definitely our best option. There's nothing else but open space for a while from what I could tell."

The next fifteen minutes are especially hard since we know our resting point is just on the other side of the trees. We weave our way around the trunks, occasionally catching our feet on a hidden root under the snow.

Kai manages to find an unexposed root and topples face first into the snow. He comes up sputtering, trying to get the snow off of him as quickly as if he had caught fire and was trying to save himself. I rush over to aid his battle, gently reaching inside his hood to pull clumps of snow out. He shivers as I work. Jack smirks at his misery.

"Want me to pelt him with a snowball for you later?" I quietly ask Kai.

"Please," he gasps as snow hits his neck inside his coat.

I wrap my arm around his shoulder and pull him to the front with me, placing him between Jack and me. When his steps fall easier, I recoil my arm and loop it through his instead so that I stay warmer.

We all give a pitiful cheer when we reach the end of the trees. Huddling at the foot of the hill, we pull out our cattails to start fires to warm ourselves.

I spilt mine open, pulling out the fluff inside. Jack lights it and it catches instantly. We add it to the pile of branches we pulled from the trees at our backs and watch it slowly start to burn. The others do the same. In the large, open space, we light as many as we need to warm everyone up.

"If I remember correctly, I think there is a lake not too far from here," Jack says. He grabs a branch and starts to draw a map in the snow. "Over here is where we need to be careful. This area has always been off limits because it's so dangerous."

He taps the snow twice as if emphasizing his point. I wonder what he and Mory have hidden in there that he doesn't want us marching through and discovering. It's probably for the best—if we find something, we'll just have to explain it away and waste more time.

"If we follow this path here," Jack draws in the snow, "and then veer off here, I think we'll make it quicker than if we go straight."

"Why?" Azra beats us all to it.

"There's a lot of hills and inclines on the direct path. In fact, we'd be climbing down at least one cliff that way."

"Definitely something to avoid in this weather," Adam agrees, taking Kalley's hand. She's still sitting on the sled, which, I imagine, is keeping her warmer than those of us sitting on the snow.

As if on cue, the snow suddenly stops. Much like the wall of rain, it comes down in a single level, like a wall being pushed into the ground. The entire group stops talking as the snow stops around us. When it reaches neck level, we notice the sudden clarity in the air, now free from flakes. The end of the snow quietly drifts down to our feet, landing on the snow banks.

"What just happened?" Zach asks, starting the conversation back up.

I look to Jack, but he looks as shocked as I do.

Without warning, it starts again, but only long enough to create a noticeable layer of snow falling from the sky. It's like the weather machine is sputtering, unable to choose whether to stop or continue.

A blanket of snow falls, one foot thick. Then it reaches us, it's only wide enough to cover a forearm's length before it ends again.

The sky repeats this once more before returning to a steady stream of snow—this time much harsher.

"Time to move," Jack proclaims, leaping to his feet.

If *he's* worried, we should *all* be worried.

We kick snow over the fires quickly and leap into action. Jack guides us, changing our direction. The team follows him without question—partly out of trust, partly due to frozen lips.

The sun only stays with us for half an hour. It's quickly frozen out by the murky gray clouds that hover over everything inside the Globe. Visibility fades into murkiness, leaving us wading around in a strange twilight.

"Which mountain do we need to be looking for?" I attempt to start a conversation to pass the time. My feet stopped tingling a while ago but the memory of the sharp pricking sensation still haunts me.

"It's the fifth one from the left, third from the right," Jack uses his hands to describe the set up. "Most of them hold pieces of the machine, the part we need to take care of is in that one."

"When this is all over," I casually look around to see who is close enough to hear, "what happens?"

"I'm not sure. If Mory can fix the machine, he might be able to save the study. I'm guessing that's not likely though. It will probably come down to figuring out how to salvage what we can."

"What do *you* plan on doing?"

"Well, I probably can't stay here even if we do get everything fixed, so I guess I'll just go wherever Mory places me. If I'm lucky, maybe I can work with Eustace or something.

"My goal is still them same. I want to make sure the world is safe. I want to make sure my parents are taken care of...and all *their* parents. " He waves at the masses behind us. "Those men and women sacrificed so much. I want to help those of them that are still out there...to make sure their sacrifice wasn't in vain."

It was a valiant goal, one I could admire. Regardless of the fate of the Globe, the world outside still needed help to survive. I could appreciate that...I'd even want to help with the efforts once the Globe is shut down.

Jack takes a deep breath, rushing to continue. "Genesis, I need to tell them."

"No, Jack, you don't." *Is he completely mad?*

"They deserve to know, Gen."

"Know what?" Red asks as he pulls Kalley's sled up to the front.

"Nothing," I snap, looking more suspicious than I meant to.

All of a sudden, Jack was trying to be the white knight he told the children about in the stories. The one who overcomes adversity and does the right thing even though it costs him in the end. I wasn't happy with him, but I also wasn't going to let him throw himself to the wolves.

We still have a mission and we need everyone to cooperate to get to the mountains and turn the machine off. If Jack wants to play martyr, he can do it another day.

"Oh, really?" Red smirks. "Nothing, huh?"

I can sense it coming.

"Hey, guys," Red raises his voice so the people around us can hear. "Jack's got a secret. I have a feeling it might have to do with a pretty girl."

His guess is incredibly wrong, but better than the truth.

"No," Jack tries to protest, but the news is already filtering back through the ranks.

"Well, that got out of hand quickly," Azra comments. "Maybe next time try not to sell your friends out, okay, Red?"

"I assume you already know since you're one of the best friends, Azra, but the rest of us would like to hear this joyous news too." He slaps Jack on the shoulder. "Come on, buddy. If you have something to share, share."

He assumes we've done something crazy like getting engaged.

Nathaniel and Adam push their way to the front, running to get ahead of the group.

"Explain," Adam demands, hands curled into fists.

"What are you doing, Jack?" Nathaniel asks, an icy edge to his voice.

Red's grin fades from his face, realizing it's not as light-hearted as he thought the conversation was going to be.

"They need to know," Jack states simply.

"Know what?" Red's voice goes up an octave. He looks around, waiting for an answer. When none of us offer one, he turns to Azra. "Azra, what's going on?"

A few people pick up the question behind us, turning it into a chorus of an interrogation. My heart starts beating faster again. This situation could get out of control.

"Enough," Adam rumbles. "We have enough to worry about without harassing one of our teammates."

No one is satisfied with that answer, but they quiet.

When I can't take it anymore, I finally burst out with, "Jack and I broke up."

The people close enough behind us to hear, gasp. We're bombarded with questions, but at least now they have something to focus on other than learning about how Jack lied to them.

The news works its way back, creating a quiet hum of conversation. Miraculously, it distracts from the cold.

"That really wasn't necessary," Jack scolds me.

"None of this was, but you started it." I roll my eyes. He knew I'd never stand around and do nothing to protect him.

"I'm still going to tell them the next time we stop," he warns me.

"Okay, *what* is going on?" Red demands.

"I'll tell you all soon, I promise," Jack says softly, as if he's talking Lilly out of a tantrum.

"Jack, I'm one of your best friends, just tell me. What is going on?" Red begs for answers.

"Soon, brother. Soon."

Jack is really going to miss this place and these people. His moves grow sluggish over the next hour, the gravity of his secret weighing on him.

There's no stopping him. He's going to tell them. I know it, Adam and Nathaniel know it, and none of us can stop him.

I take his hand, likely confusing the people behind us after my announcement, but I want him to know that I'm there for him. He holds me close as we walk.

We reach the last stop we have planned before we reach the mountains. Now that we're closer, they look far taller than they did from the bunker.

Jack waits for everyone to build their fires before addressing them. Nerves wrack my body, sending pulses of fear rushing through my entire system at strange intervals. Mixed with the shaking from the cold, I feel as though I could faint.

"I'm sure by now, you've all heard that Genesis and I are no longer together," everyone quietly nods. "There is a reason for that. I messed up."

Everyone perks up, leaning forward slightly. I sigh and Azra pats my knee.

Jack stands by me, so I can't see his face—especially since my eyes are also focused on the ground ahead of me — but he radiates strength. It might be warmer than the fire a few feet away.

In my peripheral vision, I can see everyone watching him. I wait quietly for the moment I need to stand by Jack's side and convince our friends not to abandon him.

"When we came back to the bunker yesterday, we told you we had answers, and we do. Only, I've had the answers all along."

When I look up, I find them all watching Jack closely,

hanging on his words. My breathing becomes deeper, as if my body is preparing for a war.

"There is a group that created all of this," he waves his hands around. "Far from here, there is another world, full of people who are in danger. There is a war going on and people are dying.

"This group wanted to create a way to help save them. As part of the war, people are dropping bombs. You've heard me tell some stories about these. Many of those stem from things that actually happened outside of here."

A few people blink, trying to process his words. I don't blame them. I've known for days and I'm still not sure on all the details.

"You see, everyone *in here* is part of the effort to save everyone *out there*. This company is run by my great uncle. He's studying how to fix things in the real world.

"What are you saying, Jack?" someone calls.

"I'm saying that when you were little, your families were scared for your safety with them. They brought you to Morozoko Industries and begged for you to be placed inside the Globe here. They knew what that meant for you and they chose to give you up to the study so that you would be safer inside than you were with them."

"We're not saying it was the right choice," I say from my place on the ground. I can't make eye contact with Jack. "But your families thought this was what was best for you."

"Over the years, we've all been tested to see how we adapt and learn to survive certain conditions," Jack's words start to anger the crowd. They sit up straighter and start murmuring to the people around them. "I know so much about the weather machine they used to test us because I work directly with them, reporting on what's happening here in the Globe."

"You lied to us?" the accusations start.

Jack stands quietly, taking it all. He flinches when the questions start, but he doesn't say anything. A lesser man might have yelled, trying to defend himself. Jack handles it with grace.

He answers when he can, explaining the study and his part in it. The crowd grows increasingly agitated.

"Listen up," Nathaniel finally gets involved. "Yes, Jack lied to us. Yes, we were being used. Right now, we need to set all that aside. We have a machine that's broken that *will* kill us if we don't handle it and to do that, we need Jack. So save your anger for later."

"Jack has been one of us for as long as most of us can remember." I add. "I came here after Jack did, so he's been here since my first day. We know how good he is at handling situations—"

"Because he caused them?" someone shouts.

"Even the ones he didn't cause," I yell. "We need him to help us fix this. When we're done and we make sure everyone at the bunker is safe, we'll decide what to do."

"I'll go along with whatever you decide," Jack promises. "Just please, let's work together. We can't waste anymore time."

"And what if we can't trust you anymore? What if you're leading us into some kind of trap?" someone in the back yells.

"For all we know, you could be separating the children from us to see if they can survive."

"Why would I have told you any of this, if that's what I was planning?" Jack holds his hands up, trying to calm everyone down.

"I've been inside Morozoko Industries. I just found out. Nathaniel and Azra have too. None of us believe that this is the case." I add. "From what I've seen, they really think they're helping people...but maybe they went about it the wrong way."

"We can debate ethics later," Adam finally jumps back in. He points toward the mountains. "I think we're on the clock."

In the distance, clouds are forming around the mountains, dousing it in snow suddenly. A white wave rises up, almost like a crash of water when someone jumps into the river off of the waterfall ledge, splashing a huge, consuming wave everywhere. Everything looks drastically different.

We're about to walk right into it.

CHAPTER 21

Jack sucks in a deep breath.

"We can make it to the mountain within the next two hours. By the time we get there, *that* should be over. I don't know how long we'll have until the next wave hits, but this is our last chance."

He steps forward and reaches his hand out to Red, volunteering to help him up to get people moving. Red hesitates for a moment, glancing at me, but takes Jack's hand.

"Let's go!" Red takes the first step.

We didn't have time to absorb the fire's warmth, but we crash toward the mountain anyway. If that storm is any indication, we're in deep trouble.

Jack holds my hand until we slow our pace, having run much longer than anticipated. The next hour drags by as if we aren't moving forward at all.

Then, as if the entire world had come racing at us, we find ourselves in front of the base of the mountains. They tower above us, covered in snow and rocks.

Before we can enter into their territory, we have one

final obstacle to overcome—the snow I dropped there less than twenty-four hours earlier. It crests well above our heads in a massive heap.

Nathaniel steps forward to test the bank of snow. It's so slippery that he slides back down. After several failed attempts, I try my hand at it.

Kicking my foot into the snow, I try to make a step for myself. I make it a foot off the ground before I fall back down. My foot kicks out from under me and I land on the ground with a bone-shaking crash.

"I don't think we can climb it," I grunt out. Jack and Nathaniel help me to my feet.

"That looked painful," Perrin murmurs in my ear.

"Really? Do you think?" I glance at him from the corner of my eye as he smirks.

"We'll have to dig a path," Adam announces.

"Not necessarily an entire path," Jack thinks out loud. "What about a tunnel?"

"Do you think it can support a tunnel?" Adam questions.

"It looks pretty frozen. If we can get through this first layer of ice, I think we can dig enough of a tunnel to crawl through. It would save us a lot of time." Jack crosses an arm over his chest, propping his other on it as he scratches his chin.

"If you think it can handle it," Adam replies hesitantly.

"Eustace!" Jack calls, summoning his coworker.

Together, they mutter about their plan. When they determine that it could work, we start digging out the snow. Several people work on the tunnel while the rest of us remove the snow that they're moving so it's not in our way.

Jack disappears into the growing tunnel, taking on the risk of it collapsing against my wishes. He needs to be the one to dismantle the machine, but he seems to be trying to prove a point to the group.

My back is killing me by the time we're done removing the snow, but the tunnel is constructed after an hour. Nathaniel checks it before allowing any other people inside, but once he gives the okay, we all cram inside.

On my hands and knees, I scurry through the tunnel. It's warm with all of the breathing bodies inside, and for a moment, I wonder if it would have been smart to take turns like we had over the river. Too late now.

The sound is muted inside. It would be deafeningly silent without the wind if it weren't for the noise of people forcing their way through the tunnel.

Every time I try tipping my head up, I scrape along the top of the tunnel. It forces me to bend my head low to get through. Pain radiates through my neck down my spine, but I push forward. The guys that are taller than me must find this unbearable.

The temperature rises the further I crawl into the tunnel, darkness threatening to surround me. Only a soft glow tells me there is light at the end. I have to force myself to stay focused. One hand in front of the other. One knee to the next.

When I find it hard to concentrate, I watch the bottom of Jack's boots as they move ahead of me. I focus on the tread, its pattern urging me forward.

I relax when it starts to get lighter. The second half of the tunnel is easier, though I keep a close eye on Jack's shoes.

Jack turns the moment he is clear of the tunnel walls. His hands dart inside for me, pulling me the last few feet. The open air is freedom on my lungs.

Jack hugs me close to his chest.

"Are you okay," he whispers into my hood, somewhere near my ear. My hair is tangled around my face, having fallen during the crawl.

I nod as he quickly brushes back my hair, tucking it down the backside of my hood, careful not to accidentally expose my ears to the elements while doing so.

Once he's satisfied that I'm all right, he reaches in and pulls Azra out. Red follows behind, pulling Kalley's sled, Adam taking up the backside to push as Red pulled.

Once enough people are out to help, many of us turn our attention to the mountain. It looms in front of us, fifty yards away.

The ground is brown, free of snow. It's as if the snow never touched the earth here, all collecting on the slopes of the mountain.

Jack examines the mountain for a moment, studying its slopes before taking my hand. His gaze never tears away from the fortress in front of us.

"We need to be careful," he says.

"Why?" I should know better than to ask, but I always do.

"All of that snow is resting up there, but if it's disturbed, it could come crashing down on us. We can't do anything to cause a shift in its environment."

"Isn't that the whole goal with Morozoko?" I say snidely.

Jack whips around to look at me.

"Tell them not do anything stupid. We don't need anyone getting a bright idea and rushing into this."

He waves Nathaniel and Adam over as I rush back to the tunnel. Azra spreads the word with people who are already out while I inform each new person that crawls out of the tunnel.

In silence, our entire team of people stands lodged between a mountain of snow and an actual mountain. This would be an incredible beginning to one of Jack's stories, but in his, the snow would come toppling down only to have the hero survive at the last second. I'd just as soon pass on the snow falling.

"This way," Jack shouts so everyone can hear, waving high in the air so the others would know to follow.

We tunneled through near the edges of two of the mountains. Jack leads us as we walk down the strip of dry land to the next formation.

"We're looking for a set of rocks that protrude out of the mountain slightly. They'll almost look like duplicates of each other with a few slight differences to make it look like it's actually part of the mountain to anyone who doesn't know to look for it."

My eyes trace over the rocky face of the mountain. We all spread out, looking for what Jack described as the entrance. In the end, I'm the one that finds it.

I run my gloved hands over it, checking to see if I can find a hidden door. Nothing looks unusual, but the consistencies in certain parts of the large boulders that look like exact duplicates of the other are enough to convince me to send Azra for Jack.

He examines it for a moment before running his hand along where I had touched. Jack motions me closer.

"The pendant," he murmurs as I lean close. I lower myself onto the ground, allowing my chest to get as close as it can to the area Jack is stretched out to reach.

Something clicks and we both back away as a door slides open, revealing blue light inside. It reminds me of the bunker.

Inside is a foyer area. The empty space is held up by

four large columns that support the structure. We quickly fill the room with our people.

It sounds hollow. Every breath, every shift of feet, echoes off of the walls.

"Stay here," Jack says softly to the group. "I'm going to go look for where the system is housed so I can shut it down."

"You don't know?" Adam asks.

"He was never sent inside," Eustace answers for him. "This was off limits, even to him. There's only ever been one person in here for repairs and that was two decades ago."

"I'm coming with you," I volunteer. Nathaniel and Adam quickly do the same.

"We don't need the entire team yet. It's going to take a number of us to get this thing shut down, but I have to locate all of the different rooms first."

"Jack, tell us what we're looking for and let us help," I try guiding him.

"Just us," he nods, quickly directing us to check in certain areas.

"Wait here," Adam announces. "You'll all be getting jobs momentarily. We're going to scout first."

When Adam and Jack turn, I can easily see how we had confused the two. They're basically mirror images of each other. They split off when we reach the hallway at the end of the foyer, Jack running to the right, Adam to the left. Eustace follows him. Nathaniel follows us.

Once we're out of the foyer, the lights switch from blue to red, casting an angry-looking glow as we move swiftly down the hall. The first room looks similar to the Control Center in the Morozoko Industries building. I half expect to see Mory wandering around.

Jack rushes down the stairs to the center of the platform. Instead of the screens that fill the Control Center, the room is stacked with tall towers covered in metal. Each piece has flashing lights that look like they're racing each other up and down the sides. Jack inspects them, pulling cords away from them at times.

In the next room, one large screen sits against the wall. It's connected to several tiny screens all feeding into the main one.

"This processes the information it gets from the Control Center. It tells the machines here how to work," Jack explains.

"Then rip it out," I encourage him.

"We can't yet, we have to do it in the correct order. I need to see what's in the next room."

We go through three more rooms before running into Adam and Eustace. They quickly explain what they found while Jack frowns.

Eustace and Jack step away to discuss a plan. In the darkness of the wrap-around hallway, with only the red lights to illuminate them, I have trouble seeing their faces. Adam, Nathaniel and I hover in the corner, trying to overhear.

"You understand what that means?" Eustace asks. I can barely hear him from this distance.

"It's the best plan," Jack insists. "You know it is, Eustace. Think it through."

"We have to get them all out," Eustace replies in a dark voice.

"We will, we'll make sure of it."

"You know what will happen out there," Eustace nods backward. I assume he's referring to outside of the mountain base.

"We just have to prepare them for it, that's all."

"I guess we should be grateful for the tunnel," Eustace mutters.

"All right, enough. Fill us in on this little plan," Adam blurts. "Enough with the us-verses-them secrets."

"We need to get most of them out of here. We're going to need one to three people in each room to handle different tasks," Jack responds, stepping aside to open up their circle of conversation. "According to Eustace's calculations, we need to get people back to base as quickly as possible. The weather is going to spin out of control when we shut it down for a little bit until it stabilizes."

"Our people need to be on their way back to the bunker before we pull the plugs and kill this thing. Before that though, we need them to pile as much snow onto the wall out there as possible."

"Sorry, what?" Nathaniel asks, frustrated.

"The wall needs to be higher," Eustace explains, "Just trust me on this. We need everyone outside, building up that wall. Once it's built up, we're going to pour melted snow on it to create more ice on top of it."

"Don't worry, it's just a precaution in case the device spins out of control right here," Jack assures us. "We're protecting the mountain. We're going to need to get in to fix the machine once this is all handled. We just want to help keep the elements out."

"Why do we need to fix it?" Adam requests.

"If anyone plans on living in the Globe, they're going to need the machine to live. Don't worry, no nefarious plans here," Eustace tries to offer some comfort.

"Send all but..." Jack pauses to count how many people he will need to help shut down the machine, "twenty people including us outside to build up the snow wall."

"And, Adam," Eustace interjects. "Have them take Kalley and anyone else who is injured or can't move quickly and force them to start back now. Everyone will catch up with them. Tell them not to stop until they reach the cave. They're going to need the head start, especially if this spins out."

Adam reluctantly goes outside to set up the teams

while Eustace and Jack discuss what needs to happen in each room. After a few minutes, our friends step inside, calling quietly down the hall to locate us.

"Where do you need us?" Red asks, pulling his gloves off.

Jack waits until everyone is inside before explaining. He walks around to each room, showing specific cords to pull and buttons and levers to push and flip. He leaves each person standing outside of the door to the room they will be working in.

"I'm going to check on everyone outside. Stay here and I'll be back in a minute," Jack announces. I follow him out when he motions to me.

"I'm not telling everyone everything," he says in a low voice. "I'm worried about the people outside, so we need to get them away in case anything goes wrong."

We step outside and see the wall of snow is much higher than it was before. Most of our people are on the other side of the tunnel, but a few still linger between the tunnel and the mountain's edge.

"We're going to have to crawl through," Jack says gently. "Are you okay with that?"

I nod. "I'll follow you."

Jack asks the others to go through first and then leads the way through the tunnel to the other side. I focus on his boots one more time, memorizing the treads as we go.

His hand waits for me at the end of the tunnel. I grasp

it as he allows me to climb out. I don't relinquish it once I'm upright.

"We're going to send you back to the bunker. Once we shut the system down, the machine may spin out of control for a little bit until it regulates itself.

"Honestly, I'm not sure what's going to happen, so we want to be prepared for the worst case. We need you to leave now and don't stop until you reach the cave. Rest only for a few hours and then get back to the bunker. Don't leave them alone any longer than you have to."

Jack is shouting, giving them his best rallying cry. He wants to motivate them to move quickly. I glance up at the mountain. It towers over us, beautiful and menacing at the same time.

"Once everyone returns, the group will decide what to do next, but our priority right now is to shut down the machine and keep everyone safe. Can you do that?"

Everyone nods, willing to do what must be done to protect our people.

"Go now, quickly," Jack instructs. "Stay safe."

We wave goodbye to everyone, watching as they leave. I'm glad they'll be out of harm's way.

"Now, Gen," he says, turning to me. "We're going to go back through the tunnel. Are you ready?"

"I'm fine, Jack. Just let me follow you." He gives me a strange look but drops down by the tunnel's entrance and climbs through.

"How many times have you and I walked through the tunnel back in the bunker?" he asks.

"Thousands," I smile at the memories.

"Most of those thousands were pretty fun, weren't they?" I can hear the teasing tone in his voice. He must be grinning wickedly. "You remember that two A.M. walk we took outside only to find it was pouring rain, don't you?"

"We got forced back inside and stayed in the dark corner of the tunnel for half the night." I couldn't stop my smirk.

"That was one of my favorite kisses ever," he says. "Definitely top ten."

"That *was* pretty good," I reply. I know I shouldn't, but I add, "But not nearly as good as the pond two years ago."

"Now *that* was amazing," he sighs. Jack has always been good at distracting me.

He turns around, reaching out for me at the end of the tunnel. He pulls me into his arms. He must have knocked his hood off while climbing out of the tunnel because it's no longer covering his head. The wind gently blows his hair making him the image of icy perfection. Against the backdrop of the snowy mountain, he could have passed for an ice prince.

He would have made the perfect prince in one of the stories he told the kids. I hope for his sake that his redemption arc is for the storybooks as well.

"I'm sorry for the mess I made, Gen," he kisses my

forehead. "But I'm really glad I've spent all this time with you."

I brush my hands over his arms. I can feel his muscles even through his coat sleeves.

"Whatever happens, I need you to promise me you'll do what's best for the group," Jack insists. "Don't let *me* sway you. You know what's best for those people who just left. You listen to what's in your heart to take care of *them*, *not me*, understand?"

"I will," I say frowning. "But you need to keep me accountable too. When I make my mind up about something, I'm not easily swayed, so I need you to keep me on track if I'm off base."

He leans his forehead against mine.

"You've got this, babe."

For a moment, I think he might lean it to kiss me. He breathes deeply, shutting his eyes as if trying to memorize everything the way *I* had memorized the pattern on his boot. I am his life support and he is mine...just like it's always been.

"Come on," he says, finally tugging me away. "We have to shut this thing down."

He turns to look back at me while we jog back into the mountain. The snow does wonders for his ice blue eyes.

"Jack," I stop him, tugging on his hand. I feel compelled to tell him. "Don't read into this."

He pauses, grinning.

"Read into what?"

"You..." I wouldn't normally hesitate. Ordinarily, I'd tell him flat out that I thought he was the most gorgeous man in the world and that right now, I couldn't picture a more handsome version of the man I loved, but now I live in a world where I have to be careful what I say to him.

"I just thought you might like to know," I take a breath, "that right then you looked just like one of the princes from your stories. An Ice Prince."

"So no more Dragon King, huh?" He bites his lip. I have to fight to keep my eyes from rolling back in my head.

"Maybe not," I roll my eyes, trying to pull away from him. "We should go."

He doesn't move. He's still holding on to my wrist where he caught it a moment ago. It pulls me back toward him when I move and he doesn't.

"You don't fit here, you know," Jack says lazily. "You don't belong in the ice. You're a Summer Queen, my dear Genesis. You're too fiery for all of this."

He waves around at the ice sculpture surrounding us. We're tucked away in our own little private ice palace out in the open air, all by ourselves for the first time since all this happened. Kissing him here would be incredible, but I have to wait—it's not time for us to reconcile yet.

"A Summer Queen, huh?"

Jack tips my hood off, exposing my hair. Gently, he pulls it out in front of me, getting a good look at it.

"You deserved to be wrapped in life, Genesis. You're as radiant as a sunrise in the middle of a perfect Summer day. You give life to everyone around you. You're a perfect pixie, Genesis. You're the Summer heat, to my Winter ice.

"There's also probably a very good joke in there about heat and ice creating...*steam*," Jack takes a swaggering step toward me, making me melt.

"Jack," I rest my hand on his chest, pushing him back. "Slow."

"We should get back inside." His voice is deep, daring me to walk back into the building. He holds my gaze, waiting to see who will break first.

Jack picks my hand up off his chest and kisses it before dragging me back inside.

CHAPTER 22

"They've got to be clear by now," Jack says. Eustace nods next to him. "Everyone take your places." The group shifts inside their doors.

"Gen, stand by me," Jack clenches my hand in his nervously. It's painful, but I don't let go. He needs my support right now. "Listen for our voices, we'll tell you when to go. This second you're done with your job, I want you out of this building, through that tunnel and running as fast as you can toward the cave. Do not stop for *anything*—we'll all be following right behind you."

"Don't stop for *anything*," Eustace repeats, stressing the need for a quick escape.

"One final check. Go to your stations and I'll be right in for final instructions." Jack follows Adam into the first room.

"You're sure about this?" Adam asks one last time.

"Positive. Pull that lever when you hear your code word. Wait thirty seconds before unplugging these three cables and then get out."

Adam nods.

"Don't stop for anything, Adam. Not even for us. You need to get back to Kalley and take care of all those kids." We turn and walk back to the door. "Hey, Adam? I'm sorry for bullying you when you started asking questions. I just didn't want you pulled out or to see something happen to you."

"I know, Jack, I would have done the same thing. Besides, I knew enough about what was happening and I didn't tell everyone, so I'm just as complicit as you." He gives Jack a meaningful look. "You and I are fine, Jack. Now, go handle this."

"Thanks, Adam. Stay safe."

We check in with Kris and Todd next. Jack runs through their tasks one more time before wishing them safety on their run back. They both make Jack promise to take care of me, knowing Jack will be my protector in all of this.

Azra and Red are in the next room waiting for us. I take Azra's hand as Jack runs them through their mission again.

Before we leave, Red reaches out to clasp Jack's hand, pulling him in for a hug. They slap each other on the back as Jack grows serious.

"You take care of her," he says harshly, pointing at Azra. "When you run, you watch over her."

"Always," Red says, looking a little confused. "I've always got her back."

"Make sure you do," Jack says, turning away as he rushes up the steps to the door.

"What was that about?" I mumble as we slip around the corner into the next room.

"Nothing, babe. Just my way of getting those two together finally."

We run through the next few rooms without any side conversations, quickly reminding people what to do.

Eustace stands alone in the next room, prepared to dismantle part of the machine's brain.

"I'm fine, Jack, just tell me when."

"Just be careful, buddy," Jack replies.

The two of them share a look that I can't read, but it resembles something like dread.

"Guys, this *is* going to work, right? There's not anything you aren't telling me, correct?"

"We know exactly how this will work out, Genesis," Eustace assures me.

"Don't worry about it, babe. Everything is going to work out." Jack kisses my temples again. I'm not sure how I feel about this new part of our relationship.

"You'd better hurry up," Eustace pushes us out the door. He turns his back, ready to do the most dangerous job aside from Jack's. If he doesn't do it just right, he could be electrocuted.

"You just take care of that family of yours, Eustace,"

Jack calls as we leave the room. It's a reminder to be careful enough to get back to them.

Perrin and Nes occupy the following room. I wish Perrin had left with the others—the only medical person we have and he's one of the last ones out.

They use the opportunity to threaten Jack if he doesn't look out for me. I shove them both before we leave, earning myself several over-exaggerated winks from both Perrin and Nes.

Nathaniel waits in the last room. He's standing in the shadows, nearly as dark as his hair. He steps toward us, into the red glow of the room with something in his hand.

"Are you going to threaten me too?" Jack asks with a sad smile.

"Threaten you?"

Jack nods to me.

"Ah." He doesn't hesitate before coming up with a threat. "I will bury you in that snow outside if you mess with her ever again...is that the kind of threat you're talking about?"

"It is," he confirms, taking the device out of Nathaniel's hand to inspect it once more. "And you don't have to worry about me anymore. She's safe."

"I'm glad to hear that."

Jack flinches at the words. I run my hand quickly over

his arm to let him know I'm not angry anymore. His head turns just slightly toward me with his eyes closed, like he's debating saying something.

"Nathaniel," he turns back. "Should anything happen, I need you to promise me that you'll look after Genesis."

"Of course," Nathaniel promises as I yelp.

"Nothing is going to happen to you!"

"Make sure she gets out of here. Do not let her wait for me while I'm handling the last room. You take her out and get her clear of this place, do you understand me?"

Nathaniel, acting like he knows something I don't, nods solemnly.

"I won't let anything happen to her, Jack. Don't worry about her at all while you're working in here," I relax at his words, realizing he's trying to keep Jack focused so he gets out. "I'll get her out and we'll meet you in the cave, if not before. And before you jump down my throat, I know enough not to wait for you, but I have a pretty good feeling you'll be moving so fast, you'll catch up to us before we get too far."

"Nate, I'm sorry I lied to you."

"You did what you had to do. I get it. We're fine. We'll figure it out. But you better get moving, buddy. You're starting to scare your girlfriend."

"Stay safe, Nate," Jack says, placing his hands on Nate's shoulders. "See you on the other side."

We turn to go back to the hallway.

"Ready, babe?" he asks.

"Yes, and, Jack, please don't worry about me. I know it's important that I go with Nathaniel. You just need to focus on getting out when you're done."

Even though I don't like it, I know Nathaniel is right. Jack needs to not worry about me. If that means I have to leave him here while he works, I can do that for his sake.

"Thank you, Gen, for taking care of me."

"You've always taken care of me, Mr. Extra Bread," I reply, making him chuckle.

"You have the necklace, right?" Jack asks unexpectedly.

"Yes," I answer.

"Let me see it," he requests.

I pull it out from under my collar, dangling it between my fingers. It reflects the red light in the hallway sending a shattered array of light beams around the hall. It glints off Jack's face as he smiles, looking relieved.

"Okay, good. Put it back inside your coat, and whatever you do, Gen, don't lose that."

"I'll take care of it for you," I promise.

Jack closes his eyes, nodding a few times before taking one final deep breath. He lowers his shoulders, stretching out his arms down to his fingers.

Here we go.

"On my mark," he yells. He points for me to go to my location between Nathaniel and Eustace's rooms.

Jack starts calling out commands, which I then filter down the hallway. Sirens start sounding in the hallway once the first levers are pulled and cords are unplugged. The red lights start pulsing in the hallway and rooms.

"Azra, now!" Jack calls out. After a moment, she and Red run out of the room, waving to let us know they're on their way out. I'm glad to see them racing out of the mountain.

A loud crash sounds in one of the rooms after Jack yells out a command. Knowing it was coming, I still jump. Soon only three rooms are left as the sirens grow louder. Perrin runs, leaving Nes to finish his tasks as Eustace peels out of his room.

"Hurry up, Jack," he yells before darting to the door. "Get this done before you can't."

"Just go, man," Jack commands, trying to keep everyone safe. He turns his attention back to the group. "Nes, get out of there!"

Nes makes his way through the door.

"You good?" he asks. Jack's glare prompts him to move.

At some point, the sirens and the lights have managed to sync. The whooping sound rises and falls as the lights glow and dim.

"Gen, you have to go with Nathaniel," Jack turns to me suddenly.

"I will," I say, shocked at the horror and desperation in his voice.

"Stay strong, Genesis." He turns to face the door.

"Nathaniel!" Jack whips around to the door.

Nathaniel pulls the last lever and an explosion sounds somewhere over our heads, high in the mountain.

"Did you know that was going to happen?" I demand.

"Yes, now run." He pushes me at Nathaniel as he rushes through the door. Nathaniel catches me and drags me away.

Jack steps back, out of my reach. He gives Nathaniel the most jealous look I've ever seen him give, a mix between pure hatred and gratitude. He looks like he's handing over the world and Nathaniel is about to run out the door with it.

His eyes flash over to me, locking onto my gaze. I can no longer hear the sirens even though they shriek louder and faster than before. I can't hear anything but Jack.

"I love you, Genesis!" he shouts before running back into the room Eustace just vacated.

I stumble over my feet. Running backward isn't easy.

His hood bounces behind him as he moves. Jack flings himself into the room, around the corner, disappearing as quickly as the snow had earlier today. For a moment, I hope he will reappear just as quickly and leave with us. He doesn't.

"Come on, Gen, you'll see him soon. Don't mess this up for him." Nathaniel tugs on me, forcing me to turn and run. Knowing my job is to make sure Jack isn't thinking of anything other than getting out, I run faster than Nathaniel.

That explosion worries me. No one said anything about things exploding. But I trust that Jack knows what he's doing.

The light outside is bright compared to the red and blue lights inside the compound. Nathaniel pushes me toward the tunnel.

"You're first," he says.

"I'd rather follow—"

"Not an option," he pushes the back of my knee with his foot, dropping me to the ground. "Get going."

He pushes me inside the tunnel, following so closely that he continuously hits the back of my heels.

"Nathaniel!" I shriek, trying to get him to slow down.

"Jack said to move, we're going to move," he replies, refusing to let me slow.

I picture Jack crawling ahead of me, his boot only inches ahead of me. I reach for it with each movement forward.

The air hits me forcefully on the other side of the tunnel. The difference between the two sides of the snow wall is shocking to the system.

I turn, looking up at it as Nathaniel crawls out of the

tunnel opening. He stands, looking back for only a moment before propelling me forward.

"We don't have time, Gen."

"We can wait for him," I protest.

"He said no," Nathaniel reminds me. "This is what he wanted us to do—get as far away as possible and meet him in the cave."

"How about we go far enough that we can still see when he exits? Is that fair? We've got a head start and once I know he's out safe, I'll be fine and we can run, but if I don't know, Nathaniel...."

"I know it's hard, Gen, but you and I are running if I have to pick you up and carry you over my shoulder to do so." He takes a threatening step toward me. I back up quickly, hands in the air to show I don't want to be taken by force.

"Let's go," he says.

He clamps down on my hand, worried that I might turn back. I cry out in pain, but that doesn't stop him from pulling me along. We run as fast and as far as we can from the mountain.

The snow is hard to walk in, but much harder to run in. I sink with every step, forcing my footprints to release me so I can take another step. The snow sucks me in like the ponds and pools in the swamp are said to do to the victims that actually ended up inside the Morozoko Industries building with Jack and Mory.

I fight to stay upright, stumbling every few steps. Nathaniel pitches forward too, thankfully never at the same time as me. We keep each other balanced as we crash though the icy snow.

I notice how loud our steps sound in the surrounding silence. Without the sirens lecturing us, it feels like something is missing.

Up ahead, I can see Nes running. It looks like he caught up with Eustace. Beyond him, I can see the rest of the group, all spaced out in the order we left, dark winter coats a stark contrast to the snow.

The limited light has faded since we began our assault on the weather system inside the mountain. The snow still falls, but much less than it was before.

Suddenly it sputters again, showering us in layers of snow as if it's unsure that we unplugged it and it's trying to decide if it should live or die.

"Hope that's a good sign," Nathaniel shouts.

"Me too," I say, jumping over the top edge of a section of falling snow. There's a momentary reprieve before a new layer hits me in the face.

We make it a few more yards before the snow grows quiet. Nothing moves. Nathaniel and I slow, as does the group ahead of us. Nes turns a moment before I do, looking back at the mountain.

Even the clouds seem to shift, allowing more light to filter down to us. The entire area looks brighter.

"I think we did it," Nathaniel comments, his voice echoing in the cold air.

"Did we do it?" Nes calls from behind us. The wind is the only other sound I hear.

Before I can answer, something shifts in the air.

"Nathaniel, Gen, you need to move away!" Eustace shouts in the distance.

Nathaniel sees it first, whispering my name.

When I notice it, it's a slight movement in my peripheral vision. It takes a moment for me to find it and focus on it, but it's there, a puff of white slowly moving near the peak of the mountain. For a moment, it looks like it's disappeared.

When I see it again, it no longer blends in with the snow resting high atop the mountain, but rather flies off the face of it as if it were trying to fling itself to its death. As it moves, it picks up more snow, gradually building into multiple streams running down the mountain.

It almost looks like what the waterfall would if we placed several rocks in the middle of it, creating pathways for the water to escape over the edge. The snow crashes down, building with every inch.

Nathaniel isn't fast enough to catch me this time. The entire group calls my name, throwing it around with words like *dangerous* and *avalanche.*

Surprising us, we are attacked by one final dropping of snow. It's a foot in width as it gently crashes on us. I push through the machine's final indecision, making my way to the tunnel.

As if my friends were willing it so, the avalanche's snow takes a turn, crashing to the right. It's as if a path is created, knowing I'm running toward it. This only encourages me as I rush for the tunnel.

The flood of snow continues, cascading down the mountain that Jack has yet to escape from. I know my chances of survival aren't good if I go through that tunnel, but I can't leave Jack.

I hear Nathaniel behind me, but I miraculously manage to stay ahead of him. I fix my eyes on the tunnel opening, but I'm still too far away as the snow reaches the bottom of the mountain.

I pray Jack will come bolting out of the tunnel. I wait for him, watching so that I don't miss him, but he never exits.

The snow hits the ground, bubbling up in a massive cloud. It's as if the biggest, thickest fog bank I've ever seen has just come rolling in, taking over the landscape. I can't see beyond the snow. Even the mountain disappears from my sight.

Nathaniel slams into me as the snow cloud forces its way up over the wall of snow and ice we had created. The wall blocks most of it, keeping the destruction in check, but enough showers down on us to bury us in an additional foot and a half of snow.

When I untangle myself from Nathaniel's grasp, I find the snow settling on the ground. It sparkles in the light as more of the clouds fade away, revealing just enough sun to make the world glitter.

We live in a snow globe that someone has just shaken.

Bits of snow-glitter gently fall to the ground. Trees are covered in it. The wall is buried in it. The people surrender to it.

All that's missing is the sound of music from the little wind-up box on the underside of our snow globe, though, if it's just noise we're looking for, the sound of my friend shouting is enough to fill the silence.

Nes reaches us, followed by Eustace and the others. Without coordinating, we rush toward the giant barricade keeping us from Jack.

CHAPTER 23

I know where the tunnel was. I know it is right *there*...or maybe *there*. I had tried to keep my eyes focused on it, but I couldn't.

I throw myself desperately in the general area of the tunnel entrance. The snow may have covered the wall, but inside, the tunnel would likely still be clear. That is, unless the snow entered from the other side.

It doesn't matter, it will still be loose and it's our easiest way in. I shove my hands into the snow, pulling it away. I can't help my tears—this time I can't even blame the wind. I know I'll pay for them later in this bitter cold.

Nes and Nathaniel help me, pulling away the chunks of snow that cover this side of the wall. Eustace holds back, examining the scene as Perrin reaches us.

"Gen!" Azra yells in the background.

"Azra, monitor the others," Eustace commands as she and Red arrive. "Make sure nothing else has shifted. We don't want to get caught if there is another one."

Red throws himself on the ground to assist us.

I know Kris and Todd are to my right, hopefully digging in another location.

"Hey!" Kris shouts. "I'm up. Come on!"

When I glance up, Kris is standing on top of the wall. The loose snow has covered the ice, creating a gentler slope. We can climb it.

Throwing myself onto the wall of snow probably wasn't my best idea, but I'm not thinking rationally.

Eustace directs us where to climb and we follow without hesitation. Once we reach the top, we stumble around, trying to determine where the entrance might be. We'll have to dig through all of the snow the avalanche just dropped on the once clean area.

I claw at the white stuff trying to create a new tunnel. Every time I think I've made headway, the edges of the small hole start to collapse in, a tiny version of the avalanche I had just witnessed. Tiny balls of snow crumble in, taking more and more with it each time.

"He knew this would happen, didn't he?" I finally shout, leaning back from the snow. I find Eustace a few feet away. "Jack knew this would happen and so did you. You kept this from us."

I try not to sound hysterical. I try to keep my voice even. I'm not sure it works.

I reach up and knock my hair back from my face with the back of my wrist. In my insanity, it had fallen loose and it is dangling in my way.

"Jack knew," Eustace confirms.

"He lied to me again," I whine, tears welling up in my eyes. I wasn't angry about him lying as much as the fact that he could be dead inside the mountain and there's no way for me to reach him.

"He was protecting you. He was protecting everyone," Eustace replies calmly. "He knew exactly what he was doing.

"He had to set off another explosion. I knew he'd put it off as long as possible to get you out, but if he didn't destroy the one room entirely, the machine wouldn't have died. He wanted the rest of us out of the way because he knew it would set off an avalanche."

"That's why we built the wall, isn't it?" Azra asks without taking her eyes off the other mountains. Her head swivels back and forth, looking for signs of another avalanche in progress, though even if she finds one, I doubt we can escape.

"Yes, we hoped that it would block most of it from going any farther."

"You should have told me," Adam growled.

"Would you have gone along with it if we had?" Eustace counters sadly.

"How do we get him out?" I plead, changing the subject.

"I don't know if we can, Genesis. Jack knew the risk," Eustace turns to me. "I'm sorry, Gen."

He kneels down next to me and I want to punch him. I doubt it would do much good though and I need my hands—*and his*—to help free Jack.

"Guys!" Azra shouts.

We follow her gaze up. A bit of snow has started to fall halfway up the mountain above us. It's barreling down, picking up more snow as it crashes down.

"Everyone down on the ground and huddle around Genesis, now!" Eustace shouts.

Confusion washes over me about why I would be singled out. I, of all people here, am not the one that should be saved.

I don't have a choice though. Nes grabs hold of me, jerking me toward the drop. Perrin snags my other hand and together, we jump.

I scream as we land, pain radiating through my ankle. I focus on it as Perrin tosses me to the ground and throws himself over me. Red forces Azra against me and covers her with his body. The rest of the men pile onto us, creating a tight mound of people as the snow rushes down toward us.

No one speaks for a long time. Eventually someone peels themselves off of the group.

"It's clear," Todd announces. He helps the rest of us up.

"I'm going to need a little help," Adam croaks. His lower half is encased in snow. He struggles to free himself from the giant wall of snow that has collapsed over half his body.

"What—" I murmur, taking in the sight.

"Is everyone else okay?" Eustace asks, taking control of the situation as he moves quickly to help his friend. "Todd, help dig out that side. Kris, catch him when he falls out. Nathaniel, do a head count."

Nathaniel instantly whips around, to make sure everyone is still with us. He points to each person, saying their number out loud.

Adam breaks free from the wall of snow as Nathaniel wraps up his count for the sixth time. Azra turns, getting in my face.

"Are you okay? Did you get hurt?" she demands.

"I'm fine, are you okay?" I spin her, checking to make sure there are no injuries. It's a brilliant plan because *clearly* I can see through her coat and Winter gear.

"I'm fine," she slaps my hand away. Red eyes her warily as he brushes the snow off his own gear.

"Explain *this*," Adam requests when he's free. He waves his arm to the wall of snow he just vacated.

"What just happened?" I latch on to the question.

"The pendant that Jack gave you," Eustace begins. My

world comes crashing down around me like another kind of avalanche—Jack also knew about this. "The pendant was a remote key that let the system know Jack was there so it would divert the worst parts of the weather so he couldn't be accidentally hurt inside."

If the pendant could trigger the environment to move, that means Nes was right about it moving when he lost his fingers to the cold.

"I knew he gave it to you," Eustace continues. "He told me he did. That's why we huddled around you. *You* just saved us all, Genesis. Adam was a bit too far away, which is why he ended up partially in the snow."

"How did it do that?" Nathaniel asks.

"The ground shifted enough to divert the snow. Morozoko couldn't eliminate Jack from experiencing what everyone else encountered in here, but they could realistically make sure he never got *too* close to danger."

It explained why Jack had panicked right before I ran out with Nathaniel. It explained the look he gave me too —he knew he wasn't coming out of this.

Devastation is a word sometimes used to describe the aftermath of a natural disaster like an avalanche. It is the complete and utter destruction of everything touched by the catastrophe. It is also the current state of my life. I will never recover from this.

"We can't get him out, can we?"

"No, probably not," Eustace replies sadly. "That

doesn't mean we'll stop yet, but there's a lot that went on inside that mountain after you left, Genesis, that affected what happened out here. Even if we *do* manage to get inside, I can't promise we'll find him at all, much less alive. I'm sorry."

We dig for another hour, but it feels like for every pile of snow we remove, when we turn back around, it's filled in again. More snow crumbles off of the mountain until it's too dangerous to continue. When a falling rock nearly takes out Todd, Adam decides we need to go.

Nathaniel and Perrin have to carry me away, fighting against them. Nes walks behind us, fighting back his own tears as he tries to calm me.

I FALL in and out of sleep once they shift me into their arms from their shoulders, exhausted from everything. Each time I open my eyes, it's brighter out.

Once, when I wake up for a moment, I'm inside the cave. We've walked a long way. Azra assures me we're going back to search for Jack in the morning.

WHEN I WAKE UP FULLY, it's morning. Outside the cave, the ground is covered in mud. With the weather machine gone, everything is thawing.

We return to the mountain to find that while the snow had started to melt, it has also frozen over because of the strong winds whipping around the base of the hidden structure.

The snow is frozen solid. We can't get in. Days go by and still no change. They spend two days convincing me that there is no way he survived this long without food, water, or heat. No man could survive that. I have to say goodbye.

Eventually, we return to the bunker.

NICHOLAS AND LILLY rush up to me as I drag myself in. I muster all the energy I have to be brave for them.

"Gen!" Nicholas screams as he throws himself around my leg. "Where have you been?"

He sounds ready to cry.

"Don't worry, I'm back now." I scoop him up, realizing he is much too heavy for that.

I squeeze him tightly before setting him back down. I kneel, giving Lilly a big hug too.

"Where's Jack?" Lilly asks, loud enough for the entire room of children to hear.

I look around at the little faces waiting for an answer. They search the room for him. They deserve to know.

"Come sit with me," I say, making my way to Jack's favorite spot by the fireplace.

I sit against the wall, my back to it. There's no fire now that we're experiencing Spring-like weather, but I imagine the flames roaring next to me, illuminating my face like it always did to Jack.

"Jack wanted me to share a story with you," I hear my voice crack, making Eliza duck and blink back tears. Everyone flinches, trying not to cry in front of the kids. I bite my lip before forcing a smile. "Jack has been on an adventure. He has his own story now.

"You see, Jack has been keeping a secret from us for a very long time." Several adults gasp, thinking I'm going to reveal his dark side to the children. "Jack is more magical than we thought. Jack isn't an ordinary person like you or me. Oh, no! Jack, you see, is a Snow Prince."

"A Snow Prince?" Nicholas gasps.

"Yes, Nicholas, he's the prince of all the snow. That's why he has such light hair and icy blue eyes. Jack is the Snow Prince who controls the weather.

"He uses his powers to help people. He takes care of them with the weather."

The children shift, leaning forward to hear more as I paint a picture of Jack standing dressed all in ice blue, controlling the weather to help us here in the bunker.

I describe his ice palace in the mountains and how he watches over us from there, taking care of each person in the bunker.

"He sends us flowers in the Summer to remind us he loves us. He sends us rain to grow the food we need for our tummies. And he gives us the snow to play with in Winter so that he can remind us to have fun."

"Snow Prince Jack sounds like one heck of a guy," Eliza says loudly.

"He is," I reply, keeping my tears at bay as I spin a fantastical tale about Jack's journeys as he controls the weather. Jack would be so proud that I turned him into one of his fairytales.

He will always live on through his stories now.

"What else does Jack control?" Lilly asks.

"Well, he controls the fog. When you see that, that's Jack trying to play a trick on you and sneak up to give you kisses on the cheek."

They all giggle.

"Jack brought me here," Cody announces when they quiet down. Everyone swings around to look at him.

"Jack brought a lot of you here," Eustace takes over. "He brought you here to keep you safe."

"Jack the Ice Prince has always tried to keep you safe," Adam adds. "But really, *Ice Prince*, Gen?"

"Just go with it, Adam." I roll my eyes.

"I'd say less Ice, more Frost," Nathaniel jumps in. "It

comes and goes without drawing attention, but it's just as attention-grabbing when it *is* there."

It's the perfect description of Jack. Unassuming and beautiful and perfectly deceptive.

"Jack Frost!" Lilly squeals. She starts singing until the others join her.

To the world, his stories will be that of Jack Frost, but to me, he will always be my Ice Prince, and I'm okay keeping that bit of him to myself.

CHAPTER 24

Jack's office is cool now that there is no temperature regulation in the building. His Morozoko Industries employee photo is on the screen in front of me as I stare at his file.

Inside his desk, I found journals from his time inside the bunker. There are dozens of sketches of me over the years. There are charts on each member of the bunker inside his desk drawers. All of these papers are an outpouring of the love he had for each of us.

On the bookshelves, I find many of the stories Jack brought into the bunker. From what I can tell, he still made up his own as well for the children.

"Have you made up your mind yet?" Mory asks, standing in the doorway.

"We're having meetings about it this afternoon," I tell him, finding it hard to tear my gaze away from Jack's photos. "That's why I'm here. We want you to come speak to the bunker.

"We want everyone to be able to make a fair decision on what they want to do. We don't want them to be influenced one way or the other. We'd like you to come present your mission to them—without scare tactics or you'll be kicked out immediately—so they understand what your project is and how they were involved and will continue to be involved should they choose to stay."

Mory nods.

"I'll be there."

He steps back, wandering down the hall. I don't stop him.

Turning back to the desk, I stare at the screen, looking through everything Morozoko has on him. I've learned his parents' names, where he was from, and everything about his childhood and his years working for Morozoko inside the Globe.

His pendant is and will always remain around my neck. Once the machine is back up and running, it will no longer act as a remote key, but I don't care.

Once we finish our meetings over the next few days, the group will discuss what we want to do. Together, we'll decide. Some will likely stay and others will likely go, but the choice will be ours.

Parents of the children will be brought in, presented with all of the facts, and will be asked again to make decisions about their children's lives. Many will be allowed to join their children inside the Globe and be a part of the study.

I'm still not sure what I plan on doing, but I'll be listening for Jack to keep me honest in my decision.

Jack will always be a part of my life. He's changed me in so many ways. Like the frost sliding over the ground and leaving its icy mark on everything it touches, Jack has changed this world, both inside the snow globe and out in the real world.

I'll honor him, by bringing Summer to everyone I touch.

I push back the chair.

It's time to go home.

Walking out of the building, I wave to Eustace in the yard with his wife and daughter. They'll be joining us for the meetings this afternoon.

They follow behind me as Nathaniel sidles up to me.

"How did it go?" he asks.

"He will be joining us. I'm sure he'll put on a good presentation. He wants to keep his study going, after all."

It's warm enough that we don't need coats as we walk, though the wind blows enough that for a moment, I feel an icy kiss on my cheek.

"I'm sure," Nathaniel comments harshly. "Ready for this?"

"I think so."

"A lot is going to come out today," he reminds me.

"I know." I nod to emphasize my words.

A bird sings out in the tree. I'm hoping the apples will

start to grow back soon. I'm desperate to get some fruit. Morozoko has been supplying us with food until things settle back to normal with the Globe, but it's different than what we're used to.

Maybe the bird could deliver a message to the trees for me to get moving. Or maybe I should try using the hidden compartments in the trees—that might be a better idea.

"We're all here for you," Nathaniel adds.

"Thanks. I know you are. All of our family will be there for each other today."

"Jack created a great family for us, didn't he?" Nathaniel muses.

"He did!" Eustace shouts from behind us making me smirk.

"Well, then," I grin. "Let's go take care of our family."

EPILOGUE

She is a force of nature.

She inspires things to grow all around her without even trying. She gives life.

She is a force. She is *my* force.

But in the end, it doesn't matter, because I set her free, just like blazing sunlight should be free.

One day I will see my Genesis again and she will be more brilliant than she ever was when she was with me. She's going to change the world and I have to let her.

Letting her go isn't easy, but she's safe now and the world is better for it. She's free under the stars.

One day I'll see what she's become.

For now...I just need to escape this ice prison.

ACKNOWLEDGMENTS

You thought Jack died, didn't you? I know...I'm so mean. Fear not—Jack's story isn't over yet!

Speaking of which, there's a short story about how Jack and Genesis started dating over on my website. It's my gift to you! While you're there, you can also see the World Portal for this series, get behind the scenes, and more.

Jack's story is one that I've wanted to tell for a long time—almost as much as Goldilocks and my mermaid series—and I'm so grateful to be able to create this twist on his tale. I can't wait for the next tangled retelling!

Special thanks to Jess for all of your help with Jack and Gen's story—I would be nothing without you! Thank you for your constant support and help!

Thanks to my Elites for repping for this book and all

of my different series! You are rock stars and I adore each and every one of you!

Thank you to S and J—without you, Jack's story would not have been written in nine and a half days and would probably still be sitting in my massive to-write-after-I-finish-the-rest-of-these-books list.

More than anything, thank you to my fabulous readers! Your kind words and support mean the world to me. I hope you've enjoyed Jack and Gen's journey as much as I have—writing this book was so much fun!

I hope you'll join me over at kmrobinsonbooks.com for all of the fun extras I have planned for Jack and Genesis! If you're a fan of sci-fi, retellings, dystopians, hackers, technology, steam punk, fantasy, and more, you can also get a look at my other series (and free excerpts and books) to fill the Jack- shaped hole in your hearts until his story continues!

Stay inspired!

Stay inspired!
-K.M. Robinson

WORLD PORTALS

Ready to learn exclusive facts about The Conspiracy of Jack Frost and other K.M. Robinson Series?

World Portals are now available on www. kmrobinsonbooks.com

Learn behind the scenes facts, watch videos, play games, check out our book filters, find out where to get bonus scenes, view fan art, and get access to other secrets we've hidden away inside the World Portals on the website.

The World Portals are constantly changing and information is being taken away and added all the time, so check back frequently for new content!

ABOUT THE AUTHOR

K.M. Robinson is a storyteller who creates new worlds both in her writing and in her fine arts conceptual photography. She is a marketing, branding and social media strategy educator who is recognized at first sight by her very long hair. She is a creative who focuses on photography, videography, couture dress making, and writing to express the stories she needs to tell. She almost always has a camera within reach. Visit her at her website: www.kmrobinsonbooks.com

CONNECT ON SOCIAL MEDIA

facebook.com/kmrobinsonbooks

instagram.com/kmrobinsonbooks

twitter.com/kmrobinsonbooks

youtube.com/kmrobinsonbooks

tiktok.com/@kmrobinsonbooks

Get free books and excerpts of other K.M. Robinson
books at newsletter.kmrobinsonbooks.com

ALSO BY K.M. ROBINSON

The Golden Trilogy

Book One: Golden

Forged: A Golden Novella

Book Two: Locked

Book Three: Edge

The Complete Series Boxset/Omnibus with Tempered: an
exclusive bonus novella

The Jaded Duology

Book One: Jaded

Book Two: Risen

The Complete Series Boxset/Omnibus with exclusive epilogue

The Siren Wars Saga

Book One: The Siren Wars

Book Two: Darker Depths

Book Three: Beyond The Shores

Origins of the Siren Wars: Prequel Novella

Book Four: Forbidden Waters (coming soon)

The Legends Chronicles

Along Came A Spider: A Prequel Novelette

And They'll Come Home: A Prequel Novelette

The Archives of Jack Frost Series

The Conspiracy of Jack Frost

The Redemption of Jack Frost (coming soon)

Stealing Steam Series

Book One: Lions and Lamps

Book Two: Pistons and Prisoners

Book Three: Railcars and Rulers

Top Hats and Telegraphs: A Prequel Novella

The Complete Series Boxset/Omnibus with Vambraces and
Victories: an exclusive bonus novella

Virtually Sleeping Beauty: A Novella Retelling

The Goose Girl and The Artificial: A Novella Retelling

The Sinking: A Little Mermaid Novella Retelling

Cindrill: A Cinderella Assassin Novella Retelling

Sugarcoated: A Hansel and Gretel's Witch Novella Retelling

Blood Is Silent: A Red Riding Hood Circus Aerialist Retelling

Mulan Dragon Shifter

The Holiday Court Series

Book One: Saving North (Christmas)

Book Two: Reviving Time (New Year's Eve)

Book Three: Targeting Bliss (Valentine's Day)

Book Four: Pressing Luck (St. Patrick's Day)

Book Five: Hiding Destiny (Easter)

Book Six: Tricking Fate (Halloween)

JADED: BOOK ONE OF THE JADED DUOLOGY

Her father failed in his mission to take control from the Commander, a defeat that has cost Jade her life. She will die as punishment. Now she belongs to the Commander's son—as his wife. Knowing his intent is to quietly kill her in revenge, Jade's every move is calculated to survive—until she learns her death ensures the safety of her father and her entire town.

Roan doesn't want to kill Jade, but once his family isolates her from her father and community, his only choice is to go through with the plan. Jade doesn't make it easy as she tries to sway him into falling for her. Each misstep makes him question his cause. Each moment makes every decision harder, but the Commander won't allow him to fail.

One chooses life. One chooses death. In the midst of the chaos, only one will succeed.

Now available!

Learn more about The Jaded Duology at

jadedinfo.kmrobinsonbooks.com

**GOLDEN: BOOK ONE OF THE GOLDEN
TRILOGY**

**Goldilocks wasn't naive. She was sent on a mission and
Dov Baer is her new target.**

When Auluria tricks the Baers into letting her into their
home, they have no idea she's actually been sent by the
enemy to destroy them. Intent on gathering information
for her cousin to hand over to the Society seeking to
destroy all of the rebel factions—including her own—
she's willing to sacrifice Dov Baer to save her people...
until she realizes her cousin lied to her.

Now that she's seen who Dov truly is, she has to decide
between staying loyal to her only remaining family or
protecting the man she's falling for. If her allegiances are

discovered, either side could destroy her—assuming the Society doesn't get her first

Available now!
Learn more about The Golden Trilogy at goldeninfo.
kmrobinsonbooks.com

**THE SIREN WARS: BOOK ONE OF THE
SIREN WARS SAGA**

War has hovered around the kingdom of Scylla for generations ever since the original sirens left the mer collection generations ago after nearly drowning the human prince. Over the years, select mermaids from the royal bloodline have been trained as spies to work for the reigning kings and queens, keeping the collection safe from sirens and humans.

Celena and her partner, Merrick, work covertly for the royals—not even her twin brother knows. When they discover the sirens have broken through the barriers the mer set up to keep the sirens out, Celena and her friends must race to the old kingdom of Metten to stop them from starting a war within their borders.

When she's dragged to the surface, Celena realizes that the war above the waters is as deadly as the one below the waves—and sacrificing herself may be the only way to protect her family.

The Siren Wars have only just begun.

Available now!

Learn more about The Siren Wars Saga at sirenwarsinfo.

kmrobinsonbooks.com

deadlier, and he knows he can't trust the girl who snuck into the competition this year...but Cyra might not survive his ruthlessness either in a game where only the lion's heart can win.

All wishes require sacrifice, and someone is going to pay the price for the Stourbridge.

Available now!
Learn more about The Stealing Steam Series at
lionsandlampsinfo.kmrobinsonbooks.com

ALONG CAME A SPIDER: THE FIRST PREQUEL NOVELETTE TO THE LEGENDS CHRONICLES

Little Hacker Muffet
sat on her tuffet
destroying her cords and Way.
Along came a hacker named Spider,
who sat down beside her
and frightened his opponent away.

When Fet, one of the most skilled hackers in the Legends, discovers her best friend and leader of her group has been abducted and held for ransom, she must escape unnoticed and find Peep before it's too late.

.   .   .

WHEN SPIDER, a new recruit training to join her hacker ring, slips out with her and claims to have a plan to save her friend, Fet is forced to bring him along. As she discovers he's not who he claims to be, she faces grave danger and learns just how deadly a spider bite can be.

Now available!

Learn more about The Legends Chronicles at
acasinfo.kmrobinsonbooks.com

VIRTUALLY SLEEPING BEAUTY

T*o wake her up, he has to enter the game and help her beat it...*

SURELY THE CLASS president wouldn't illegally over-juice to stay in the virtual reality game citizens are allowed to play for four hours a day, but when Royce's aunt calls in a panic because her goddaughter hasn't left the game yet, his only option is to go inside the game and drag the girl out.

THE GOLDEN KNIGHT quickly discovers the princess' absence in the real world isn't of her own doing—*she's trapped inside the game by unknown forces*—and if she can't escape soon, she could die for real outside of the game. He's even more shocked to discover that Rora outranks him inside of the game, which means she'll have to fight to *protect herself* from the evils locking her inside a dangerous world.

CAN Rora and Royce work together to outsmart a vicious queen and evil magician, and defeat digital dragons, or will Rora slowly fade away until there's nothing left but an empty shell and the game ranking she will leave behind?

Now available!

Learn more about Virtually Sleeping Beauty at
vsbinfo.kmrobinsonbooks.com

THE CONSPIRACY OF JACK FROST

No one inside the snow globe knows that Morozoko Industries is controlling their weather, testing them to form a stronger race that can survive the fall out from the bombs being dropped in the outside world—all they know is that they must survive the harsh Winter that lasts a month and use the few days of Spring, Summer, and Fall to gather enough supplies to survive.

WHEN THE SEASONS START SHIFTING, Genesis and Jack know something is going on. As their team begins to find technology that they don't have access to inside their snow globe of a world, it begins to look more and more like one of their own is working against them.

. . .

GENESIS SOON DISCOVERS MOROZOKO INDUSTRIES, but when a foreign enemy tries to destroy their weather program to make sure their destructive life-altering bombs succeed in destroying the outside world, only one person can shut down the machine that is spinning out of control and save the lives of everyone inside the bunker —Jack.

Now available!
Learn more about The Conspiracy of Jack Frost at
jackfrostinfo.kmrobinsonbooks.com

SUGARCOATED

Hansel and Gretel's witch was actually on their side...

Annika's job is to create a cake to match the candy-colored rooftops, nightly firework shows, and daily parades ending in unexpected executions for the mad king's ball, but her true mission is to sneak a thirteen-year-old assassin into the palace using her gift of illusions.

Hansel's job is to protect his little sister, Gretel, once she assassinates King Levin and ends the destruction in Candestrachen, using his power over light to rescue the young girl from the chaos her influence over life and death will create.

. . .

WHEN THE ENTIRE forest reconstructs itself under Gretel's command while trying to save herself from a king's guard, Hansel and Annika must put their feelings aside and ensure their plan holds true—even if it means one of them has to sacrifice themselves to protect the mission.

Her illusions were meant to save her....but not everyone will survive the assassination attempt.

Learn more about Sugarcoated at
sugarcoatedinfo.kmrobinsonbooks.com

THE GOOSE GIRL AND THE ARTIFICIAL

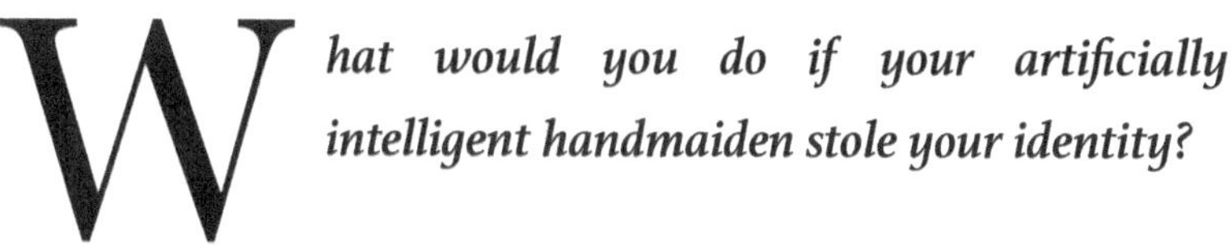

What would you do if your artificially intelligent handmaiden stole your identity?

THREATENED BY HER ARTIFICIAL, Arta, Princess Goselyn is forced to switch places and pretend she isn't human when she reaches Prince Corinth to negotiate a treaty they both need to be able to take their respective crowns one day. If she doesn't comply, her Artificial, controlled by her evil cousin, will not only kill Goselyn's mother, but Prince Corinth and his father as well.

. . .

Can the quiet princess outsmart a machine created to be more intelligent than she is, all while surviving the other Artificials and robots working against her in the foreign palace, or will Corinth and his father find out and destroy her chance to save them all?

Learn more about The Goose Girl and The Artificial at goosegirlinfo.kmrobinsonbooks.com

THE SINKING

**The sea witch wants to silence her, but not for the
reason you think.**

When a quirky older woman pawns a fancy seashell necklace at her mother's antique shop on the pier, Cara doesn't think much about the story the woman spins about the wearer turning into a mermaid.

ON HER WAY HOME, she accidentally drops the necklace into the ocean and is swept out to sea where she meets—a merman who volunteers to take her to his mother, the sea queen, to help her get her legs back.

. . .

CARA SOON LEARNS that it's Quay's eighteenth birthday—a day that has been a curse for his family—and is meant to be one for her too. Now she must fight to survive the sea with Quay at her side.

Fans of The Little Mermaid will love this twisted take on the beloved story.

Now available!
Learn more about The Sinking at
thesinkinginfo.kmrobinsonbooks.com

CINDRILL

C inderella is an assassin out to murder the prince...*but he's hunting her too.*

THE NANOBOTS CINDRILL'S master gives her to use as a mask allow her to slip into the ball wearing a face that isn't hers, but when the assassination attempt goes sideways, Prince Davian doesn't understand why her face changes when he injures her, slicing her foot open around a unique pair of shoes as she runs away.

WHEN CINDRILL RUNS into the prince the next day without her nanobot mask on, he doesn't recognize her, but immediately decides her skills will be useful on his hunt for the would-be-assassin woman who nearly killed his father and his fiancée the night before.

Both are tasked with the job of murdering the other, but things don't quite go as they had planned when Cindrill's master and Davian's fiancée interfere as the two try to decide whether or not to kill the other.

It's hard to recognize a woman when she uses technology to change her appearance, but Cindrill is going to use that to her full advantage as she destroys the prince. ***Will either survive?***

Now available!

Learn more about Cindrill at
cindrillinfo.kmrobinsonbooks.com

BLOOD IS SILENT

Red *Riding Hood is a circus aerialist and the wolf is ready to cage her.*

SIENNA HAS GROWN up working for the circus, dangling off her signature red silks every night. Her grandmother has been known to wander off to train new acts for their boss, but when Sienna tries to find her to bring her back to the show, she doesn't expect the dashing and dangerous Elijah to join her.

WHEN they finally find Grandma Ida has been trans-formed deep in the heart of the woods, Sienna will stop at nothing to save her—but the wolf has her right where he wants her, and she won't be able to escape his claws.

SHE WAS TOLD NOT to go into the woods alone.

Now available!

Learn more about Blood Is Silent at
bloodissilentinfo.kmrobinsonbooks.com

MULAN DRAGON SHIFTER

There are no female dragon shifters in Yan Liu...except Mulan and her family. Only the enemy province has women with scales, so when they attack the Center as Mulan is dropping off her twin brother for his assignment with the army, she's forced to play the role of a non-existent brother after she shifts and rushes into the battle to protect her real twin.

TOGETHER, they must lie to their commanding officer—Mulan's secret boyfriend—and the entire army to protect her from their wrath should they find out and consider her an enemy, but Mulan's special gift might be too great to keep her secret hidden for long. She may be the only one that can save the kingdom and return the black jade blossom to the emperor.

Can Mulan survive the war, navigate two men vying for her attention, and keep her scales hidden long enough to return the province's life source to her people, or will dark, hidden forces destroy everything and cause her plans to burn hotter than her scale-melting dragon flames?

Now available!

Learn more about Mulan Dragon Shifter at mulaninfo.kmrobinsonbooks.com